Playing by the Rules

Playing by the Rules

A Novel

ELAINE MERYL BROWN

ONE WORLD | BALLANTINE BOOKS
NEW YORK

A One World Books Trade Paperback Original

Published in the United States by One World Books, an imprint of The Random House Publishing Group, a division of Random House, Inc., New York.

ONE WORLD is a registered trademark and the One World colophon is a trademark of Random House, Inc.

Reader's Circle and colophon are trademarks of Random House, Inc.

LIBRARY OF CONGRESS CATALOGING-IN-PUBLICATION DATA

Brown, Elaine Meryl.
Playing by the rules : a novel / by Elaine Meryl Brown.
p. cm.
ISBN 0-8129-7034-9 (trade pbk.)
1. African American families—Fiction. 2. Mountain life—Fiction.
3. Blue Ridge Mountains—Fiction. 4. Virginia—Fiction.
5. Orphans—Fiction. 6. Kidnapping—Fiction.
7. Domestic fiction. I. Title.
PS3602.R696P57 2006
813'.6—dc22   2005055477

Printed in the United States of America

www.oneworldbooks.net

1 2 3 4 5 6 7 8 9

Book design by Dana Leigh Blanchette

In loving memory of my father,
Elmo Ronald Brown,
the inspiration for my climb,
the last of the Mohicans

ACKNOWLEDGMENTS

I'm grateful to my agent Victoria Sanders, and my editor Melody Guy, both insightful and wonderful women who have made this journey an enjoyable one. Just as important is my gratitude to Random House.

I'm grateful to Alice Peck, Danielle Durkin, and Tammy Richards, and to all the people who have had fun passing through Lemon City who believe that the characters and the town live on.

Thank you to my family, friends, and colleagues who have inspired and encouraged, especially Henry, Bob, Gerri, Adriane, Shelley, Pat, Debra, Farrell, Toni, Olivia, Marsha, Rhonda, Sandra, Sam, and Ben.

For Mom, David, Erica, and Madison, thank you for the love and support and for understanding the time I had to take away in order to get things done.

Playing by the Rules

"The role played by the Negro woman in the development of her race in America is a history worth recording. In education she has been a pioneer in her club life, she has set the clock forward for hours in the ameliorating conditions of Negro children in all sections of the country—yes, largely out of the pockets of washer women, domestic servants, day laborers. She has gone into the alleys, the slums of our cities north and south and gathered up children, legitimate and illegitimate, and brought them out into God's great sunlight."
—Charlotte Hawkins Brown, *The Charlotte Hawkins Brown Papers*
    "The Role of the Negro Woman in the Fight for Freedom," from a
    speech delivered June 1943 in Madison Square Garden, New York
    City. (Founder, Palmer Memorial Institute, 1902)

Thirty years later:

LEMON CITY CHRONICLE,
Classified Section
December 25, 1973

"Medford Attaway, seeking his birth mother. Wants to know who she is before starting his own family, not leaving any rocks, box, or socks unturned. Send information or picture to Lemon City P.O. Box 411, or contact the sheriff directly. No questions asked."

Lemon City Rules

1) NEVER MARRY AN OUTSIDER. IF YOU DO, THE BOLL WEEVIL WILL BITE YOU BACK.

2) IF YOU CAN'T BE HONEST, YOU MIGHT AS WELL BE DEAD.

3) AIRING YOUR DIRTY LAUNDRY OUT IN THE STREET WILL SMELL UP THE NEIGHBORHOOD.

4) DON'T LET THE MOJO LADY KNOW YOU GOT TROUBLES. IF YOU DO, SHE'LL GIVE YOU MORE.

5) CHEATING MAKES YOU LOWER THAN A DOG SCRATCHING UP A WORM IN THE DIRT.

6) WHAT GOES AROUND WILL ALWAYS COME BACK AROUND AND HIT YOU IN THE HEAD.

7) HELP THOSE IN NEED AND NEVER JUDGE THEM BY THE HOLES IN THEIR SOCKS.

8) DO BUSINESS AT HOME FIRST, THEN WITH OUTSIDERS YOU CAN INVITE INTO YOUR HOME, AS A LAST RESORT.

9) MIND YOUR OWN BUSINESS PERSONALLY AND PROFESSIONALLY.

10) SUPPORT THE COMMUNITY IN EVERY WAY POSSIBLE AND IMAGINABLE.

If you know anyone who has broken the rules and fallen by the wayside, immediately contact the Ladies of Mt. Zion Baptist Church for reformation instruction, council circle demonstrations, or renewal training.

Prologue

The fall rain came down with such force it felt like tiny daggers plunging into her body through the plastic poncho. The flimsy hood could protect her from getting wet, but not from the pain the sky was causing, and she considered it punishment for what she was about to do. What was worse was the way the Blue Ridge Mountains stood still, making her feel they were staring at her, watching her every move.

Splashing through puddles, her heart pounded louder in her chest and her breath became quick, not from the weight of the crate she held tightly against her belly covered by the poncho, but from the burden she would carry with her for the rest of her life. Inside the crate was a sweetgrass basket holding precious live cargo. Finding a destination would be her last act of protection for the infant, and guilt ran over her as easily as the water sliding off her plastic outerwear. Feeling she had no choice but to commit the crime, the thought made her cry harder than the skies. She wished the circumstances had been different, but there was no turning back.

The wailing from inside the basket became unbearable, and she resigned herself to the fact it was time to let go and stop walking in what seemed like circles and find the baby a home.

There was a light on in the house up ahead despite it being way past midnight, when most Lemonites had their heads hard-pressed against their pillows. She tiptoed up the steps to the wooden porch, confident the sound of heavy rain would conceal the creaking. As a last precaution, she scanned through the darkness to make sure she wouldn't be noticed. Suddenly the rain slowed down, turning into a drizzle, and she took it to be a sign that this was a good porch—that the life she was about to abandon would grow to become calm and one day be at peace. Convinced this was where the baby belonged, she gently lowered the basket onto the floor.

Pulling back the blanket, she uncovered the tiny face. "Forgive me," she said, looking into his teary deep brown eyes. With trembling hands, she made sure the layers of blankets were tucked tightly around him so no cold from the westerly wind could penetrate the sturdy straw of the basket. She moved her fingers around the crate until satisfied she found the diapers and extra milk she had packed to get him through the week. She wasn't a bad person. It was the most she could do.

Her hand stayed on the basket handle longer than it should have when it was time to say good-bye, and she began to rock the infant to sleep so it wouldn't witness her cowardly escape. Enough time had passed to give her second thoughts, but the only thing she lingered on was how she'd got herself involved in this mess and that it was hard to raise a child without a husband. Even though she was convinced she had made the right decision, she had to keep repeating that to herself.

She hummed a quiet lullaby until the baby's eyes finally closed, then withdrew her hand slowly, reluctant for the separation. Against her will, she made her head turn toward the dark road. As she stood up, her legs felt like they would collapse underneath her, but she managed to hold onto the railing, walk down the steps, and keep her eyes focused front. "No regrets," she kept mumbling under her breath; then she recited the first thing that came to mind, which was Matthew from the Bible. "For if you forgive men when they sin against you, your heavenly Father will also forgive you. But if you do not forgive men their sins, your Father will not forgive your sins." She shoved her hands beneath her poncho to keep them dry and wipe them of this shameful business that she only hoped wouldn't come back to haunt her one day. Then she folded her hands in prayer, remembering Mark: "And when you stand praying, if you hold anything against anyone, forgive him so that your Father in heaven may forgive your sins."

As she stared into the darkness, the mountains now looked like ghosts hunching over in the night, ready to pounce to protect its citizens, if necesssary. But she knew Lemon City was a friendly town and despite its strong opinions of strangers, she felt it would have a big heart for the tiny memory she'd left behind. Once she was certain her legs were strong enough to carry her, she picked up her pace and began to flee from the scene as fast as she could. The sides of her plastic poncho spread and flapped like wings as she gathered up speed until it sounded as if she were a bird taking off in flight. Her plan was to be long gone before the Lemonites saw daylight.

Chapter One

Louise couldn't figure out what Medford's problem was, which made her feel as angry as a Virginia tiger beetle stuck on its back. For the past week, he had been more restless than a church bell waiting for Sunday to roll around. To say that Medford was acting strangely was an understatement. Lately, whenever she and Medford were together, it seemed to Louise that his mind was preoccupied with something or someone else. In fact, just last week she'd called him several times during the evening and the phone just rang and rang. Usually he picked up the receiver no later than the third ring, because normally at that time he'd be home. Normally, he'd already be in bed, stretched out flat on his back, talking to her in a relaxed state of comfort. The other thing that made her eyebrow raise was when he came to visit her at the library last week and he walked right past her office in a daze as if he had forgotten the room where she worked. If it was another woman he was thinking about, and he had changed his mind about her, Louise thought she'd rather hear about it now, when they were only six weeks into the start of their relationship, than later.

She wondered whether or not she had done something to put him off, but that was a question she wasn't going to ask. She wasn't going to get involved in one of those "let's talk it over" conversations that usually carried on like crickets chirping endlessly into the night, that quieted down for stretches of time, then started back up again—same song, different day. She wasn't going to talk about his mood change at all, she decided. Well, maybe she'd be willing to participate in a conversation about them being together on a long-term basis, but she wasn't going to bring it up first.

At best, Louise told herself they'd had fun while it lasted and if it were over between them, she was ready to accept the end was near and move on.

It was Christmas Day and she wanted to crawl back into bed, but that wasn't an option because Nana and Granddaddy were preparing a holiday feast, having her and Medford and the family over for dinner along with several of their friends. Besides, Medford would be coming to her house to pick her up soon so she had better get ready, and she had better not be too evil by the time he got there. The good part was, they didn't have to travel too far for dinner since her grandparents only lived across the street.

Rummaging through her closet for something to wear, Louise turned her thoughts to her grandmother. She knew Nana would be expecting Medford to present her with a diamond ring for Christmas, since Nana had hinted at that on more than one occasion. But Louise also knew that as far as gifts went, Medford was as practical as straws on a broomstick, and more prone to giving long johns or socks at best, things that were useful and had a purpose, and that was fine with her.

Even so, Louise understood her grandmother's desire to bring Medford into the family. Nana thought that Medford would make a wonderful husband, not only because he was the son of Clement, Granddaddy's best friend, but because he was the perfect example of a rule-abiding Lemon City citizen. For over a hundred years, Lemon City's Rules were the foundation of its success and prosperity, with their purpose being to establish a strong sense of community and moral way of life. Lemon City's last rule, Rule Number Ten: SUPPORT THE COMMUNITY IN EVERY WAY POSSIBLE AND IMAGINABLE, was the soul of the town and the heart of its people.

Lemon City never took kindly to strangers and discouraged the influences that unknown forces brought along with them from stepping inside its borders. "Outsiders," as they were commonly called, were as unwelcome to Lemon City as a heat wave hovering over a crop of tobacco ready for harvest. Following The Rules was essential to the town's survival, and Medford was as devoted to Lemon City as the morning mist was to the Blue Ridge Mountains. Consequently, Louise knew that Medford, the perfect great-grandson-in-law, would be Nana's ideal Christmas present. It was too bad Nana would be disappointed, Louise thought. In fact, she was too, in a way. After giving in to Medford's advances, he was turning out to be weird, and Louise wanted to be as far on the other side of disappointment as she could get. Besides, six weeks wasn't enough time to warrant a commitment, even though it was something that had crossed her mind. In the beginning she was undecided about Medford, but before she knew it he had begun growing on her like Virginia creeper up a black oak tree. She had never been this wishy-washy about anything before, feeling as if she were sitting on a fence unable to climb down on either side. It was annoying to have someone catch her heart's attention. But if Medford was going out with other people, so could she. Nothing was stopping her from doing it, especially since being loyal to one man had never been her style to begin with. She had tried it before and it didn't work. At least Medford could have had the courage to tell her to her face, she thought to herself, and not mess around behind her back so she had to figure things out on her own.

How could she be so stupid? Louise asked herself as she snatched a wrap dress, held it up for scrutiny, and flung it back into her closet. She did the same with her black-and-white dress with squares, arranged in a geometric design that she hated now because it looked like a checkerboard and made her dizzy. She pulled out a suit with a belted, slim-fitting jacket and pleated skirt, held it out in front of her for a few seconds, then jammed it between the rest of her clothes hanging on the rack. Nothing appealed to her, and she resigned herself to not having anything to wear. She wasn't in the mood to show her legs, so she went to her drawer to pull out a crew-neck knit sweater to match a pair of flared woolen slacks, and hoped that her sister-in-law Elvira wouldn't show up too overdressed for Christmas dinner. If she weren't so upset with two-timing Medford, she'd go downstairs to the ground-floor apartment to ask Elvira in person, what she was going to wear, but the way she was feeling she didn't even want to pick up the phone and make holiday attire a big deal. She would leave that to her grandmother.

The last thing on Elvira's mind was putting on clothes as she and Billy lay naked in bed trying to make a baby. She and Billy lived downstairs from Louise, in the two-family house that Granddaddy built to keep his grandchildren close. Since her husband was the Lemon City Sheriff, and it was a holiday, she was taking full advantage of monopolizing his time on his day off.

For the six years they had been married, Billy and Elvira had tried to get pregnant. Enjoying an active sex life, they soon learned that frequency had very little to do with egg fertilization, yet they didn't let the odds discourage them from maximizing the process of bringing forth life. After spending several minutes between the sheets, Billy was becoming more exhausted as his wife was becoming more desperate. Reaching between his legs, Elvira attempted to inspire him back into the mood, but Billy gently grabbed her hand and pulled her to the floor. Excited that her husband might be interested in trying a new position, Elvira soon realized that she had misunderstood. Instead of more lovemaking, Billy joined her on the floor, getting down on his knees, putting his hands together to pray, "On this day, when a great gift was born into the world, please help us give birth to our own little baby." Then he folded his wife's hands into his and added, "Maybe this is the best way to get what we want." Billy clasped his hands over his wife's as they prayed for several minutes. When they finished their divine request, they were so filled with joy that they jumped back into bed and made more love, doing whatever they could do here on earth to help their prayer come true.

Nana and Granddaddy were careful not to get in each other's way. As he was making his traditional eggnog and she was preparing her special ambrosia, they were mindful to give each other adequate space in the kitchen.

In the Dunlap house, Christmas was the time for treats. On the counter and in the pantry, and wherever there was room on trays and tables on the back porch, Nana had baked lemon desserts—all presents she delivered to family and friends. There were lemon tarts, lemon cookies, lemon cakes with lemon icing, plain lemon cakes, lemon cupcakes with yellow frosting, lemon meringue pies, lemon marmalade, and lemon squares. The individual cups of lemon pudding and frozen homemade lemon sherbet that she couldn't wrap in a box, she saved for after dinner. Nana had almost as much fun with lemons as she did growing tomatoes in her garden, which everyone knew she was devoted to, and took quite seriously. For Outsiders, lemons were bitter and sour, but not for Lemonites. When they bit into lemons, they felt they were savoring history and swallowing sweetness.

Granddaddy was feeling cramped, surrounded by what he perceived to be a clutter of desserts that were more plentiful this Christmas than they had been in previous years. His wife had invited more people to dinner than usual.

"I hope we have enough room at the table for all the people you having here for dinner," Granddaddy said, taking four egg cartons from the refrigerator and placing them on the counter. "I hope we don't have to sit someone on the floor with the cat."

Saint, who was curled into a ball underneath the kitchen table where Nana was peeling lemons for her ambrosia, poked her head up at the sound of the word "cat." Then she lowered her head back into its original position and closed her eyes the way they had been before her nap was interrupted.

"I only invited Vernelle and Sadie and Theola—only three Ladies from Mt. Zion Baptist Church, and Clement and Bootsie." Nana paused, making sure she'd included everyone, then added, "Oh, and Ole Miss Johnson." She made a sour face that wasn't caused by the lemon juice that had squirted onto her cheek. "With the table extensions and the folding chairs, we'll all fit."

"Fit as tight as a big foot crammed into a little shoe," said Granddaddy, cracking eggs, separating the whites from the yokes. "Fit as tight as Clement is with his money, squeezing it so hard he could flatten out a nickel and turn it into a quarter."

"Including family, there'll only be twelve of us," said Nana, ignoring her husband, licking the juice that rolled down her arm from the lemon she had just peeled.

"Our shoulders will be kissing and our elbows will be knocking folks out the way. Loving shoulders and hating elbows. There'll be conflict at the table . . . love, hate . . . love, hate. All that emotional back and forth ain't right on Christmas day."

"Oh, Willie." Nana laughed. "Quit fussin'. It's only seven more people than usual for a few hours on one day. Stop acting foolish. We'll fit fine."

"It's only you that I'm thinking 'bout. If Faye didn't leave home last month, I know we'd only have our family over for dinner. Not that I have anything against inviting friends, I just think that you're overcompensating."

"What you mean by that?"

"Inviting all these people over to substitute for Faye's absence is making more work for yourself than you need to be doing."

"It's no trouble, spreading the joy and the love of the Lord on this day."

From what Granddaddy could tell, his wife had been spreading more than good tidings lately, putting on a few pounds in the past month since their youngest grandchild, Faye, had left Lemon City. Faye's decision to move away from home and leave town altogether was as unnatural as a black bear fleeing hibernation from the mountains in winter. No one had ever left Lemon City. There was no reason to. All the people had whatever they needed. The inheritance provided by their ancestors who were of the mixed blood from plantation owners, slaves, and Powhatan Indians, left a legacy that insured everyone a good education, a lifelong job, a wholesome family upbringing, and a supportive community. But Faye had her own ideas. She had made the decision to go against his wishes because she claimed Black Power was her calling and she had important dreams of her own. His wife had talked him into giving his granddaughter his blessing to go. The next thing he knew, Faye was on the train to New York City to start her own hair-care business, and he fought back the tears at the memory of waving good-bye to the back of her newly permed hairdo. Just when he had gotten used to her natural Afro, now she had gone and changed up on him again. Young people nowadays were fickle, he thought. He just didn't understand why they didn't appreciate life being predictable—like waking up to the sight of the Blue Ridge Mountains every day and having the skyline view be the same.

They had raised their grandchildren, Billy, Louise, and Faye, after their parents were killed. The tragic accident made them become tighter as a family and Nana even more determined to keep her loved ones close, which made her decision to let Faye go all the more difficult. She didn't want to sacrifice her expectations at the risk of her granddaughter's happiness, and now Granddaddy saw his wife's payback for the results of her generosity. Over the weeks he watched as she filled the gap with cooking, cleaning, crocheting, quilting, and doing whatever else she could find to plug the void.

Reaching up to the cabinet, Granddaddy grabbed the crystal punch bowl and set it down on the only empty space on the counter, which served as his makeshift work station since his wife and her lemons had taken over most of the kitchen.

"Faye is gone and she's not coming home anytime soon," Granddaddy said, hoping to help his wife move on.

"She ain't gone, gone. Don't talk like she's dead," Nana snapped. "At least she sounded happy this morning when she called to wish us a Merry Christmas." Examining the peeled lemons stacked in the bowl that were marinating in their own juice, Nana took inventory of the other items she had organized on the table for her ambrosia. The pecans and walnuts were cracked and mixed in one container, the pitted cherries were in their open cans, the peaches were swimming in their Mason jars, the bananas were sliced on the cutting board, and the miniature marshmallows were waiting inside their plastic bags. All she had left to do was cut open the fresh coconut and pineapple.

"But I just couldn't help myself, and told her 'I don't know what's so merry about it. You ain't here,' " Nana continued. Grabbing the hammer, she slammed into the coconut, making Granddaddy jump and drop a piece of eggshell into his mixing bowl.

"Aw, Ernestine. The girl don't need to feel guilty, especially today." He fished around with his finger in search of the missing eggshell. "She just got to New York City and settled down only a month ago, so you might as well start getting used to her being away. Besides, there ain't nothing you can do about it now. You're the one who gave her permission to go in the first place."

Granddaddy smiled as he recovered the eggshell and wiped it on a paper towel. As he continued stirring the eggs and adding milk to the mixture in the bowl, a mischievous look appeared on his face. "Did you remember to tell Faye that you were feeling so lonely without her that you invited Ole Miss Johnson over for Christmas dinner?" He glanced over his shoulder to catch his wife's reaction.

"You know that ain't true. If Lurleen were the last person on earth I wouldn't feel the need to share my table with her." Nana took the butcher knife and hacked the top and the bottom off the pineapple. "It just so happens that the only reason I invited her to dinner was 'cause she's our neighbor and I decided to be neighborly. In fact, there are exactly three reasons why I invited her." Nana put down the butcher knife and held up one finger. "One . . . she's recovering from the tree accident she had last month." She held up a second finger. "Two . . . I don't think it's right for *her* to be alone." She held up a third finger. "And three . . . just 'cause I don't like her don't mean I can't look beyond her meanness and be friendly, especially today."

Granddaddy shook his head, still cracking eggs, careful to separate the yokes from the whites so he wouldn't have to engage in another runaway-slippery-eggshell search mission. To say that his wife and Ole Miss Johnson didn't like each other was being kind.

Their intense rivalry in the tomato competition at the Annual County Fair made them relate as politely as two bull moose charging each other, ramming their antlers, protecting what was theirs. Granddaddy hoped that Christmas would provide a day of truce.

Ole Miss Johnson lived next door to Nana. In their youth, they had been close friends, but time came between them and split them apart like a half shadow across a full moon. Some would say it started when Ole Miss Johnson's husband, Easely, died. Others would say it started with tomatoes.

Doing her best to get dressed, Ole Miss Johnson was moving slowly in her bedroom getting ready for Christmas dinner. The storm that raged through Lemon City last month and cut through her backyard like a mini-tornado had caused a tree branch to fall on her, breaking several ribs, making it more painful than usual to get around. She had no family and usually ate her holiday meals at Mt. Zion Baptist Church. But since the storm, it was difficult to maneuver, and she didn't feel like going far from the house and was grateful that her next-door neighbor extended a Christmas dinner invitation. As excruciating as it was for Ole Miss Johnson to get dressed, she knew it had been even more painful for her neighbor, Ernestine, to invite her into the Dunlap home. Besides hunger, the pleasure of seeing Ernestine's discomfort was the only reason she was making an attempt to match her neighbor's effort to be sociable.

Ole Miss Johnson grabbed the left side of her body as if that were the only means to holding her ribs into place. Although the bandage had come off a week ago, she was still extremely miserable and it hurt whenever she attempted to accomplish the least of things. Putting her arms through the sleeves of her dress, and pulling the front around her, she knew it would be a while before she could manage through all the buttons. To lift her spirit and pass the time while sitting on her bed, trying to get her fingers to work in unison, she began humming "Joy to the World," hoping that would help her to find the joy in the day.

Well into the holiday spirit, Nana was tossing the nuts, fruits, and marshmallows into the larger mixing bowl, like she was bringing together old friends. "I wish I had some deerstongue or calamus to sprinkle into this ambrosia to make Clement pay some attention to Theola."

"Why don't you leave those two alone?" Granddaddy said, pulling out the drawer, looking for the electric mixer. "Clement can handle his own business. He's a grown man and if he's interested in Theola I'm sure he'll find a way to let her know." Mumbling into the bowl, he added, "Besides, you're on the edge of breaking Rule Number Nine: 'Mind Your Own Business Personally and Professionally.'"

" 'Umph . . . all it seems to me is that Clement needs a little help with taking some initiative." Nana stopped slicing the pineapple and glanced upward as if she spotted something on the ceiling. "Now where did I put that mistletoe?"

Nana wiped her hands on her apron and felt the thumbtacks she had put into her pocket. Before Granddaddy could begin another sentence, she was headed through the kitchen door. She walked into the dining room, knowing she'd taken the mistletoe out of the storage box but not remembering where she put it. Moving into the living room, she spotted it on the mantle above the fireplace. Fishing around in her apron pocket, she removed a thumbtack from the cardboard and proceeded to hang the mistletoe on the archway over the entrance of the front door.

"I bet you he's shy," Nana said, returning to the kitchen, going to the sink to wash off the sticky fruit-juice residue from her hands.

"Ain't nothing bashful about Clement, so stop making things up to keep yourself occupied 'cause your granddaughter ain't here," Granddaddy said, turning off the electric mixer so he could hear himself speak. "That's exactly what I mean about overcompensating. You've got two other grandchildren. I'm sure they'd appreciate your noticing them instead of mourning the missing." He unscrewed the cap to the Old Crow Kentucky Straight Bourbon Whiskey and poured it slowly into the mixture.

Nana knew her husband was right. She had to focus on what she had instead of what she lacked. It wasn't that she was missing herbs to make Clement pay more attention to Theola. She was missing her granddaughter, Faye. Her other granddaughter, Louise, still lived in Lemon City and would be bringing that fine young man Medford to Christmas dinner, and she was hoping to have a new addition to her clan. Her grandson Billy was her heart and Nana hoped his wife, Elvira, was doing everything possible to make her a great-grandmother, which would make her family expand even more. Yes. Everything was perfect, she thought to herself. She should think about her family growing and not diminishing. It was time to think about tomorrow instead of yesterday.

"Wouldn't it be nice if Medford proposed to Louise and gave her some karats for Christmas, and I don't mean the kind you eat?" Nana took the small hammer from her apron, held another hairy coconut shell firmly in place, and cracked it open.

"No, it wouldn't," said Granddaddy, stirring in the whipping cream. "They just started courtin' seriously last month. Don't rush things. It's bad luck, and Lord knows we don't need any more of that." He poured the egg whites into a separate bowl and started beating them until the peaks were stiff.

"At least that way," Nana added, "I'd have two of my grandchildren guaranteed to be here with me. Louise would stay because Medford wouldn't dare think of leaving Lemon City," she said with confidence. "And Billy ain't going nowhere 'cause he and Elvira are gonna have their babies born and raised right here." Nana's smile took over her face, thinking about the future. Then she mixed the ingredients in the ambrosia and with every movement of her arm, she increased her strokes as if the power she put behind the wooden spoon would help make the marriage proposal she had predicted and the grandbabies she wanted come true. "Don't you want to see your oldest granddaughter married?"

"Of course, I do," said Granddaddy. "But she's gotta see it first." He sprinkled nutmeg and cinnamon to his milky batch, then added a dash of anisette. Proud of the outcome of this year's holiday tradition, he poured himself a small glass to sample.

"They've been together practically every day since the storm," Nana confirmed. "That was before Thanksgiving."

"And that's a start," said Granddaddy. "Let's just wait and be patient and see how things turn out." He saved a small taste of eggnog for his wife and put the glass to her lips for her approval.

"But you know they've been secretly sweet on each other for years." Nana took a sip and frowned at the taste of whiskey. "Ever since she was little and he was a little bit older."

"That's the truth, and we know it. Let's just hope they realize it too." He licked a spot of eggnog off the corner of his wife's mouth, and that not only made her blush, but seemed to put her at ease.

Two women were on Medford's mind right now as he was driving along Route 23 behind the wheel of his 1972 black Ford Bronco, four-wheel-drive pickup truck alongside Clement on their way to the Dunlaps for Christmas dinner. They weighed so heavily on him that he didn't have enough energy to put together words and form them into sentences, and this had made him quiet lately, so quiet that he hadn't been himself. One woman he wouldn't know if she dropped out of the sky and landed at his feet; the other he knew all too well, and he was aware that she was beginning to think there was something not right between them. Even though he had been distant lately, the last thing he wanted was to send Louise the wrong message. Tomorrow he decided he would tell her what was on his mind, so she wouldn't think he was losing interest, or worse, seeing another woman. Tomorrow he'd tell her about the search for his mother and how he felt it was important to uncover the truth before he could ask for her hand in marriage so they could start their own family. Despite the fact he had only been dating Louise seriously for the past six weeks, he had known all along that she was the one for him. And now that he was on a serious, life-changing mission, he hoped the love of his life would understand. Certain the ad that he'd placed in today's *Lemon City Chronicle* would generate responses from the public about his birth mother, Medford was optimistic he'd get results fairly soon.

The wool turtleneck sweater he was wearing irritated his skin, making him itch. He slid his finger alongside his neck to scratch and realized he was rubbing his kidney-bean-shaped birthmark. It was the only place on his body that was a souvenir from his birth. It also happened to be the same spot on his body that was sensitive to Louise's touch. He always saw the irony in his birthmark, which he considered to be the one thing the two most important women in his life had in common because it was the point of intersection, like lines on a road map, the place where they connected, but would never meet.

In contrast to uncovering the mystery of his mother, Medford didn't feel the same passion to find his biological father. As Clement's adopted son ever since he could remember, there was no mistaking the man who'd saved his life and raised him like his own. Medford doubted his birth father could have done a better job than Clement. It was finding his mother that became a priority and the older he got, the more he was being consumed by curiosity. It haunted him to have no knowledge about the woman who had abandoned him forty-four years ago on Clement's porch. With every passing day, it became more and more an obsession.

Medford glanced at Clement. There was a thin white cloud swirling around his derby hat from the cherry pipe tobacco he was smoking. Clement had as many hats in his closet as a millinery, or at least as many hats as some women have shoes. His everyday hat was a porkpie, but he had an assortment of other headwear that included Panama hats, buckets, and fedoras. The way Medford saw it, Clement wasn't deliberately stylish. He was as bald as a rock on top of his head, with hair that clung like moss to the sides, giving his hairline a horseshoe kind of shape. The hats he wore were intended to cover his vanity and as Clement would be the first to say, his "head-toppings" also made him more appealing to the ladies, like sprinkles across a scoop of ice cream.

Taking a puff off his pipe, savoring the smell of his cherry tobacco, Clement blew smoke out of the crack of the opened window.

"I been noticing that you and that gal been seein' a lot of each other lately," he said, clenching his pipe between his teeth. "Seem like she's been enjoyin' herself being with you too." He waited for his son to add on to the conversation, but Medford continued driving as if he were alone in the car. "I know you been waitin' a long time for her to come 'round, had your eye on her since she was young . . . how old's she now? Twenty-six or so? If you ask me, that's just ripe for marryin'."

"Yes," agreed Medford, wincing at the age difference between him and Louise. "But please don't make me sound like I'm robbing the cradle."

"I don't mean it like that." Clement smiled at the response

from his son. "It's just, I see the way you two been lookin' at each other over the years. And at forty-four, you's old enough to get married. Matter of fact, son, you's old as hell. You been round long enough to be married and widow'erd and married again, if you ask me. Don't want people talkin' about you like you was your Uncle Bootsie."

Bootsie wasn't a blood relative, but since Clement and Bootsie had been friends since high school, he might as well be family deserving of the title.

"It doesn't bother me what people say," Medford added. "They're supposed to be minding their own business anyway."

"As you know, Bootsie sings in the Pursuit of Happiness Jubilee Choir. At least all your singin', as far as I know, is done in the shower."

"What's that supposed to mean?"

"Ain't 'spose to mean nothin'. You know Bootsie is like a brother to me . . ." He paused to take a puff on his pipe. "Just want to make sure you still like gals, is all." He slapped Medford on his knee, creating a reflex reaction that made it jerk against the steering wheel.

Medford looked at his father as if he were crazy. There were times when Medford thought he actually was.

"I know which way Bootsie likes the wind to blow, but I don't think he's decided on which direction to follow," Clement continued, pushing another stream of smoke out the window. "What I wanna know is why you been so quiet lately and what's goin' on with you."

"I just have something on my mind, that's all." Medford was hoping he didn't sound defensive. The last thing he wanted to do was hurt Clement's feelings. "I'm sure I'll bring it up some other time . . . later, when it's not Christmas . . . maybe tomorrow. But right now I just want to enjoy the holiday."

"Then tell your face it's enjoyin' the holiday, 'cause it looks like it's going to a funeral."

Medford finally forced his mouth into a smile, and Clement took another draw on his pipe, happy to get his son to talk even if it wasn't about the thing that was bothering him. Clement already knew, based on experience, that whenever a man was quiet, the silence usually had something to do with a woman.

With the eggnog chilling in the refrigerator, Granddaddy went upstairs to take a shower. While Nana was waiting for him to finish, she counted the number of boxed lemon desserts to make sure she had the right amount of gifts for her guests. Making a few trips, carrying the boxes to the living room, she organized them neatly under her fully decorated red spruce tree. As a final touch, she plugged the cord into the outlet and the lights came on, making her feel her tree was now completely dressed. She put the Nat King Cole Christmas album on the stereo and set the needle down easy, because it wouldn't feel like Christmas until she heard him sing "The Christmas Song."

Turning her head toward the fireplace, Nana looked at the stockings that were hanging and stuffed with smaller items, each embroidered with the names of her grandchildren: Billy and his wife Elvira, Louise, and Faye. Despite Faye's absence, Nana appreciated the memento of her granddaughter and held out hope that she might arrive home for a surprise visit.

Walking to the front of the house, Nana stood on the enclosed porch overlooking the snow-capped mountains that looked like their peaks had been dipped into Granddaddy's heavy whipping cream. The porch extended half the length of the house, with windows that gave her breathtaking views of the extraordinary beauty that lay before her. No matter how many times she stood in this position looking in the same direction, she never tired of the glorious scenery, and with the winter upon them and the dogwoods standing naked, she could see clear through the branches to the rambling mountain vistas. Land that God made that stood the test of time, that she could depend on being there every morning when she awoke, provided her with a sense of safety and security.

Yet she felt there was something slightly unsettling about this day as she stared at the Blue Ridge. The smell of tobacco was unusually heavy in the air, which was strange because the plantations had been long gone and it was winter. When she inhaled more deeply, she also detected a sweet smell trailing the pungent thickness, which was odd because there weren't any flowers in bloom. But there was no mistaking that the scent that lingered smelled like a combination of cured tobacco leaf and rose.

When Louise opened the door, Medford stood there greeting her with a smile that looked as if it had been painted on with a brush. Behind the grin she could tell he was withholding something, like a secret that was crumpled up on paper and tossed into a dark corner of a closet. As he leaned forward to kiss her, she grazed her lips against his, touching more air than skin.

"Is that all the Merry Christmas I get?" he asked, stepping into her living room.

"Don't worry, I've got your present right here." Louise picked up a shopping bag filled with gift-wrapped boxes and gestured toward one of the packages.

"That's not what I mean."

"It could get merrier later." She attempted a smile that rivaled his for phoniness. "That all depends on you." She grabbed her coat from across the arm of the couch.

"I've got something I need to tell you," said Medford.

"Speak," Louise said as if giving an order.

Medford put his arms around her, giving her the attention she deserved. "But I can't tell you now," he said. "It has to wait until tomorrow. It's too deep for Christmas conversation."

"Don't bother." Louise pulled away from his embrace. "It doesn't matter."

"Louise, what are you talking about?"

Medford looked confused, but Louise didn't care. "Come on . . . it's time to go," she said as politely as she could. "Nana's expecting us."

Chapter Two

It was raining on Interstate 64 as Jeremiah Richardson headed west in his 1964 white two-door six-cylinder Dodge Dart 270. Squinting through the windshield, the last thing he needed was for the temperature to drop so the roads would freeze. Those conditions would be disastrous for driving, he thought, and it could get worse if the rain in the mountains turned to snow. It was bad enough the law wasn't on his side, now he had to contend with the weather being against him as well. With Lemon City almost a hundred miles away, it wasn't the lack of sleep that was bothering him, it was making sure the same pair of headlights weren't on his tail for an extended period of time. It wasn't hunger making the growling noise in his belly either, it was the feeling of not knowing whether or not they'd make it safely to the mountains that was churning his stomach. Driving through the darkness and the pouring rain wasn't what he had in mind for Christmas Day, and he lit a Winston as if that would help him to see better. He heard some stirring behind him in the backseat, and the next thing he knew his nine-year-old sister's head sprang up like a jack-in-the-box.

"After Lemon City, then where are we going?" Ruby Rose asked, waking up from her nap. As the end of her question transitioned into a yawn, she flung one leg over the other and climbed into the front seat. "Why's it named after lemons anyway? That's a funny name for a town."

"A long time ago the people named the town after the color of their skin."

"Why? Were they yellow?" she posed as if she were afraid to ask the question, having a hard time seeing people's faces the same color as the crayon she used to fill in the sun in her coloring book.

"They were a mixture of three races, which made most of them light-skinned."

"Oh," said Ruby Rose, unsure of how that would occur, but willing to accept it as fact.

"We're only going to pass through Lemon City," Jeremiah explained. "That will give us some time for all the attention to blow over so we can throw the cops off our trail. If we stay put somewhere for a while, hopefully some of the heat will die down. Then we can drive north to Massachusetts." Jeremiah took a hit on his cigarette and blew out the smoke. "I hear that's where Dick Gregory plans to move."

"Who's that?"

"You haven't heard about Dick Gregory?" He glanced at his sister.

Ruby Rose shook her head.

"He's that famous comedian and civil rights activist who also ran for president in 1968, who's now thinking about buying a four-hundred-acre farm in Plymouth, Massachusetts." Jeremiah paused to make sure Ruby Rose had absorbed all that information. "I've come up with the perfect plan. Check it out." He took another hit off his cigarette. "With what I know of healing with herbs and crystals combined with Dick Gregory's knowledge of holistic nutrition, with any luck, maybe I could interest him in a deal and we could go into business together. How'd you like jumpin' into somethin' like that?" He looked in the rearview mirror, then returned his eyes to the road. "The other cool thing is Dick served in the Army too. Our paths never crossed in Vietnam, but that's something we also have in common." Glancing over his shoulder he could see his sister was sitting quietly, intrigued by the story, expecting to hear more. "I read somewhere in a newspaper that there are five houses on his property. If we play our cards right, maybe we could work something out, and he'd let us live in one of them."

"Are we gonna become farmers?"

"I guess that's what you might call us. You're not afraid of a little hard work and getting up early in the mornings, are you?"

"No." Ruby Rose wasn't completely convinced, but she thought it would make Jeremiah happy if she agreed. "Sounds like fun." Ruby Rose began humming the "Old MacDonald" song. A few minutes later, she interrupted herself. "What are healing herbs and crystals?" She wrinkled her forehead and pulled a string of yarn that was already unraveling on her glove to expose the tip of one of her fingers even more. After finding a pen on the floor, she began to draw a face on her finger to make a puppet person. "How can you heal with rocks?"

"I'll explain all that to you later." Jeremiah was wondering how long it would take her to ask that question. "I'm gonna stop the car and pull over on the side of the road in a little while, so we can eat. I'll show you then."

Ruby Rose continued humming the "Old MacDonald" song, making her puppet person dance to the tune.

Putting out his cigarette, Jeremiah thought how great it was to finally be reunited with his sister. Driving along Interstate 64 in the pouring rain as the windshield wipers moaned and struggled to clear his view, he started seeing pieces of his family, broken into fragments, and thought about how there was nothing he could have done to put it back together.

Jeremiah and Ruby Rose had never really lived together. They had the same mother, but different fathers. Their mother died four years ago, the same year Jeremiah turned eighteen and got caught in the tail end of the draft and sent to the United States Army and shipped out to Vietnam. He arrived in the jungle just before Cambodia was invaded and the National Guardsmen opened fire, killing four young people at Kent State in Ohio and two at Jackson State in Mississippi. Two years was all he served, because he developed an arrhythmia and temporary hand paralysis that no one could explain, other than by exposure to napalm. But Jeremiah didn't recall being near that chemical and the cause of his infliction remained undiagnosed. However, receiving this unfortunate news from the doctor in the infirmary wasn't all bad. After losing over half of the brothers in his infantry, being spared from front-line combat actually gave him back his life. He was assigned to nonactive duty in the pharmacy, where he learned about medicine. But it was the herbs that he researched and experimented with, like the chicory he ate to steady the beating of his heart and the snakeroot tea he drank to shrink the tumor that the doctors finally located against his spine, that provided his cure. Unlike his prescription medicine, which constantly made him vomit, the herbs had no side effects. Ultimately they made his heart grow

stronger and gave him back the use of his hands. When he finished his tour of duty, the Army discharged him shortly after he
turned twenty in 1972, the year the B-52s bombed Hanoi and
Haiphong, around the same time the President started withdrawing the troops from Vietnam and conversations for a cease-fire
and peace talks began. That was when he wound up in Mattoxville, Virginia, outside Portsmouth, and Dr. Handy gave him a
job.

It wasn't purely coincidence that brought him to Mattoxville.
After his mother passed away, he called neighbors from his hometown in Livingston, who said that his sister had been taken away
by a social worker and transported two hundred miles to Mattoxville. Jeremiah was hoping that Ruby Rose would still be there.

It was a good thing he got a job with Dr. Handy, because it was
time well spent. The older man, who appeared to be fiftyish but
could have been in his early seventies for all Jeremiah knew, was
conservative-looking for his nontraditional and unconventional
ways. He was a licensed physician, as well as a self-proclaimed
doctor of life who had the amazing ability to fix, cure, and heal
with or without prescription medicine. As the proprietor of the
drugstore on Old Kings Street and Main, Dr. Handy taught Jeremiah, who already had some knowledge of herbs, to heal with organic materials, such as crystals and precious stones. Between the
Army and Dr. Handy, Jeremiah learned a variety of survival skills
ranging from living in the wilderness to executing renegade rescue
prisoner-of-war missions, from reducing severe arthritis pain to
caring for the maimed and critically wounded. One thing he
hadn't learned, however, was how to escape the law and avoid becoming a felon on the FBI Most Wanted List, but he was always
up for mastering a new trick and taking on a new challenge.

It was also at Dr. Handy's where Jeremiah learned about Ruby

Rose. One day a woman was talking so loudly to her friend while he was filling a prescription that he couldn't help but overhear the conversation. He heard a lady describe how she felt sorry for a young girl about nine years old who was as cute as a button with honey-brown pigtails and tiny polka-dotted freckles who was living with a foster parent who was questionable. According to the woman, the foster parent probably treated that child the way she would kick around a mangy homeless dog if she had one. Not that one had anything to do with the other, she added, but she believed that the way people took care of their pets was an indication of how they provided for their own. Jeremiah knew it was a long shot, but the girl fit the description of what he remembered about his sister and was about the age Ruby Rose would be. When he heard the woman mention Miss Molly Esther Reynolds as the kind of example that gave foster parenting a bad name, he went straight to the telephone book. When he flipped through the pages, almost immediately he found an M. E. Reynolds on Chickahominy Road.

After surveying the house for several months, he didn't like what he saw, and knew it was only a matter of time before he'd rescue his sister from the prison the state called a home.

"Are we almost there yet?" Ruby Rose squinted her eyes to see through the rain, sliding against the window to identify anything recognizable on the interstate.

"Almost."

Turning to Jeremiah's profile, she asked, "What took you so long?" She made her hands climb one over the other as if they were stepping up an invisible ladder, her bare fingers touching through tattered gloves.

"I wish I could have come sooner," Jeremiah said, keeping his

eyes on the road. "But I had to wait for the right time to get you."
He glanced at Ruby Rose, who turned her head toward the window and wiped her face with her sleeve.

"Trust me, I tried to adopt you legally, but I had just turned eighteen and the courts wouldn't let me do it without a proper home and decent-paying job with health benefits. Then I went into the Army for two years. When I got out, it took just as much time to realize I wasn't going to get help from the stupid system to gain legal custody. Confidentiality laws made it impossible for me to get the documents I needed to make a case to become your legal guardian. Then I found out that when Mama knew she was sick, she signed papers that released you to state authorities, which meant I no longer had any legal rights to claim you as my sister. With Mama dead and the fact that we have different fathers, we might as well have been total strangers in the eyes of the law. The fact that we were once a family had been taken away by the state, and I'm just as likely as any real kidnapper to go to jail because taking you from Miss Molly Esther Reynolds is considered a crime. Yet I had no choice but to steal you away." He glanced at his sister, who wiped her face again with the back of her sleeve. "And now you're stolen state property, and I'm stuck with you." Jeremiah chuckled, hoping to make his sister smile, but she wasn't in the mood. "We'll have to stay undercover for a while," Jeremiah said seriously. "But it's worth it, since the only people we have in this world are each other."

He wished he could think of something to say to make her feel better. "Are you up for an adventure?"

Ruby Rose didn't answer right away; the lump in her throat was still there and she couldn't stop her bottom lip from quivering. But after a while she turned to face her brother and hugged him as best as she could without making him swerve the car in the road and change lanes and get into an accident.

"I know how to play that song on the piano," she said, turning her attention to the radio as if her fresh new start in life required a whole new subject.

"What song?" Jeremiah asked, relieved she was returning to good spirits.

" 'You Are the Sunshine of My Life,' by Stevie Wonder," she said, pointing to the radio.

"*You* are," Jeremiah smiled and winked.

"No. *You* are," Ruby Rose countered, playing the game.

"No. *You* are." Jeremiah elbowed her in the ribs.

"I said it first." Ruby Rose poked him on the side of his stomach.

"So what. I said it second. Plus, I'm bigger than you," Jeremiah added, jabbing her back with his finger.

"If you're lucky, maybe I'll play it for you on the piano one day."

"You can actually play the piano?" Jeremiah caught himself sounding surprised. "Quit jivin', girl. You any good?"

She fluttered her fingers along imaginary keys, playing make-believe scales. "I'm already in the *John Thompson's Modern Course for the Piano Fifth Grade Book.* I bet I could be in a recital soon, if I practiced . . . if I had the chance . . . if I continued playing." When she turned to the window, her words drifted into the glass.

"Let's try to make that happen," Jeremiah said. "That's one thing about the future . . . you never know what to expect. So let's hope that when it gets here, it offers nothing but the best."

"Do you think what's-his-name . . ." Ruby Rose tried to remember, and then as if a lightbulb went off in her head, "Dick Gregory has a piano?"

"If he doesn't have a piano you can play *on*, I know he's got lots of kids you can play *with*."

Ruby Rose crossed her fingers and her legs and her arms. The past four years had been the worst time of her life, and the period before that hadn't been exactly fun either.

Sitting in the front seat next to her brother, Ruby Rose's thoughts drifted to their mother. When Mama wasn't drunk and passed out, or high on whatever kind of drug was convenient and affordable at the moment, she'd tell Ruby Rose stories that would make her laugh, especially the one of how she got her name. This would usually occur around bedtime, when her mother felt guilty about one thing or another, like opening up a can of vegetables and serving them for dinner cold. Or because her mother thought it would help relieve the pain from the slap she'd received when she refused to call one of her mother's many boyfriends "uncle." Then Ruby Rose's mother would playfully pull her to the couch and wrap her arms around her. The story would always start the same way: "I named you Ruby Rose because the day you came into the world, your lips were pink, your cheeks were flush, and your hair looked like amber wheat kissed by the sun. Your birthstone was a ruby, because you were born on the seventh of July. And I could tell by the freckles that were mere buds on your face that you'd have a beautiful reddish tint to your skin. With the way your little fists were balled up tight and waving back and forth, I could see you'd have a spirit as intense as fire. And when I put my nose against your little neck, I smelled a soul as fresh and as sweet as a rose in full bloom. Since you were such a cute little ruby-red gem, when the doctor asked me what I was going to name you, I told him I would call you Ruby Rose." Then, in one of those rare moments when her mother was actually loving and fun, she tickled Ruby Rose, who laughed and laughed, forgetting about her hunger or her pain. That was one of only a few good memories that Ruby Rose had of (*their*) mother. The others she tried to push back into the shadows of her mind.

Jeremiah hardly ever came to visit Ruby Rose when she lived

with Mama. He didn't like Mama taking all those pills, smoking those rolled-up cigarettes without white-tip filters that didn't smell like Salems. He didn't like her drinking and staying out late at night, being with all those different men. Ruby Rose didn't like it much either, but since Jeremiah was fifteen years her senior and ran away from home as soon as he was old enough to read a map, he didn't have to put up with their mother's unscrupulous, unpredictable ways. He didn't even come to see their mother when a handful of strangers from the Faith Redemption Ministries said a prayer, cremated her, and put her in a cardboard box that was buried in Potter's Field.

Little did Ruby Rose know that the sadness was just beginning. The day the child-welfare lady came, and led her by the hand to her 1960 eight cylinder four-door hardtop Oldsmobile sedan, Ruby Rose started sobbing so hard that she couldn't wipe the snot away fast enough.

By the time she arrived to mean Miss Molly Esther Reynolds' house in Mattoxville, Ruby Rose had changed. She had grown up on the car ride that took her two hundred miles away from her home in Livingston. Mama had given her no choice but to leave her childhood behind.

Standing at the top of the stairs with her arms outstretched like a lifeguard come to rescue someone drowning in deep water, Miss Molly Esther Reynolds was all fancy in clean clothes, with a smile that had been pressed on with an iron. When Ruby Rose went inside the house, she could tell Miss Molly Esther wasn't used to having children around. There wasn't a single toy in sight and everything was perfect in its place. The sofa and chairs were covered in stiff plastic and lots of porcelain knickknacks were perfectly arranged on glass coffee and end tables. There wasn't any noise in the house either—no laughter, no music, and no TV. Ruby Rose doubted that the phone even rang often. Trusting her senses, she took what she saw as a warning that she should watch her step around this stranger whom she hoped wouldn't ask to be called "Mother."

For two months everything was fine with Miss Molly Esther, until one day Ruby Rose's stomach started hurting at school and she came home without an appetite. When she couldn't finish her dinner, Miss Molly Esther threw a fit complete with foam forming in the creases of her mouth. Ruby Rose told her she had a stomachache, but Miss Molly Esther didn't listen and didn't care, saying there was a huge famine in West Africa with starving children eating leaves and roots of trees. These children would give their right arm for real food; then she added that Ruby Rose was gonna eat those peas one by one until her plate was clean. Ruby Rose wished she could mail her peas to the hungry children in West Africa, along with a few other meals Miss Molly cooked. She forced down one more pea and couldn't help it because it was too late, her stomach had already revolted, and she heaved back and hurled a stream of green all over Miss Molly. The next thing Ruby Rose knew she was sitting in a chair in the corner, facing the wall for the rest of the night.

After the upset-stomach incident, things got worse. When she came home from school, Miss Molly would make Ruby Rose clean the floors and scrub toilets. Ruby Rose spent so much time on her knees that her skin became raw and began to bleed. Miss Molly Esther was careful to cover Ruby Rose's knees with bandages. When the neighbors asked about the gauze that was wrapped with adhesive tape around her legs, Miss Molly Esther would laugh and say, "This is the fallingest child I ever did see, so clumsy this one is. I think she's better off just sitting still in a chair." Some days Ruby Rose thought she was better off alone; other days she thought she'd be better off dead. Regardless, she didn't understand how someone who carried a Bible to religious study and sang in the church choir on Monday nights could be so cruel. If one night wasn't enough, Ruby Rose concluded, probably Miss Molly should go see God every day of the week.

Sometimes Miss Molly Esther would take a break from herself and be nice. Thankfully that would happen for long stretches at a time—for about six months to a year. But then her eyes would get wild, her laugh would turn into a snort, and her eyebrows would connect into one hideous bushy line, and Ruby Rose knew she would get extreme punishment whether she did something wrong or not.

Ruby Rose couldn't wait until she got old enough to punch Miss Molly Esther in the face and snatch off her wig, and run away. However, before Ruby Rose had a chance to seek revenge, Jeremiah had shown up at the back door to help her make her escape.

For four years, Ruby Rose had tried to break out of the prison the state made her call home. Besides the time living with Mama, it was the hardest sentence of her life.

Peering at Jeremiah out of the corner of her eye, she decided she liked having her big brother around and didn't want to let him out of her sight.

Early in the afternoon, Jeremiah turned off the interstate onto a dirt road and put the car into "park." Opening the trunk, he grabbed a few sandwiches and a can opener for the corned beef hash and baked beans. He handed the late lunch to Ruby Rose, then went back for the plates, utensils, Thermos, and cups.

When he and Ruby Rose finished their picnic, Jeremiah carefully put all the trash in a garbage bag. Walking around the car, he inspected the ground to make sure he wouldn't be leaving any evidence of their presence behind. He threw the remains from lunch into the trunk, then searched around for his backpack. When he found it, he removed the wooden box and got back into the driver's seat.

"Ruby Rose, take a look." Jeremiah opened the wooden box to reveal pouches made of soft yellow cloth with sharp edges bulging from the fabric. "These are the healing herbs and crystals I mentioned. These are what I refer to as my 'small bags of miracles.' "

As he opened one of the bags, Ruby Rose's eyes widened when she saw the sparkle.

"Gracious day!" she exclaimed, taking a few crystals from his hand. "These are the prettiest rocks I've ever seen." She held the stones toward the ceiling to admire the brightly colored glass even more.

"They're called crystals." Jeremiah emptied the contents of the pouch onto a cloth he had draped over his hand.

"They look like you just found them in a treasure chest," Ruby Rose said, with her jaw dropping at the sight of the gleaming gemstones.

"Well, I'm not a pirate, that's for sure." Jeremiah smiled. "I use these for healing." He removed another pouch. "And these are medicinal herbs." He handed her the *grobus benzoin,* to give her a quick lesson. "The popular name for this herb is jumbo bush. It makes hair and fingernails grow, sort of like gelatin does." He put the pouch underneath her nose so she could not only learn to see the difference between the herbs, but know that each had its own distinctive smell.

"Smells like black licorice," said Ruby Rose. "It makes me want some candy."

Jeremiah handed her another pouch. "And this here is snake-root."

Ruby Rose caught a whiff of the contents of the pouch even before Jeremiah opened it, and she pulled back as if she were about to come into contact with rancid trash. Not only was the odor strong, but thinking about the name of the herb she wasn't completely certain there wasn't a snake slithering somewhere inside the bag.

"Whew. That stinks." Ruby Rose fanned the putrid air away from the pouch.

"Snakeroot is one of the most potent herbs of all. It's got properties similar to penicillin." Jeremiah handed Ruby Rose the pouch. She pinched her nose as if she were caught in the crossfire between two skunks.

"Even though it smells bad, this herb is pretty amazing. It can treat anything from asthma to respiratory infections." Then he presented her with another pouch. "And this is prickly ash. It relieves toothaches." He paused long enough for her to examine the plants, then added, "These are only a few of my herbs. I have dozens more inside my backpack and never leave home without them."

Ruby Rose was quite impressed with her brother, but his introductory lesson to crystals and herbs didn't compare to the presentation that was about to happen next.

"And this, my lovely lady, is for you. Merry Christmas."

She watched as Jeremiah leaned over to put a fourteen-karat gold chain with a ruby pendant around her neck. No one had ever given her anything this precious and valuable before.

"I've been waiting to give this to you for a long time."

Ruby Rose stammered, the words having trouble passing through her throat, tears forming in her eyes. "But . . . but I . . . I didn't get you anything."

"You didn't know that you would see me," Jeremiah offered. "You don't need to get me a gift," he added. "Besides, just being with you is Christmas present enough."

Ruby Rose decided at that moment that wherever she and Jeremiah wound up wouldn't matter as long as they were together.

There was no hell worse than living with Miss Molly Esther Reynolds. She had a raised burn mark on her arm that had turned into a darkened keloid to prove it.

Jeremiah returned his gemstones to the trunk and jumped back into the car, anxious to get back on the road. He turned the key in the ignition, but nothing happened. He tried starting up the car again and the 1964 Dodge Dart let out some loud knocks followed by a sickly sputter. Looking at Ruby Rose, Jeremiah took in a deep breath and let it out. Pumping the accelerator this time, he turned the key, held it firmly in place, and the car finally turned over, but not quietly. The loud knocking noise that sounded like a pipe banging against metal began again, and the more he pressed down on the gas pedal, the louder it got. He shifted the gear into "drive" and the car moved forward, then jerked to a stop. Frustrated, he pounded his hand against the steering wheel and muttered to himself. The only thing that prevented him from yelling out curses was the sight of his sister.

"Uh-oh," Ruby Rose said, recognizing the sound of trouble.

"Let's just sit and wait a few minutes," Jeremiah offered, trying to relax. "She's been driving for a long time," he said, patting the steering wheel, attempting a more gentle approach. "She isn't ready to get back on the road just yet." He leaned into the seat and placed his hands behind his head. "It's a chance for us to take a nap. Let's relax and close our eyes for a minute."

But Jeremiah and Ruby Rose couldn't sit still long enough to rest. In less than a minute, Jeremiah lurched forward and turned the key, and Ruby Rose sat upright, anxious to learn what would happen next. Finally the car started and they were on their way, driving west again on Interstate 64. Jeremiah couldn't remember when the knocking noise had stopped, but he noticed his gas was low and it was time to fill up his tank. He spotted the familiar dinosaur through the trees and was glad to know there was a Sinclair station up ahead. Because of the nationwide gas shortage, he prayed the prices wouldn't be too high and the lines too long. He had seen signs along the interstate as high as one dollar and twenty cents per gallon when it had been only thirty cents about a year ago, and just last week he had waited over an hour at an Esso station. But since it was Christmas Day, maybe he wouldn't have to worry. Hopefully most people would be at home, celebrating with their families.

Chapter Three

The doorbell rang. Nana patted her hair into place, straightened her festive new red dress with mistletoe print, and smoothed down her white lace collar with matching lace attached to the sleeves that looked like doilies wrapped around her wrists. When she opened the door, there stood Billy and Elvira.

"Merry Christmas," Nana said, throwing her arms open wide as a mountain gap for a big hug and kiss.

"Merry Christmas," Billy and Elvira replied.

"Oh, good. We're the first to arrive," said Elvira, stepping into the room, placing bags filled with gifts by the tree. "Nana, do you need any help?"

Billy slid his wife's coat off her shoulders and hung it in the closet.

"You can take the crystal cups out of the china cabinet and set them on the table for Granddaddy's eggnog," said Nana. Admiring Billy in his double-breasted charcoal knit suit, she added, "Looking mighty handsome today. It's real nice to see you out of uniform."

"Thank you, Ma'am. You're kinda fly yourself," Billy teased as he jokingly eyed his grandmother up and down like he would a young woman if he were single.

". . . And Elvira." Nana didn't want to leave her granddaughter-in-law out of the conversation. "That's a cute dress you're wearing, dear . . . very festive . . . red, the color of passion." Nana winked, as she usually did when hinting at what Elvira needed to do or to wear to make a baby. Elvira was a big woman, but she wasn't fat. She was solid like bedrock yet had curves in all the right places, like a bluebell in early spring.

Elvira smiled wearily as she distributed gifts under the tree.

"Where's Granddaddy?" Billy asked, starting toward the kitchen.

"Here I am. I'm just stirring up the eggnog so that it stays good and fresh. Y'all ready to have some?"

"Yes, sir," said Billy. "I've been waiting for this all day." He rubbed his hands together with anticipation. "In fact, I've been saving a taste for this eggnog since last Christmas."

The doorbell rang. This time it was Clement, Medford, and Louise at the door. After an exchange of holiday greetings, the first thing Nana noticed was that the oversized, neatly wrapped gift Medford was holding was way too big for a tiny diamond ring, and the second thing was that her granddaughter was inappropriately dressed for the occasion. Because both matters required her immediate undivided attention, she was torn. Thinking quickly, she concluded that Medford was a smart man and there was probably a smaller box inside the one he was carrying. Inside that box, there was probably another box that was smaller still, and so on, and so on, all the way down to the tiny diamond-ring-sized box just waiting to be revealed. Of course he couldn't possibly let on to Louise that he was carrying something small; that would be a dead giveaway, Nana thought to herself. He'd have to trick Louise so she'd be pleasantly surprised. "Medford, just put that present underneath the tree along with the rest of the gifts." Then she smiled at him much longer than she should have, which she could tell made him feel uncomfortable.

While Medford placed his gift underneath the tree, and Clement found Granddaddy drinking eggnog, Nana pulled Louise aside.

"Girl, what you got on there?" Nana pointed at Louise's slacks and turtleneck, talking in a sharp whisper. "Why didn't you put on something nice for Christmas? This is a special day. You don't want to walk up in here like you going to work."

Louise tried to respond, but Nana wouldn't let her.

"I raised you better. How you 'spect to get a husband looking like this?" Nana tried to keep her voice down, but it started going up, and when Medford looked in her direction, she calmed herself, nodded, and smiled.

"What's wrong with the way I'm dressed?" Louise defended.

"Come on back here tomorrow so I can give you something," demanded Nana.

"Give me what?" Louise asked. "Money to go shopping?"

"No. I ain't giving you no money," Nana said, as if her granddaughter had turned into a fool. "I'm not gonna talk about it right now; we got company."

"Nana, you can't be serious."

"Serious as the stroke you're gonna give me if you don't see that Medford is the right man for you and you better start acting like it."

"Where is everybody?" asked Louise to no one in particular, in an effort to escape her grandmother. "I'm starving." She politely excused herself to join everyone in the dining room gathered around the eggnog bowl. Louise was relieved when the doorbell rang and Nana had to redirect her attention.

When Nana opened the door, in walked Vernelle, Theola, and

Sadie, Nana's friends, members of the Auxiliary Committee of the Ladies of Mt. Zion Baptist Church. They all greeted each other with the enthusiasm of women who hadn't seen each other in years, even though they had just been together in their quilting club the day before.

Vernelle Hopkins was the shortest of the three women and as fate would have it, she also happened to have the smallest voice and the least to say. Some folks suspected it was because she was overrun by her husband, Rufus, who had a voice as loud as thunder, making it hard for Vernelle to get a word in without shouting up a storm. After giving herself migraine headaches from trying to have regular conversations with him, she gradually became more quiet over time, until one day she felt like she hardly needed to make her presence known at all because Rufus had enough volume to represent them both. Vernelle already had religion but it got to the point where she joined the Ladies of Mt. Zion Baptist Church just to have her own friends to talk to, which made the time she spent with her husband less frequent. The only time she didn't mind him yelling was when they were in bed together and the level of his voice became a barometer of his pleasure. But today Rufus was at home sick in bed. Normally he spent Christmas Day at the church serving the elderly, but this year he had opened his mouth too wide and a flu bug must have flown in. Vernelle had given him a chest rub made of a combination of whiskey, lemon, and turpentine, which made his condition improve. He was at home, just getting over the chills, well enough for Vernelle to feel it was okay to leave him alone. Before she left the house, she promised to fix him a plate from Ernestine's since he was at the point in his illness where he could actually appreciate and keep down his food.

As Vernelle waddled over to the eggnog, she heard Nana complimenting Theola on the fine outfit she was wearing. Then she saw Nana throw her eyes in the direction of Clement just in time to catch Theola blushing like a sixteen-year-old.

Theola Dempsey was the tallest of the three women and just the opposite of Vernelle when it came to talking. Theola's husband died in May 1968, a month after the death of Martin Luther King, Jr. Theola thought it was the assassination that killed her beloved, but the townspeople felt that she had talked him to death. Theola had an answer for everything, including why she was having a hard time winning Clement's affections. She would say he was "crotchety," and while to most people that meant "cranky," to Theola it meant he needed some crotch to even out his temperament and hers was available. Many townspeople suspected that Clement couldn't be with Theola because he'd rather die of natural causes or from consumption than be assaulted by an attack of words. What Theola had going for her was her beauty. She had long, wiry hair that would challenge a wide-toothed comb, a modest nose, and a broad mouth with thick lips that people specifically attributed to being the motivation for her talking. She was born with a shock of white hair stemming from the crown of her head, making a thin trail all the way past the nape of her neck. It had always been a source of teasing when she was a little girl, being called "skunk" more times than she could remember. But her mother told her to tell the children that her hair had been dipped in glory and baptized with light in the name of the Lord, and that seemed to get them to stop teasing her for a while, and it made her feel special. Nowadays when people looked at her and stared above her eyes, she took for granted that they might be thinking something but knew to keep their comments to themselves. What helped Theola age gracefully was following the exercise program on TV in the mornings and making her bicycle her primary means of transportation in the afternoons, weather permitting. Her looks usually attracted a variety of men, but the only one she wanted was Clement. When Nana told Theola to help herself to eggnog and her friend went off to follow her suggestion, she couldn't help but think that the white streak running through Theola's hair reminded her of the white line drawn down the middle of a tar-paved road.

As Nana helped Sadie take off her coat, she nodded in the direction of the piano, letting Sadie know she was welcome to make herself at home.

Sadie Washington was descended from one of Lemon City's five Founding Fathers. Coming from a long line of religious leaders, she was dedicated to the church. In a way, Sadie was a woman ahead of her time, hanging on to her maiden name even after her marriage to Dugga Junior Dowdy in 1930. As much as she loved her husband, she refused to have a surname that reinforced her body type and frame. She was also a widow, but unlike Theola, she'd been happily married for thirty-six years. Despite being quick to keep the name she was born with, Sadie Washington was basically slow. Not slow thinking, but not quick or up to speed at anything else, either. And it didn't seem as if it was always her fault that she was usually left behind.

No matter the circumstances, it seemed instead of *taking* time; Sadie was always *dragging* time along with her. Even menopause for Sadie was ten years late. When most of her friends had finished "the change of life," she was just starting. Because of her hot flashes, Sadie always traveled with her church fan so she could wave it over any part of her body as needed, and was constantly pulling her clothes away from her as if she were afraid the fabric would melt her skin. The only part of Sadie that didn't move slowly was her fingers, which graced the piano keys swiftly and with such dexterity that it seemed as if her hands belonged to someone else.

Nana hung up Sadie's coat and when she turned around, her

friend had pulled out her blouse like a tent and was flapping it like she was airing out sheets so air could circulate and dry out her bosoms.

"Now we're just waiting on Bootsie and Ole Miss Johnson," said Nana. "Go on inside and enjoy some eggnog while I try to organize this tree."

As Nana was arranging gifts underneath the Christmas tree, she listened while her guests made polite conversation.

"I don't know what started this whole dern gas shortage in the first place," said Clement, biting into one of Nana's deviled eggs. "It's a pain in the butt if you ask me."

"It was the Arab nations that imposed the oil embargo," replied Granddaddy, pacing himself on his eggnog. "They call that oil group OPEC. It stands for Organization of the Petroleum Exporting Countries. Betcha didn't know that."

"What do those people way over there have to do with us anyway?" Clement asked, wiping his mouth with a napkin, shaking his head.

"It's where we get a lot of our oil," said Louise, looking at Medford without smiling. "Oil is the lifeblood of any industrialized country. It's almost impossible to function without it, unlike other entities that can exist on their own." In her own way, Louise wanted Medford to know that she would be fine by herself.

"Well, let's get it from someplace else," said Theola, trying to get Clement's attention by joining in the conversation. "Don't they have oil up there in Alaska? Some down there in Texas?"

Clement looked at Theola and made the sides of his eyes turn up instead of his mouth, as if he was squinting at something that bothered his vision.

"All I know is I can't take those long lines anymore," complained Elvira. "It cost almost twenty dollars to fill up that tank in that big old school bus. Not only that, sometimes I have to wait as long as an hour before I can even get close to the pumps."

Elvira had a way of going on and on with her stories like a leaky faucet that had no way to turn off the drip. Sometimes she even got her tales twisted into knots and while in conversations, whether in person or on the phone, had to write things down to keep the details straight. Exaggeration was beyond her control, but because everyone knew she was well intended, they gave her their patience and undivided attention. "I remember one time I forgot to get gas and I had all my kids in the bus on my way to take them home," Elvira continued, shaking her head. "And I was in that line and oooh, golly, goodness, gracious . . . those kids couldn't sit still if I strapped them into their seats and chile, finally I just had to let them out the bus so they could run around along the side of the road—out of the way of traffic, of course." She took a breath as if she was exhausted recalling the incident. "I will never take them with me again. Next time I get gas for that big old bus I'm going first thing in the morning, by myself, before I pick up any kids. Whooo-we . . . getting gas was really somethin'. I think it would be easier digging for gold in Nana's tomato garden." Elvira had the kind of laugh that made other people follow.

"Now they're talking about getting gas on odd and even days," said Medford, finally able to get a word in.

"What does that mean?" asked Vernelle softly.

"Excuse me?" asked Medford, unable to hear.

Billy was sitting next to Vernelle and explained. "That means that if your license plate number ends with an odd number you can go to the gas station every other day. And the people who have even-number plates get to go and get gas on alternate days."

"And I just heard they're asking for gas stations to voluntarily close down on Sundays," said Granddaddy.

"Now you're talking. That's a good thing," said Sadie. "Maybe it'll get more people in church."

"Guess I sold the Shop right in the nick of time," Granddaddy added. "Who would want to be involved with all of this mess?"

The Shop was the car repair and gas station that Granddaddy had bought for Faye's husband Harry when they got married. He thought he was doing Harry a favor by setting him up with his own business, but when Harry turned out to be bad news and turned up dead one day, Granddaddy had no reason to hold on to the Shop and got rid of it quicker than he would a lighted stick of dynamite. He sold it to the first person who gave him half the down payment in cash.

"Got that right, Granddaddy," said Louise. "The other thing they want us to do is keep the thermostats down low to conserve energy."

"Ain't that a blip. Not during these mountain winters," said Theola, sucking her teeth, throwing her arms around herself, pretending to keep warm, hoping that Clement would get the hint to wrap his arms around her too. Clement glanced in her direction, then lowered his eyes to the floor.

"It's all part of the President's conservation plan," continued Louise.

"The only part that makes me happy is that daylight-savings time happens all year 'round now to save fuel," said Granddaddy.

Everyone smiled and cheered and saluted with their eggnog, nodding their heads in approval.

Bending under the tree, Nana happened to glance toward the front door to see Billy and Elvira talking while standing under the mistletoe. She stood up and yelled out, "Kiss, kiss!" and they did. Later, when Louise and Medford happened to be near the mistletoe, she shouted out, "Kiss, kiss!" They hesitated a moment before they made their lips finally meet, and Nana picked up immediately that something else was terribly wrong beyond the way her granddaughter was dressed.

To get into the kissing game, Theola meandered underneath the mistletoe while Sadie prepared to sit down at the piano. As Sadie began to play "Silent Night," Theola pretended to be listening to the song while shooting glances of encouragement at Clement.

Clement turned away and started up with Granddaddy.

"Willie, who you think is gonna be in the Super Bowl this year?" Clement asked, feeling Theola's eyes on him.

"I'm not normally a betting man." Granddaddy usually said this before he was about to make a wager. "But if I were, I'd put my money on the Dolphins. They lost to Dallas last year, but they showed the Redskins a thing or two, and I betcha they're hungry for another taste of trophy."

"The Vikings got themselves a good appetite too," chimed in Billy, easing into the La-Z-Boy, pushing the arms forward to make the leg rest come up so he could take the pressure off his bad knee. "Tarkenton's been doing a mean job quarterbacking this season."

"Yeah, but Miami's got a tough defense, which will make it hard for the Vikings to break through," said Louise. When it came to current events, especially sports, Louise made a point of being as knowledgeable as the men. She couldn't help herself. It was a natural feminist reaction.

"I'll tell you this," said Clement. "If Miami gets to the Super Bowl, they'll rip the Minnesota front line to shreds."

"In that case, it don't matter how much better Tarkenton is getting; he ain't got a chance." Billy finished his eggnog, then rested his cup on the arm of the chair.

"All this talk going on," Granddaddy said, still standing, holding the pitcher of eggnog, giving his grandson a refill. "I wanna know if y'all mean what you say. Who's willing to bet that these two teams will be in the Super Bowl in the first place? I'm a nice guy, but I'm willing to take your money." Granddaddy paused, staring down at his fellow football fans. "Anyone just want to bet on the Dolphins making it to the Super Bowl?"

Billy and Louise shook their heads.

"Nah, Granddaddy," said Billy. "I just spent all my money on Christmas."

"Me too," Louise added.

"All I got to spend are words," said Clement, putting his hands inside his pockets. "Money is something I keep to myself."

The doorbell rang and Bootsie walked in with Ole Miss Johnson trailing behind. While Bootsie had been in the house just last week, Ole Miss Johnson hadn't been under the Dunlap roof in over thirty years, even though she lived right next door. It seemed as if everyone stopped what they were doing to take in the spectacle of the fragile old lady emerging on foreign soil, which was as strange as witnessing concrete floating on water or seeing a mayfly in June. Judging by the quiet in the room, after welcoming her guests, Nana thought it was a good time to sit down to eat.

Once everyone was seated, Granddaddy folded his hands and said grace: "Dear Lord, thank you for bringing this family and their good friends together." He squinted through one eye at Ole Miss Johnson. "Bless the food before us on this Christmas Day, and the fact that we don't have to deal with Outsiders anymore. Amen."

Granddaddy's sensitivity to Outsiders increased about two years ago when his youngest grandchild, Faye, married one and all hell broke loose. Faye's husband, Harry, had brought more problems with him than horseflies swarming around cow manure, and one day he turned up dead. His demise created even more chaos because Granddaddy and his family were under house arrest, considered suspects in Harry's murder. Everyone at the table knew what Granddaddy was talking about as far as Outsiders were concerned. If another Outsider never showed up on his doorstep, it would probably be too soon.

When the clamor of sterling silver utensils against porcelain serving bowls, platters, and plates began, Louise launched into conversation. "Have y'all heard of the NBFO?" she asked, looking at Vernelle, who was the most likely to be on top of women's and health issues. Everyone at the table seemed to quiet down in order to hear Vernelle speak.

Vernelle was a midwife who had birthed many healthy Lemon City babies. She had big, steady hands, and her arms looked as though they could extend through a long, dark tunnel and grab whatever was on the other side.

"Can't say I have," said Vernelle, reaching for the salt and pepper. "What's that stand for?"

After hearing her response, the clatter at the dinner table returned to normal.

"Does it stand for New Brotherhood For Officers?" Billy offered. "For some kinda new police organization?" He stretched out his leg and the joint was so stiff that it popped on cue, as if adding punctuation to his sentence.

"It stands for . . ." Louise didn't get a chance to finish her statement.

"No, no . . . don't tell me," Billy interrupted. "Let me guess." Then he turned to his grandmother. "What you think, Nana? New Bread From Oven . . . Nothing But Fresh Olives."

"Billy, quit acting stupid," said Louise, giving him a disgusted look.

"Wait a minute. I'm not done."

"Yes you are," Louise replied.

"Medford, this one is for you, brother. "What about . . . New Boyfriend Follows Obsession."

Medford looked at Billy and wondered if he not only read people their rights, but also read their minds. Maybe he'd seen the ad in today's *Lemon City Chronicle*, Medford thought.

"Nana, can you please stop him?"

Medford wanted to tell Billy to let his sister talk, but he knew better than to interfere with the siblings.

Billy was on a roll. "Clement, try this one on for size . . . Nicotine Burns Foul Odors."

"Now that don't make no kinda sense," said Clement, looking beyond Theola, who was in his line of sight, all the way to Billy. "Now be a gentleman and let your sister tell her story."

"Nana?" Louise pleaded.

"Alright . . . alright. Billy, quit now. Behave yourself."

"NBFO stands for National Black Feminist Organization," said Louise finally.

"I should have known that's what it was about," said Billy. "Something boring. Who cares?"

"Since when did colored women become feminists?" asked Ole Miss Johnson, intrigued by the notion, trying not to let the pain of sitting upright in a chair reflect in the sound of her voice. Nana nodded her head in agreement, but stopped when she realized she was taking sides with her neighbor.

"Since Flo Kennedy founded the Feminist Party in 1971 and Eleanor Holmes Norton helped start the NBFO in November last year," declared Louise, who cringed whenever she heard the word "colored" and flinched at the word "Negro," but accepted the fact that old folks might never get used to the change of labels. Although that wasn't the worst of it. What really sent her over the top was being called Afro-American, because she couldn't imagine a race of people being named after a hairstyle.

"Flo who? Ain't she the one from New York City who wears those big pink sunglasses and a cowboy hat?" asked Sadie, who suddenly became more interested in her mashed potatoes and asked Bootsie to pass her the gravy. Smiling, she thanked him with a grin that showed as many teeth in her mouth as there were keys on a piano.

"Did she say Kennedy?" asked Bootsie, who was slightly hard of hearing despite being a tenor in the Pursuit of Happiness Jubilee Choir. "Which one is she talking about, John F., Robert, or Ted?" He leaned in closer to Sadie so he could hear her response.

"Flo," said Sadie.

"Who's that?" Bootsie looked confused.

"I believe she's a black feminist." Sadie was anxious to get back to being occupied with her mashed potatoes.

"Oh," said Bootsie, as if he finally understood. Then he contemplated the idea. "We got them now too?" Perplexed by the concept of black women and feminism, which seemed like a contradiction in terms to him, he became confused all over again and decided to focus on his food.

"Oh, yeah. That's right. She's that lawyer, ain't she?" recalled Vernelle, getting back her memory. "Always cracking jokes while taking care of business. That's what they say."

"Both these women along with several others decided to organize the NBFO, to get equal rights for women," added Louise.

"I don't know why they bothered," said Ole Miss Johnson, squeezing out her words with whatever air she could force out her lungs through her cracked ribs. "If you ask me, ain't no colored women being oppressed by colored men."

"I don't know why colored women need to separate themselves from the men to begin with," said Theola, directing her comment to Clement, trapping him with her eyes.

"One reason for the need for separation between the sexes is that women overall still get paid less than men," said Louise.

"You get paid pretty well as head librarian, don't you, dear?" asked Nana.

"This is not a complaint about *my* salary, Nana. I'm just talking in general. But I've always wondered, if they put a man in my spot . . . let's say, you, for instance, Billy." Louise turned to her brother. "They'd be more likely to pay you more money."

"Damn skippy, they'd pay me more money. Because I'd be worth it. No offense, Sister, but I'd better get paid a higher salary than you. I got a wife to take care of, and at some point in the near future, kids to feed, Lord willing." Billy nodded his head as if agreeing with himself.

"See what I mean? That's exactly my point!" Louise exclaimed. "The Department of Labor statistics show that women are more reliable and absent less frequently than men in the work force. But the status quo thinks the same way Billy does, and that's not fair, which is why we need an NBFO."

"Don't get yourself riled up over nothing, young lady," Granddaddy mumbled to his plate. "You don't need more money. You got plenty of money. Just looking for trouble finding things to worry yourself about for no reason."

"All I can say is, put the community first," offered Ole Miss Johnson, taking a break from her food as if she had just lost her appetite. "The rest will take care of itself. Ain't no need in dividing folks, splitting something in two when it's got more strength as one." She patted the corners of her mouth with her napkin as if her cheeks hurt. "Don't be fooled by nobody."

"I'll say amen to that," said Sadie, trying to keep the food inside her mouth.

"Me too," agreed Theola, winking at Clement.

"Depends on what you mean by oppressed," said Vernelle. Thinking about what Ole Miss Johnson said earlier in the conversation about colored women being oppressed by colored men. "Rufus with his loud self tries to keep me down with the volume of his voice, shouting over me like what he got to say is more important, like I'm standing in a room on the other side of the house. That man makes me half-deaf, forcing my ears to put up with that racket. I need the right to peace and quiet. Shucks. If I can get them rights, now that's something I'll sign up for."

While everyone fell out laughing at the table, Medford leaned over and whispered to Louise.

"I don't oppress you, do I baby?" He was having a sudden need for her attention.

It seemed to Nana as if this was the first time the two had spoken since they arrived.

"Not at all," Louise replied, trying to put on a smile. "I'm not talking about you." She playfully nudged his arm, forgetting about her attitude. Regardless of his having another woman in his life, she still wanted a friendship between them.

"We've always been liberated," said Nana. "As far as I'm concerned, I don't know why in heaven's name we need an organized group to take on that mission."

"The bottom line is, y'all are just trying to avoid being in the kitchen," Billy said to his sister. "That's what it all boils down to. That's all it is . . . just admit it. Well, if you want to know the truth, kitchen work is y'all's job." He waited for the backlash to hit him. There were gasps from the women, including Nana, who was scowling, but he didn't care; he was just getting started. "And y'all are better suited for that kind of work than us men. Y'all got them little tiny hands that can get the grease out of the corners of pots real good, arms slim enough to reach in and out of ovens, find food in the back of the refrigerator. Y'all are better at organizing all those cans and jars in the cabinets, polishing the silverware, putting it back into place, and it's our job to come along and mess everything back up. Ain't that right, fellas?"

None of the men at the table dared to agree with Billy. He was on his own.

Elvira nudged her husband hard with her elbow.

"Ow," said Billy.

"Can you punch him for me too?" asked Louise.

"Hey, if the system works, it don't need fixing."

Elvira hit her husband again.

"Ouch!" exclaimed Billy.

"Seriously," said Louise, when she caught Nana's attention. "The double standard on the sexes is problematic—even here in Lemon City."

"If you're complaining about how sex is," Billy snickered, "your boyfriend ain't taking care of business."

"I'm speaking in terms of compensation and promotion," added Louise.

"Not at the dinner table, Billy. Not in front of company," said Nana. "Not on Christmas Day. You know better."

"Sorry, Nana." Billy sat back in his chair, making an effort to cover his laugh behind his napkin.

Nana just shook her head. "Bootsie, you still singing with the Pursuit of Happiness Jubilee Choir?"

"Yes, Ma'am. In fact, we have a concert New Year's Eve at the church. Would love for y'all to come."

"We'll be there," said Nana. "So will Medford. And Louise will be wearing a dress," she added with conviction, which Louise took as a signal that it was time to change the subject.

After dessert, when the clanking of forks began to slow down, the sighs became heavy, the men expanded their belts another notch to accommodate their stomachs, and the ladies patted their bellies as if they needed consolation, Nana announced it was time to move into the living room. She asked Louise and Elvira to help her clean the table. Louise pulled Medford by the hand for assistance, and Elvira grabbed her husband, tied an apron around his waist, and led him to the kitchen without meeting too much protest or resistance. While Billy had a lot to say in front of the fellas in public, at home where it was private he was as helpful as he could be, checking his male ego at the door.

Granddaddy entertained the remaining guests with conversation while Sadie played Christmas songs until everyone gathered into the living room.

When they settled into position around the tree, Nana gestured to Elvira to present the first gift since she'd been the first one to arrive for dinner. Elvira searched for a present underneath the branches and when she found it, she proudly handed it to Billy.

Taking the package from his wife, he put his ear against the box and started to shake its contents.

Elvira's eyes grew large, and she grabbed his arm to prevent any potential damage. "You'll break it," she explained. "I just got the doggoned thing fixed. Be careful." Her voice was sweet in spite of its warning.

"I wonder what it could possibly be?" Billy asked while tearing off the paper and opening the box. "I hear it ticking . . . could it be a bomb?" Billy started laughing, then looked inside the box and was pleased.

"Come on, let's see," said Nana, anxious to know what had her grandson's attention. "We want to see too."

Billy held up the Seth Thomas Stephan mantle clock. It was the same antique mantle clock he had found on Route 23 a year ago, broken, that someone had tossed and left as junk. Elvira had repaired it, and in addition to the ticking sound, he could see that it was working because the second hand was moving. It was polished and looked brand-new. "I just love you, baby." He hugged Elvira, then handed her his gift after locating it under the tree.

Elvira opened the box slowly, knowing that her husband hated shopping, which made him unpredictable at picking out gifts. Instead of hurting his feelings whenever he bought her a present, she was always prepared to look surprised and then grateful, no matter what. She pulled a lovely pink-and-white summer tent halter dress with a matching jacket and belt from the box.

"See, baby. You can wear it either way," said Billy, excited. "You can wear it with the belt now, tight around your waist, when you ain't pregnant and when the stork is on its way you can wear it without. The saleslady at the store said it has versatility." He grinned with a great sense of accomplishment.

"Thank you, baby. I just love it. This is so beautiful. It's just what I wanted." Elvira held up the tent dress to take a closer look at the pattern of large pink begonias against white cotton for all to see and then smiled at her husband in approval of his fashion selection. She was actually relieved to be pleased with this year's gift.

"How thoughtful," said Nana, thinking how nice it would be for Elvira to fill out that dress by summer.

"Yeah, Billy. You think of everything," said Louise. "It's a two-for-one deal," she added. "How clever."

"You should have gotten something like that for your sister too," Nana said to Billy. "She could use a dress."

Louise made the corners of her mouth rise for her grandmother, while telling herself she'd never be caught dead wearing anything like that in her life.

"I got a little something for you," Granddaddy said to Nana, making an effort to ease the unexplained tension between his wife and his granddaughter.

"Let Louise and Medford exchange," Nana replied, anxious to see what was inside the big box Medford had wrapped for Louise.

"Okay," conceded Louise, handing Medford his gift while passing a sly look at her grandmother. Nana scowled at Louise for depriving her of seeing what Medford had bought her first.

Medford quickly unwrapped his present and pulled back the

tissue paper. "Just what I needed." Inside the box was a heavy flannel red-and-black plaid jacket, the kind that lumberjacks wear. "How did you know I needed one of these?"

"I just figured since you work outside on your construction jobs you could use something warm."

Medford was grateful and gave her a hug and kiss. "My turn." He handed his present to Louise, and Nana gave the opening ceremony her undivided attention.

Louise ripped off the wrapping paper, and there on the side of the cardboard box was a picture of a Sunbeam blender.

"You said you needed a new one the other day," Medford announced, happy that he'd paid attention.

"I sure did say that," Louise responded, opening her gift, thinking she should have kept what she needed to herself. "Look, Nana, it's got a one-piece blade that twists off for easy cleaning, fourteen speeds, and it's easy to operate." She read the description that was next to the picture on the side of the box. "I can make milk shakes, salad dressings, grind up baby food for Elvira when she gets pregnant, stretch out leftovers if I need to."

"Humph." Nana forced a smile, trying not to show how horrified she was at the sight of the gift.

"Do you like it?" Medford asked Louise.

"As far as blenders go . . . I think it's really cool," Louise replied, not knowing what else to say. "It looks like it does everything except prepare the ingredients for you." She hugged him, not letting on that she was expecting something different, perhaps a little more personal. The truth was, even though they had known each other for most of their lives, they had only been together for six weeks. "Thanks."

Nana wasn't only disappointed that Medford hadn't bought Louise a ring, she was also annoyed that he'd given her a gift with a picture on the box so she didn't even have to open it to find out what was inside. Then she heard strange noises coming from her husband's direction, like hogs snorting at feeding time. When she turned to face him, he was covering his mouth with his hand to hide the snickering underneath.

"What's wrong with you?" Nana asked Granddaddy. "Your throat itch and need scratching or something? You catchin' a cold?"

"Nothing," said Granddaddy. "Just thinking about something funny, that's all."

"You want to share the fun with the rest of us?"

"No. I prefer to keep it to myself," he said, trying to calm down. "I know that's rude, but the only thing I want to share right now is this gift." He handed his wife her present. "Here's what I got for you. Open it up and don't try to predict what's inside." He started laughing again. "You know you ain't too good at guessing."

"Humph," Nana said under her breath. She opened her present and pulled out a shiny set of garden tools small enough to fit into the individual pockets of the brand-new canvas belt that she could wrap around her waist when it was time for her to go outside and plant her tomatoes.

"This here garden belt is for good luck to kick off a new year to compete in the Annual County Fair," Granddaddy said, loud enough for Ole Miss Johnson to hear.

"I love it. I just love it." Nana snapped the belt around her waist and strutted like a model walking down a runway to show off her new accessory to her guests.

"You'll need more 'an new tools to take away my crown next year," said Ole Miss Johnson, half-joking. "In fact, now that I think of it, beating me is dern near next to impossible, like holding back a copperhead from biting when it's made up its mind to strike. And by the way," she said, pointing her finger, "for as many years as we've been growing tomatoes, that important piece of information should have sunk in real deep by now, as easy as a pick-axe driving into fertile earth."

"Now, ladies." Granddaddy was diplomatic. "It's not springtime yet. You've got a few more months to go before you start hurling insults at each other."

Nana had had about enough of her neighbor. Now that dinner was over, she felt she had lived up to her charitable Christian obligation and was ready for the old lady to leave. But Ole Miss Johnson stayed in her seat, and it looked to Nana as if evil were her anchor.

However, the truth was, Ole Miss Johnson was in so much pain that she couldn't get up without assistance. She wanted to go home, but part of the problem was that she was too stubborn to ask for help to rise out of her chair, the other part that she found a small sense of satisfaction in making her host feel a tinge of discomfort too.

After all the presents were exchanged and opened and the various lemon dessert gifts handed out, Sadie took her place at the piano and Bootsie began singing "Away in a Manger." When he finished that song, everyone launched into "Hark, the Herald Angels Sing," totally throwing themselves into the Christmas spirit because they wouldn't get another day like this until next year.

Jeremiah and Ruby Rose followed the road to Lemon City like the smell of tobacco hitchhiking a ride on a gust of wind.

"Are we there yet?" Ruby Rose asked, staring out the window.

"Yep. There's the sign up ahead," Jeremiah pointed out. "We're here."

The modest announcement carved from wood stood proudly alongside the road. It read: LEMON CITY, POPULATION 6,596.

For the first time Jeremiah felt relaxed enough to enjoy the beautiful scenery that the Blue Ridge Mountains provided. They had been driving for most of the day, and it seemed the sun was setting fast. As he looked through his windshield, the snow-covered peaks and high summits of the great mountain range surrounding them made him feel small upon approach. As he scanned the sprawling chain of magnificent rock, he was easily reminded that there is a God and that only He could create such a masterpiece to welcome them with expansive arms and a long embrace. Looking up at the sky, he admired the hawks soaring overhead, flapping their wings, rising with the drafts on motionless flight, making travel look effortless, a stark comparison to the life journey of him and Ruby Rose. Even though the forest was still, the bare trees that opened up to extraordinary vistas also exposed him and his sister to the officials that might already be on their trail. Rescuing Ruby Rose from her unforgivable situation made him feel more like an escaped convict than her savior.

"You know what Dick Gregory did?" Jeremiah asked.

"What?" Ruby Rose answered, unable to peel her eyes away from the new view.

"He actually ran nine hundred miles from Chicago to Washington, D.C."

"Was he running from the law, like us?"

Jeremiah smiled. "Nah, he was running to protest world hunger."

"What sense does that make?"

"It was his way of getting attention in the newspapers and on TV, to make people aware of the crisis and hope that they would care and do something about world hunger too."

Just as Jeremiah said that, smoke came out from underneath the hood of the car. The sound of a pipe banging against metal started up again, but this time it was louder and made the car shudder as if something were about to break. The car stalled, then shut off and sputtered to a complete stop.

"What happened?" asked Ruby Rose, leaning into the dashboard as if that would get her closer to the hood to locate the source of the problem.

"I don't know." Jeremiah turned the key in the ignition, but the 1964 Dodge Dart knocked and clattered and refused to start. "Damn it!" He put on his gloves, got out of the car, cleared the smoke away with his hands, and carefully lifted the hood. Coolant started spurting at him from every direction. He looked underneath the car, only to find liquid pouring out—a major leak. He checked the hose. It was cracked. When he unscrewed the radiator cap and looked inside it was drained—no antifreeze left. With no coolant flowing through the engine and radiator, two major systems were down. He checked the fuel pump, which he determined wasn't delivering properly to the carburetor, which was also causing part of the problem. Lifting the fan belt, he could see that it was worn. After testing the spark plugs one at a time, he could tell the ignition system was shot.

"Ruby Rose," Jeremiah called to his sister.

She rolled down the window and stuck out her head.

"I'm afraid I don't have good news."

"By the looks of things, I wouldn't think so," Ruby Rose replied.

"We're gonna have to continue our journey on foot." Jeremiah looked at the sun to see how much farther it had to go before it disappeared. There wouldn't be much daylight left. Then he glanced at his watch. "Let's grab a few things from the trunk and get moving. It's going to get dark soon."

Jeremiah opened the trunk and placed the essentials on the road. He took a screwdriver from his tool kit to remove the license plates from the car and tucked them away safely inside one of the bags. Shifting the car into neutral, he gave it a shove from the rear and watched as it rolled off the side of the road down a cliff into a thickly wooded ravine. He stayed until the car came to a halt and vanished into the shrubbery and trees.

"How far are we walking?" Ruby Rose carried the bag with the food.

Jeremiah flung the backpack around his shoulders and picked up Ruby Rose's suitcase. "We'll stop at the first friendly house that gives off any sign of warmth and holiday spirit."

Before they got to the last chorus of "Hark, the Herald Angels Sing," the doorbell rang. Everyone thought it was Sadie playing the C note three times during the "glory to the newborn king" part, but it was followed by three very distinctive knocks. The room went silent as they stopped singing and everyone stared at one another, wondering who the late, uninvited guest could be. Nana looked at her husband for a moment, then a wide grin captured her face. "It's Faye!" she shouted, racing to the door. "Bless her heart, she decided to come home for Christmas after all."

However, when Nana opened the front door, her face turned to stone. She let out a gasp, then put her hand to her chest, which seemed to prevent the words from coming out of her mouth. There were two people standing on her front porch who were not from Lemon City, two Outsiders, to be exact. One grown man and one young girl. Granddaddy saw his wife's reaction and responded. Watching her expression transition from complete joy to total shock, he came to the front door to see what had caused her transformation.

Granddaddy was taken aback by the two strangers standing before him, but managed to collect himself and speak. "Can we help you?" Granddaddy asked the man since his wife was unable to exercise her vocal cords. He couldn't help but examine the strange pair in the same way he would a sideshow at a circus.

"Sorry to bother you good people." Jeremiah took off his hat, trying to make a favorable impression. Despite the cold, he did his best to turn his frozen mouth into a smile. "But we've been walking for quite some time and though I'm not one to seek charity, my sister here, as you can see, is really cold and I was wondering if you might have someplace warm where we could take shelter for the night. We don't need much room and we're not particular."

Jeremiah pointed to the sky with clouds moving from west to east, suggesting there might be snow, or worse, a mild storm coming. "From the look of things, I'm afraid the weather may take a turn for the worse."

Granddaddy said nothing to the strangers. Gazing at the sky, he was thinking that whatever nature had decided to do wasn't his problem. He was trying to figure out why Outsiders always seemed to wind up at his front door and looked down at his feet to the welcome mat. He wished that certain folk wouldn't take it literally.

"It's Christmas Day," Jeremiah reminded them. "It's late, and everything is closed," he continued, one step away from begging. "We're sorry for the imposition, but we have no place to go." When he put his arm around Ruby Rose she seemed to reinforce his story; her muscles contracted and her body began to shiver as her lips and the fingertips poking through her gloves were turning blue.

Billy came to the door to see what had captured his grandparents' attention. When he caught sight of the two Outsiders, he instinctively stepped between them and his family in case he had to block any sudden moves. Lemon City was a long way from home for Outsiders, and his professional assessment was that these two weren't lost. Looking around the older Outsider's shoulder to check out his car, he was surprised to discover there was none in front of the house. Sizing them up, he concluded that a man with a child traveling on foot late at night, the two of them appearing as if they hadn't had a change of clothes in at least a day, literally smelled like trouble. Trusting his instincts, despite the fact the two had a look of innocence about them, the trouble he detected was that they were probably fugitives running from the law.

"I'm sorry, sir. Please forgive my rudeness," Jeremiah said to Granddaddy, Nana, and Billy, as if reading their minds. "My name is Jeremiah Richardson, and this here is my sister, Ruby Rose Wilkes."

"Rose," Nana repeated. "Ruby Rose." Then she remembered the smell of flowers early in the day and wondered if it was this child's scent being carried by the wind.

"Come on in. Come on in," said Nana. "You've been standing outside in this cold long enough. Forgive me for forgettin' my manners."

Jeremiah and Ruby Rose were relieved to hear those words, as well as to enter the house and be greeted by the warmth coming from the fireplace.

Granddaddy's and Billy's jaws dropped at Nana's sudden friendliness toward the Outsiders, but they also knew it was cold outside and it didn't make much sense to let the people freeze to death on their front porch. If they did, then they'd have a whole other problem on their hands. They could dispose of the bodies, but it would be difficult to rid themselves of the guilt.

Nana turned to her guests, who had witnessed the unimaginable scene and were now staring in disbelief because she had invited Outsiders into her home who had nothing to do with business. Confused about whether or not she was violating Rule Number Eight: DO BUSINESS AT HOME FIRST, THEN WITH OUTSIDERS YOU CAN INVITE INTO YOUR HOME, AS A LAST RESORT, Nana was confident she was adhering to Rule Number Seven: HELP THOSE IN NEED AND NEVER JUDGE THEM BY

THE HOLES IN THEIR SOCKS. Even though she couldn't see the condition of the material inside Ruby Rose's shoes, the little girl had holes in her gloves, and as far as Nana was concerned that was close enough. That was all the proof she needed that she was following The Rules.

"Everyone." Pausing to get their attention, she scanned the room and discovered it was the least of her worries; she already had all eyes on her. "Everyone," Nana repeated. "This is Jeremiah Richardson and his sister, Ruby Rose Wilkes. They've come to join our Christmas celebration." Nana never imagined that silence could be more quiet, and she sensed the stillness in the room was begging for additional information to release her guests from their catatonic states. "Keep in mind that Christmas is a time of great joy, good tidings, and giving." She was nervous about how her audience would receive this presentation, but she moved on. "A time to remember that all the inns in Bethlehem were closed to the baby Jesus, and thank God that someone was kind enough at the stable to take him in and provide a place of warmth and comfort." That little Outsider introduction had just popped into her head, and she hoped it helped to make her family and friends feel more comfortable with the intruders. If nothing else, at least it helped her to justify her own actions. "For without that place of warmth and comfort, our lives would not be the same. Who knows what would have happened to the baby Jesus had there not been that stable to receive him?"

"He would have been born someplace else," offered Ole Miss Johnson.

"That's not the point," shot back Nana.

Ole Miss Johnson wanted to ask Ernestine if she'd gone clear out of her mind comparing these vagabonds to the baby Jesus. Lemon City didn't take kindly to Outsiders, no matter what. No matter if it was Christmas Day and they were the last people on earth. One thing had absolutely nothing to do with the other, but it wasn't her house. She was in enough trouble with her neighbor as it was, so she kept her mouth shut.

Everyone in the room was torn between watching Nana and her neighbor or the two Outsiders, as if each couple commanded a certain level of attention and scrutiny.

Granddaddy couldn't believe what his wife had just said about the Outsiders and the baby Jesus either. But because she released the words as easily as a spring breeze blowing through an opened window, he knew exactly what was on her mind. With over thirty years of marriage, he could make a calculated guess, knowing just where she was planning on putting the two for the night. He could tell it was the little girl who got to her, and with that being the case, he also knew his wife's generosity might outweigh her good judgment and common sense.

Everyone stood up surrounding the two as if they were rare creatures at a zoo. Bootsie and Clement were suspicious, believing the Outsiders standing before them might be con artists. Sadie, Theola, and Vernelle thought the young man was handsome despite his disheveled clothes and unshaven face, which judging by the way he looked was nothing a good washing machine and sharp razor couldn't cure. The little girl was cute, with her nutmeg-colored freckles against cocoa-butter skin, but Sadie was the only one who noticed her hands with fingers long enough to embrace the keys on a piano. Elvira didn't know what to make of the two, and it wasn't her place to say, but she would have given them blankets and food and led them to the shed and thought twice about letting them in the house. Ole Miss Johnson thought that any Outsiders in Lemon City meant trouble, but she sensed one good thing about the man, and that was recognition. The moment he walked into the room, she could tell immediately she was in the presence of another healer. She hadn't had a whiff of snakeroot in over twenty years, and the bitter scent was emanating from his leather backpack on the floor like the smell of swamp water on a hot summer day. It had a distinctive odor, with properties almost as strong as penicillin. The plant was extremely rare, she thought to herself, and she knew he must be exceptional to have gotten access to the root. On the other hand, after examining the little girl, Ole Miss Johnson could tell by looking through the tunnel of her dark young eyes that life had already dealt her a series of heavy blows, and she felt sorry for the young thing.

There was something about the male Outsider that rubbed Medford the wrong way, and it had to do with how long he fixed his eyes on Louise and vice versa when Nana made the introductions.

Temptation sneaked up on Louise and she didn't have a chance to step out of its way. She stood apart from the circle of family and friends to get a better view of this stranger, unable to take her eyes off him. Although she knew he was off-limits and she was halfway involved with Medford, she wasn't married to him. More important, they obviously didn't have the kind of commitment that would prevent her from being available to someone else.

Once the introductions were made, Sadie started playing the piano again, trying to create a sense of getting back to normal. Nana stayed in the room to finish the second verse of "Hark, the Herald Angels Sing," just long enough to see that the Outsiders knew the words to the song, so she could verify they were Christians. Satisfied that they sang along, Nana went into the kitchen to fix them both a plate.

Granddaddy joined her, knowing that whatever opinion he had about the situation wasn't going to do any good.

"I know what you're gonna say." Granddaddy started waving his hand to his wife to express himself first, but it was too late.

"They can stay in the cottage," Nana pleaded. She nodded her head repeatedly, as if the motion would trigger him to do the same.

"For goodness sake, Ernestine. They're Outsiders."

"I know, but the little girl can't remain out in the cold. She needs some food in her stomach and a warm place to sleep. Ain't nothing of value in the cottage for them to steal, if that's what you're worried about."

"We don't know these people, Ernestine," Granddaddy said, trying to get her to be practical.

"I know, but I don't think anything bad is gonna come of it." She patted his chest to soften the emotions inside. "We just gotta trust it'll be okay. Besides, it's just for overnight." Nana laid her hand against his chest again; hoping it would warm her husband's heart.

As Granddaddy looked at his wife, he was well aware that it wasn't going to be "just for overnight," just like he knew he had lost this fight. "I'll meet you halfway," he compromised, which he felt was much better than being defeated. "Let's hear what they have to say for themselves, and the kind of explanation they give us for how they landed on our front porch. We'll hear their story first, then we'll make a decision. Agreed?"

"Agreed," Nana said with a look of satisfaction.

"Depending on what they say," Granddaddy continued, "we either put them in the shed or they can stay at the cottage. But only for one night."

Nana hugged her husband with the complete knowledge that a person could always change his mind.

The cottage down the street from the Dunlap house was barely visible from Tuckahoe Road in spring and summer, but in fall and winter, when the leaves that normally clung to the sycamore trees left their branches, it was exposed like an eastern white pine without its needles. It was the three-room house that Granddaddy had built for his family in case anyone wanted to get away for a while or feel like they were on vacation, needing only to venture down the road. There were even times when he rented the cottage to the young adult children of friends who craved to experience life independent of their parents before they purchased or built their own homes. Since the cottage was comfortable living quarters, when his wife said it was where she wanted to put the strangers, Granddaddy suspected it would be for more than just one night.

Nana took the plates that she was warming for the Outsiders out of the oven. Delivering their hot plates to the dining room, she called Jeremiah and Ruby Rose to the table so they could enjoy their meal. Everyone tried to be polite and let them have their privacy, but they couldn't help but notice how the two devoured their food like wild dogs.

Granddaddy wanted to be sure the Outsiders had satisfied their appetites before questioning them. When Jeremiah and Ruby Rose finished eating, he requested that Jeremiah explain in detail to everyone in the room how he and his sister happened to come to Lemon City, and even more important, how they came to select their house.

When Billy sensed some resistance in the Outsider and saw he was reluctant to share his story, he felt an obligation to offer him words of encouragement. "As the Lemon City Sheriff, it is my duty to tell you The Rule—like reading you the Miranda Act— that means your rights, and inform you of the consequences. Rule Number Two: 'If You Can't Be Honest You Might as Well Be Dead.' Which means," Billy continued, "if you're lying about your story, it could result in death at the hands of myself, or by Jefferson County Sheriff Beaureguard Taylor. Take your pick."

Jeremiah held his breath, and he thought it was in his best interest to hide nothing. Instead of sitting, Jeremiah felt he should stand to present his case. "We share the same mother," he began nervously. "But we have different fathers." He paused to give them time to react. "Our mother was a junkie and an alcoholic and liked men more than she loved her children."

"Oh, no," said Nana, Sadie, Theola, and Vernelle, all looking at each other. Everyone else in the room wanted to hear more before taking the time to react.

Jeremiah continued. "As I got older I ran away from home and when I got old enough, I joined the Army. Around that time, Mama gave Ruby Rose here to the state of Virginia." He gestured toward Ruby Rose as if she were the evidence supporting his case. "And there was no record of us being brother and sister . . . and then our Mama died."

"Oh, no," repeated Nana, Sadie, Theola, and Vernelle. Everyone else in the room wanted to hear more before formulating a response.

After Jeremiah told them the truth about his family, their mother, and his sister's foster care situation with Miss Molly Esther Reynolds, including the part about him now being wanted as a kidnapper by the law, their hearts went out to the Outsiders. They had never heard a story so sad. It cut through their emotions so deeply they could feel the stabbing of someone else's pain. A situation like this would never happen in Lemon City. Lemonites were people who always took care of their own.

Sadie, Theola, and Vernelle were close to tears. Nana stayed steady and chose to hold on to her strength. Ole Miss Johnson was mesmerized by the tale. Louise was intrigued, and for the first time in Billy's career he felt justified in not handing over a criminal to Beauregard Taylor, an old family friend at the Jefferson County Sheriff's Office. The way the Outsider stood up and told his story, Billy believed he was telling the truth, but he wasn't going to let the Outsider know he could be taken so easily.

"Is that so?" Billy smirked. "Are you sure you've told us the real story, and there's nothing more to add?"

"It's the truth," said Jeremiah. "I swear it." Then he remembered he was face to face with the law and stammered. "Are you . . . are you going to arrest me?" Jeremiah was terrified and couldn't believe his luck had gone from bad to worse.

"Not now . . . not yet," Billy replied, still hedging, keeping the Outsider on his toes, not letting him feel too comfortable, admittedly receiving some enjoyment from being in a position of authority and watching the Outsider squirm. In spite of that, he decided to give the pair the benefit of the doubt and at the same time to keep a close eye on them both. Billy locked eyes with the male Outsider. "My grandmother seems to have taken a likin' to your sister. As long as that continues, consider yourself safe for the time being." Billy held his gaze on the Outsider to let him know he meant business.

Granddaddy and Nana looked at each other, giving themselves a knowing nod that the Outsiders should stay.

Walking to the mantle, Nana reached for Faye's stocking and handed it to Ruby Rose. As tears of joy streaked down the girl's face, Nana knew it had been a long time since anyone had given her anything.

Ruby Rose was grateful for the stocking, but it was the brown horn-blowing angel ornaments that she saw hanging on the Christmas tree that brought tears to her eyes. She had always wanted a real tree decorated like that. Miss Molly Esther Reynolds always had miniature artificial ones with a bulb or two, with hardly any presents underneath. Then she noticed the piano in the corner and thought there might be hope. If her fingers weren't still frozen, maybe the lady they called Nana would let her play.

When the last guest left for the evening, Nana packed up two bags of leftovers, handed them to Billy, then instructed him to take Jeremiah and Ruby Rose down to the cottage. At the last minute, Louise volunteered to go with them, with no regard for leaving Medford behind.

Surprised by her granddaughter's rudeness, Nana yelled after her. "You make sure you stop by here tomorrow, ya hear? I got one more gift to give you. Ya hear me? Don't forget . . . I'll see you tomorrow."

There was no response. Louise was long gone out the door.

Chapter Four

The day after Christmas, Louise woke up wondering if she had dreamed about the Outsiders or if she had really encountered them in her grandparents' living room. Like a camera lens coming into focus, her mind began to see a clear picture of Jeremiah and his sister walking down Tuckahoe Road to the cottage. Yes, it was true, there were Outsiders in their midst and on the premises, and she began thinking about the young girl's big brother, remembering that he was kind of fine.

After pouring herself a glass of orange juice, Louise made breakfast before taking a shower. She had promised to see her grandmother today and then expected at some point to listen to what Medford had to say. Whatever it was, she had a feeling it wasn't going to be good.

She couldn't think about Medford without acknowledging their odd history. They first got together five years ago at the Soul Mate Auction at the Annual County Fair, which raised money for the Town Council's charities. Since 1968, it became their tradition to have a yearly fling around auction time, until she got the

idea that she might consider something serious. That opportunity
came after the big storm that blew straight through Lemon City
the weekend before Thanksgiving Day. Medford chose to ride out
the bad weather at her house, and the close quarters provided the
perfect condition for intimacy and comfort in exploring a potential relationship. Although Louise was reluctant to let him into
her life, she thought she might become open to the possibility and
give it a try.

She'd had a bad experience about ten years ago back in high
school, but it seemed like only yesterday. She fell in love with
Carter Lightbrook, who was the first boy she surrendered to. It
was love at first sight and she allowed herself to experience eupho-
ria, but Carter eventually broke her heart. One day, she woke up
with a couple of bug bites on her arm, which the doctor later told
her was chicken pox. It just so happened that she'd kissed Carter
after school that afternoon, and he came down with a dreadful
case. The virus nearly killed him and he never forgave her for passing along the disease, never believed that she didn't do it on purpose. He not only quit her; he stopped talking to her altogether
and started spreading vicious rumors, telling nasty lies. Eventually
Granddaddy had to speak to his parents to prevent Carter from
tarnishing his granddaughter's reputation. The Lightbrooks took
the warning seriously and moved to the other side of town. The
incident made Carter Lightbrook Louise's benchmark for relationships. She'd learned early on that words could easily walk
away, especially when it came to the subject of love. Even though
that happened twelve years ago, whenever she thought about that
time of her life, the pain was still sharp like a fresh wound that
opened all over again. Some people got over that kind of thing
quickly, but Louise guessed she was slow to recover. Trust was
something she didn't know if she would ever find again. For her, it

was an object as deep as buried treasure and she was doubtful if her shovel could expand long enough to reach it.

Now that she and Medford had been seeing each other for over a month and he was acting strange, Louise was beginning to think getting serious was a mistake.

She went to her drawer and pulled out her Afrobabies sweatshirt, the one with the short brown stubby cartoon character holding a talk sign that read "Keep On Trucking" on the front side, and the word "Peace" on the back. It was obvious that she and Nana had a different interpretation of what it meant to dress casual and if her grandmother thought that yesterday was informal, then she would probably describe today as being downright shabby. Sliding into a pair of Landlubber bell-bottom jeans, she thought about how clothes had never meant much to her except as a means of covering up her private parts and keeping warm. How anyone could make such a fuss about wardrobe other than for going to church was beyond her. She attributed her detached feelings to the fact that when she was twelve years old and her parents died in that horrible car crash, she'd had more important things to deal with than apparel. At an age when most girls were beginning to care about how they looked and what they wore because of boys, for Louise it just wasn't a priority. At the time, death had become her obsession, and she was trying to manage the best way she could to handle the worst pain she hoped to experience in her entire life.

Standing in front of her bathroom mirror, Louise untwisted the four big braids in her hair that she made each evening to prevent it from getting tangled in the morning. Using a plastic pick with a Black Power fist carved into its wooden handle, she proceeded to comb her hair and spray on a little Afro Sheen to make sure all was in order. Then she headed over to Nana's to get some

Christmas leftovers and whatever else Nana had in mind to give her.

She found her grandparents relaxing in the living room. Saint was curled up on the floor, taking advantage of the heat generated by Nana's slippered feet. Nana was working with yellow yarn to complete the baby sweater and booties she was making to add to her hope-chest collection of clothes for the grandchild she was praying would come along one day. Knitting was what she did to take her mind off anticipation. In fact, with the variety of clothes she was creating in the event of a pregnancy, she felt she had enough inventory to easily maintain stock in the Montgomery Ward mail-order catalog. Granddaddy was reading *Black Scholar* magazine with *Ebony* and *Jet* stacked on the floor, dozing on and off, while the afternoon movie on the TV was playing in the background.

After kissing her grandparents on the cheek, Louise went into the kitchen and opened the refrigerator. As she began to place the large Tupperware containers with the leftover food on the counter, Nana came into the room.

Carrying a small hardcover book, Nana handed it to Louise. "I told you I had something for you. I found this on the bookshelf upstairs in your room. Now does it look familiar?"

Louise read the title on the cover. "*The Correct Thing to Do, to Say, to Wear*, by Charlotte Hawkins Brown."

Nana pointed to the book her granddaughter was holding. "Charlotte Hawkins Brown was a famous teacher who founded the Palmer Memorial Institute for Negroes back in 1902. She was a woman with great pride in herself and her people. Because she was in education some folks say that she might have been related to us, but she was from North Carolina and they got the Great Smokies, not the Blue Ridge, but it's all part of the same mountain chain, like one big long fence, and who knows the way everybody is all spread out and connected, we could have kin down there too." Nana looked at Louise to make sure she was taking it all in, still pointing to the hardcover. "That's her book on etiquette, on proper behavior, wardrobe, and manners."

Louise groaned.

"It's the first book of its kind for Negroes. I ain't gonna lie to you, there are things in there that might be a little old-fashioned, but all you need is the general idea."

"Nana, I really don't think I need it." Louise thumbed through the chapters, reading a few of the headings out loud. " 'Boy and Girl Relationships,' 'The Earmarks of a Lady,' 'Dress for Girls,' 'Grooming.' Oh, Nana. This stuff is nonsense. You can't be serious about me reading this." Louise passed the book to her grandmother, but Nana shoved it back into her granddaughter's hands.

"Yes I am. You did when you were young, and you need to refresh your memory. I said it might be dated, but the message in there still works and it needs to be delivered to you." When Louise didn't respond, Nana continued. "You don't want to be as old as me and by yourself."

"Being old and alone doesn't scare me," Louise responded. "Besides, I'll always have you."

"No you won't. I'll be dead."

"Then I'll have Billy and Elvira."

"Who's gonna put their arms around you at the end of a long day, after you done worked so hard and are tired?"

"I can't worry about those kinds of details." Louise found some aluminum foil and began the process of taking food from the containers and wrapping it up for herself.

"Who's gonna cuddle up with you at night and make you feel safe and warm?"

"A security blanket."

"Blankets don't hug back."

"Yes they do. They wrap themselves around you."

"You use that fresh mouth around Medford? No wonder he gave you a Sunbeam blender; the motor's probably loud enough to drown out your wisecracks."

"Nana, I'm not worried and I don't want you to be. I'll find someone. But it doesn't mean I'll have to be married to him."

"Oh, girl." Frustrated, Nana threw her arms to the air. "It's so easy for me to be through with you, but I ain't giving up." Then she softened her tone when she saw resistance leaving her grand-daughter. "Dear, this book may help you think about dressing a little better so you can go on, get engaged, and get married, like you 'sposed to."

Louise's eyes grew large. "I hope Medford won't make a deci-sion to marry me based on the clothes I wear."

"It won't hurt to make yourself presentable. You're twenty-six years old, and instead of dressing like a tomboy you should be looking more like a lady. Look at you now, with that sweatshirt on." Nana threw up her arm at Louise as if the extra-large sweat-shirt over her medium frame exemplified the kind of sloppiness she was talking about.

Louise felt her grandmother had gone too far, and it was time to go. "Nana, I love you. I'll read the book. Just promise me you won't quiz me on it. Besides, I don't know if I want to get married. I don't believe marriage is necessarily part of the natural order of things, nor is it the answer to loneliness, boredom, or even happi-ness for that matter. It didn't work for Faye. And I know you may find this hard to believe, but not everyone wants to have chil-dren." Louise grabbed more aluminum foil and finished wrapping up her leftovers. After packing up the food, she kissed and thanked Nana, then did an about-face so her grandmother could see the reverse side of her Afrobabies sweatshirt sign that displayed the word "Peace."

As Louise turned the key and opened the outside door to her house, she heard the phone ringing. Taking two steps at a time, she reached the second floor and answered it.

"Hello," she said out of breath.

"Who's chasing you?" Medford asked.

"No one. I just came from Nana's," Louise managed to get out.

"Will you be home for a while? I'd like to come over."

"Sure. I'll be here for the rest of the day," she said, still panting.

"See you shortly." Medford hung up. He didn't like the way Louise had left him last night, but it wasn't worth bringing up. He had more important things to discuss with her.

Louise didn't know what there could possibly be to talk about that couldn't be communicated over the phone, and questioned whether or not Medford's change of heart was even worth having a conversation about at all. Yet whatever was on his mind, she guessed it must be important. Breaking up was hard enough to do without scheduling a meeting about it. She would rather she and Medford just see less of each other or have the whole thing fade away like ink on an old newspaper long forgotten in an attic. Eventually they'd be back to just having sex like they usually did around the time of the Annual County Fair, and that would be just fine with her.

She turned on the oven to warm up the leftovers to eat.

By the time Medford arrived, she had finished washing the dishes.

They sat down at the kitchen table. After noticing the intense look on Medford's face, Louise stood up and offered him a drink. Taking a glass from the cabinet, she poured some Boone's Farm Apple Wine for herself and a shot of Johnny Walker Red for her guest.

Medford took a swig and let out the sound he usually made when the first taste of Scotch went down warm, creating a burning sensation. He reached across the table for Louise's hand, and she allowed him to take it.

"I've known you and your family for a long time." He cleared his throat. "If you don't mind my saying so, I've watched you grow into a fine young woman. It's a fact that I'm a lot older than you but age ain't nothing but a number, and I've always wanted to care for you. Not take care *of* you, mind you, 'cause I know you're a liberated woman. It may bother some of these brothers out here, the way you are, but I ain't scared of you, so don't think you're gonna run me off." He took time to catch his breath. "I'm not threatened by a strong woman. A woman who's got the courage to keep her power appeals to me, and you're a big part of what I need in my life."

"A big part of what you need in your life?" Louise repeated, making sure she had heard him correctly. "What's the other part?" she asked, half-joking.

"That's one thing I need to sort out for myself. I can't talk about it right now, but let's say I've got some searching to do and when I'm done we can be together. I just need to know that you'll be waiting for me."

"Waiting?" Louise repeated. "I don't like to be kept hanging."

"Louise, you know I was adopted, right?"

Louise nodded her head.

Medford didn't know how much he should tell her about his mission, mainly because he didn't know that much about it himself. "I can't tell you the details right now. But I need you to be patient. And then I need you to say yes."

Louise didn't respond on purpose, since she couldn't think of any promises at that moment that she could keep.

Medford knew that marriage was something to be taken seriously, and he wanted to delay making his proposal official to Louise because he didn't think the timing was right. He poured himself one last shot of Scotch and slugged it down immediately. When he stood up, he put the red-and-black checkered jacket back on that Louise had given him for Christmas. Taking his gray wool hat out of his pocket, he lowered the flaps down over his ears, then kissed his girlfriend tenderly on the lips to let her know how gentle his persuasion could be. "I love you," he said, waiting for Louise to reciprocate.

She cleared her throat. "I like you too, Medford," was all Louise could offer. "It's all happening way too fast for me anyway." She looked at the table, then lifted her eyes to him again. "Remember, we haven't spent enough time together to talk about love."

"If you think about it, you've known me all your life, and I've known you for damn near half of mine. Not many folks get to spend that much time together. So don't sweat the clock, baby. Look at what's real." He smoothed back her hair with his hand and kissed her on her forehead. "Have a good day, Louise." After that, he closed the door.

Louise felt like Medford had left her with too much to think about, which wasn't fair. She didn't like guessing games and couldn't believe he was asking her to commit to something he didn't even bother to explain. It wasn't like him to mess with her head, but if he didn't want to discuss what was on his mind, that was his problem and she shouldn't care. Life shouldn't be so heavy, she thought as she got up from the table; it should be more about having fun.

Confused by the encounter, Louise needed a distraction from what had just taken place. Torn between doing an activity like making fruit juice in her new Sunbeam blender or reading *The Correct Thing to Do, to Say, to Wear* to take her mind off the conversation, she opted to sort through her albums and listen to Marvin Gaye. Stretching out on her couch while finishing her glass of wine, she tossed and turned trying to relax and get comfortable. When she finally did, it was "Let's Get It On" that was coming through the speakers, and the image of Jeremiah that was entering her mind.

When the song ended, Louise got the urge to call her sister-in-law. It was so quiet in the two-family house she could hear the phone ringing downstairs. While she was waiting for it to be picked up she thought about Rule Number Three: AIRING YOUR DIRTY LAUNDRY OUT IN THE STREET WILL SMELL UP THE NEIGHBORHOOD. But she was comfortable that this would be an exploratory conversation.

"Hello," answered Elvira.

"Is Billy there?" Louise asked in a loud whisper.

"No. He had to work today. What's going on? You sound funny."

"I have to talk to you about Medford."

"Wasn't that a nice gift he gave you?" Elvira asked, making small talk.

"No," Louise said flatly.

"You didn't like the Sunbeam blender?" Elvira was surprised. "Girl, what's wrong with you? That was expensive. That was the hottest-selling kitchen appliance in the stores this year. Those type a' things hardly ever go on sale, and I know they ran out of 'em downtown 'cause I was looking for one for myself. If you don't like it, give it here. Matter of fact, I could use it tonight to experiment with a recipe I found that makes a cracker dip out of vegetables and ground beef."

Louise rolled her eyes. "Vi, listen. I've got to talk to you about Medford," Louise repeated with a sense of urgency.

"Oooh. Sorry, girl. That's right. You called me. You know sometimes how I can get carried away." Elvira laid the phone flat against her ear, then sat down and propped her legs on the chair at the kitchen table. "What happened? What'd he do?"

"To answer both your questions, 'I don't know,' but he says he's searching for something and I still think he's seeing someone else even though he ain't saying." Louise let out a big sigh. "I don't know why he won't just come out with it. He doesn't have to beat around the bush. 'Sides, the only thing a grown man searches for is women or whiskey, and Medford drinks Scotch."

"Naw, he ain't with another woman, Lou," said Elvira. "Why you say that?"

"He ain't been himself lately. He's been distant, like his mind is always someplace else. There's something going on that he's not telling me, and I hate secrets. Something just ain't right."

"Aw . . . it's just the holidays." Elvira didn't want to be dismissive, but at the same time she didn't want Louise to worry.

"You mean running around shopping? Being stressed out? I don't think that's it," Louise said, frustrated. "This is different."

"You know that man loves you. You got his nose wide open, can put a big ring in it and tug on it like it's a leash." Elvira giggled.

"What do you think about Jeremiah?" Louise shifted gears.

"Who?" Elvira stopped laughing.

"You know, the Outsider."

Elvira took her feet down from the chair and sat up straight. "Girl, you got to be out your mind! You better quit thinkin' 'bout that. You know what happened to Faye messin' 'round with one of them. You know better. That ain't right. You can't go 'round with no stranger you don't know. Didn't you learn that lesson last year? What does it take to get somethin' through your head, now? You better stick with Medford like you got some sense. At least you know what you're getting into. You know you got a good thing, girl. He's just going through a phase, that's all. Whatever it is, it's only temporary. Don't you worry. He'll come around."

"Alright. Alright. I just asked a simple question. You don't have to go on and on over the deep end. Forget I ever mentioned it, and don't tell Billy."

"You don't have to remind me. I won't say a word. I ain't no fool. You just don't go and do nothing stupid."

Elvira tried not to get excited when she heard something she thought would be of interest to others, but she couldn't help herself. She didn't mean to share as much information as she did, but words would bubble up inside her like lava in a volcano and before she knew it, everything would spill out.

As soon as Billy got home from work, Elvira told him all about what was on his sister's mind. Billy just sat in his favorite chair and listened. Under these kinds of circumstances, he usually kept his thoughts to himself. Since his sister was grown and there wasn't any imposing threat, he didn't feel a need to take any action. The only thing he hoped was that he wouldn't have to repeat what he'd experienced last year with his other sister, Faye—a bad situation with an Outsider, in which he finally had to intercede. He no more needed another murder investigation than Joe Frazier wanted to be hammered by George Foreman again, or Hall of Fame player Frank Robinson wanted to be passed over for a manager's position in major-league baseball.

Chapter Five

It was a cloudless day in 1867 when Pastor Lucas T. Walker ventured up to Mt. Overpeck, where he meditated for a day or two. As the legend goes, it was the sacred place where God delivered him The Rules to pass on to all the Lemonites. It was a document that they should abide by in order to provide guidance to the town and its people. Everyone knew that the pastor had terrible handwriting and debilitating arthritis and that the parchment with the expert lettering could not possibly have been crafted by him. After much examination, the townspeople deemed the gift a miracle, and from that day forward they accepted The Rules as a guide for living because the dogma also made perfect sense.

The mountains created an ideal environment to support The Rules. Since the townspeople were surrounded by massive rock, it provided a natural barrier to keep strangers out while serving as a wall of protection to keep the Lemonites in. The Rules warning about Outsiders in general had merit. There was no doubt that the doctrine was responsible for making Lemon City the success it was today, but as Nana stood on her porch admiring her view, she was conflicted. She couldn't help but think about these two new Outsiders in particular, why they blew onto her porch on Christmas Day, why everyone was touched by their story, especially that of the little girl. Ruby Rose needed to be around some good women to find her example, Nana decided. Traveling on the road with her older brother, running from the law, was no way for a young girl to grow into womanhood. There would be no harm done if they remained in the cottage until the Annual County Fair in September, she thought—just long enough for them to collect their bearings and let a little time pass. Since she had talked her husband into letting them stay for these two nights, eight more months wouldn't hurt, and she laughed at the wide range of comparison. She'd tell Granddaddy she was making an exception for the girl, that it was in her best interest, and with a little arm twisting, she hoped he'd understand. Now she wanted to know what Jeremiah thought about her idea and she picked up the phone to find out.

"Hello, Jeremiah?"

"Yes."

"This is Mrs. Dunlap. I mean, this is Nana callin'. You can call me Nana. How y'all doin' today?"

Jeremiah and Ruby Rose were sitting down, getting ready to eat breakfast. "Just fine, thank you. You have a nice place here."

"I thought you'd like it. That's why I'm calling. How'd you like to extend your stay?"

Jeremiah couldn't believe his ears and tried to contain his excitement. "That would be mighty kind of you." He glanced at Ruby Rose and without speaking, mouthed Nana's offer, hoping that his sister could read lips. When she clapped her hands silently and jumped up and down in her seat, Jeremiah knew that she understood Nana's invitation.

"Hello?" Nana said, making sure Jeremiah was still there.

"Oh, sorry, Nana," Jeremiah said respectfully. "I think we'd like that very much."

"Well, feel free to stay if you like, until the Annual County Fair. That's in September. Don't ask me why I picked that date. I guess because it's a big event and the most fun you'll have in town all year, and Ruby Rose would enjoy herself. Speaking of Ruby Rose, don't worry about her schooling between now and then. Elvira can tutor her in all subjects, and Sadie can give her piano lessons. I'll speak to both of them about it."

Either Nana was talking too loud or Ruby Rose had good ears, because she heard the young girl hootin' and hollerin' over the phone.

Jeremiah's face went from being lit up to losing its luster. "Nana, I don't want to put your family in jeopardy or anything," he said seriously. "I'm still a wanted man and I don't want to get you into trouble."

"That don't worry me none. We got Billy on our side. If the police start poking around Lemon City, Billy will be the first person Jefferson County Sheriff Beauregard Taylor will call." Having said that, Nana added, "See y'all later," and hung up.

Seen from on top of the Blue Ridge, the snow-covered houses of Lemon City were arranged in no pattern in particular. The smoke from the chimneys swirled up in a steady stream to meet the sky as if it had cabin fever and needed to escape cramped quarters. Winter was the time of year when the town had no choice but to let down its guard, giving the unsuspecting the impression that it was open, but in reality, it extended no invitations. With bare trees and no leaves to cover it up, it became the object of exposure, making the snow its only blanket of protection, an accomplice to its privacy. When it was released from the sky with relative frequency, the snow came down so fast there was no time to leave footprints behind.

Ruby Rose looked out the bedroom window and saw a deer near the sycamore trees. It nibbled at the ground and searched for any grass generously left by winter, just as it had every morning for the past several weeks. She liked living in the cottage and was so happy that Nana Dunlap had said she and Jeremiah could stay. It was the first time in years that she felt like she had a home.

She was also happy about the nice clothes hanging in her closet and stuffed inside her dresser since Nana Dunlap had taken her downtown shopping at Thalhimers and Kresge's and then at the Sears and Roebuck in Jefferson County the other day.

Stepping into her brand-new slippers, Ruby Rose shuffled to the living room, where her brother was sleeping on the pullout couch. As far as she was concerned he was sleeping way too long, and she couldn't stop herself from waking him up. She started percolating coffee to see if the smell of Maxwell House would make him stir. When that didn't work, she turned on the TV and adjusted the volume high. Then she laughed as loud as she could at the cartoons, but he still didn't move. Finally, she took a pillow from her bedroom and threw it on his head. That got him going. He sprang up quickly, like one of those deer outside when it was minding its own business, then suddenly heard something unexpected behind it. She could tell Jeremiah didn't appreciate being disturbed, but she also knew he wasn't mad when he started chasing her around the room and tickling her until her sides felt like they were going to split and she yelled "uncle."

After they settled down from their playing and Jeremiah splashed some water on his face, he and Ruby Rose made breakfast. It was Ruby Rose's favorite part of the day, when they become a team, she as the helper and Jeremiah as the head cook. As Ruby

Rose passed her brother the eggs, he cracked them into the bowl. Jeremiah made the bacon and she made the toast. He prepared the grits and she poured the juice into the glasses and set the table. Every morning they practiced this routine until they no longer bumped into each other and tripped over each other's feet. It was the same way when they did laundry and folded clothes together. After a few weeks they had become as coordinated as two professional dancers. There was very little that they didn't do together, including tasks as simple as going outside and bringing in firewood. Ruby Rose was like Jeremiah's shadow, not letting him get too far out of her sight.

When they finished eating, Jeremiah rubbed his arms, feeling a sudden chill. He turned around to see the fire in the fireplace dying and realized that their wood supply was getting low. After he and Ruby Rose washed and dried the dishes, he took twenty dollars out of the envelope he kept hidden on the top shelf of the closet and told his sister to put on her coat. Then they walked to the Dunlaps' house to see what they could do about replenishing one of their main sources of heat.

Nana opened the door. "Hey there, Jeremiah and little Darlin'," she greeted. "Come on in. How y'all doing today?"

"Fine, thank you, Ma'am," Jeremiah and Ruby Rose answered, wiping the snow off their feet before following her into the kitchen.

"Louise and I just got back from the Piggly Wiggly," Nana said. "We're in here putting away groceries. Come join us."

When they entered the kitchen, Louise looked up and smiled at Jeremiah. Over several weeks she had seen him only in passing. This was the first time she'd got a good look at him since Christmas, and now that he was groomed and polished, he was even more appealing. He was brown like the color of ground coffee, with eyes as intense as coals and a hint of a dimple on one cheek that warmed his face when he smiled. He was taller than she was, but not quite as tall as Medford. And now that she could see his face, he seemed much younger than she had originally thought. Her best guess would put him in his early to mid-twenties.

"How are things going for you at the cottage?" Nana asked as she stacked the canned goods on the table, all the while noticing he and Louise were paying more attention to each other than she would like.

"Couldn't be better. Thanks for asking."

"You're not having any trouble, are you?"

"No, Ma'am. No trouble at all. I'm here because we're running out of firewood and I come to see if I can buy some more." When Jeremiah glanced at Louise, she looked down and focused on the fruit she was taking out of her bag.

"Help yourself," said Nana. "There's a wagon and a wheelbarrow out back, and plenty of cords. Take what you need."

"Thank you," he said, handing Nana the money on his way out the door. "Will this do?"

"This is more than enough. I'll only take half." Nana took two fives from Jeremiah and put them into her apron pocket.

"How are you doing with food down there?" Louise asked, to start a conversation and detain Jeremiah in the kitchen a little longer.

"We're all set. Ruby Rose knows a little about cooking and I've been doing my own for quite some time. I even bake." Jeremiah tried not to sound like he was bragging. He only wanted to make friendly conversation.

"Let me know if you need help," Louise offered.

"I'll certainly keep that in mind." Jeremiah started to head out the door again, but something made him speak. "In the meantime, we'd appreciate your company if you'd like to come for dinner or just stop by to say hello." He smiled and looked at Louise in a way that made Nana feel uncomfortable.

Louise picked up on his choice of pronouns, the fact that he said *we* and not *I*, and Nana picked up on Louise being a bit too forward in making herself available.

"Louise, you ain't got no time, chile," Nana reminded her granddaughter, then turned to Jeremiah. "Louise and Medford are often running around, here and there, doing things together, this and that, don't you know." Nana paused to give herself time to think about how much information she wanted to reveal. "They're a busy . . . a busy couple," she said. "They've been seeing each other for months now." Nana counted the time between Thanksgiving and Christmas. "Well, almost that long, but they've known each other since they were young, and now they're constantly together. If you need any help with anything or if you're in the mood for company, you can call on Granddaddy and me anytime."

"Nana, we ain't all that busy," chimed in Louise, annoyed that her grandmother was not only speaking for her, but telling all her business. "In fact," Louise continued to Jeremiah, "if there are any groceries you need, I can pick them up for you. I've got a car, or we could go together. And I can even cook you a wonderful 'welcome to Lemon City' meal. I'll bet you've never had one of those before."

"He had one," said Nana. "Don't you remember? It was Christmas."

"That doesn't count," said Louise. "That one wasn't planned."

"Well, you don't need to drive Jeremiah around. He can borrow the 1970 eight-cylinder, two-door white hardtop Pontiac GTO coupe to run errands in. It ain't doing nothing but sitting in the driveway anyway, deteriorating like its owner is probably doing in the ground." Catching herself mumbling toward the end of her sentence, Nana raised her voice to a normal speaking tone again. "Oh, excuse me," she said to Jeremiah. "The original owner, my ex–grandson-in-law, passed on a few months ago. He's dead and buried and won't be needing any transportation. His car's available. God rest his soul."

Medford was the perfect man for her granddaughter and Nana wasn't going to let anyone, especially an Outsider, come between them. She was tempted to call Medford right then and there to ask him what was taking him so long to ask her granddaughter to the altar.

"So what would you like from the store?" Louise persisted.

Jeremiah felt uncomfortable causing the two women to fuss, but couldn't figure out a way to avoid answering Louise's question. "Cereal, milk, juice, sausage, pancake mix, the usual—and, oh, and Scooter Pies for Ruby Rose."

"What about for you?" asked Louise.

Ruby Rose felt she was being passed over by Louise and didn't like that she was flirting with her brother.

Louise closed her eyes, pretending to read his mind. "Don't tell me. Let me guess."

"Just some meat and vegetables, that's all. I'll leave it up to you. You look like a person I could trust."

Nana was confused by her granddaughter. One day she was a feminist, the next day she was acting simple, chasing after some man.

Ruby Rose thought Louise already had a boyfriend because she'd met him at the Christmas party, and wondered why she wanted two.

Nana rummaged through a drawer until she found what she was looking for. Pulling out a set of car keys with the letters GTO on the chain, she handed it to Jeremiah. "Here you go. Now you can take yourself to the store."

"Are you sure you want to do this?" Jeremiah took the keys from Nana's hand.

"Don't give it a second thought." Nana smiled.

"How much do you want for this?" Jeremiah offered. "I've got money."

"Don't want nothing, young man. In fact, I should be paying you. Trust me. You're doing us all a big favor."

"Thank you, Mrs. Dunlap." Jeremiah shook Nana's hand.

"Call me Nana, please. You too, Ruby Rose."

"Yes, Ma'am." Ruby Rose smiled at Nana, but when she looked at Louise she straightened her face.

"Since you don't know where the Piggly Wiggly is, I'll go for you right after I finish helping Nana."

"You don't have to do that," said Jeremiah, dangling the car key on the chain.

"Listen to the man," Nana advised. "He's making sense."

"Jeremiah and me can go ourselves," chimed in Ruby Rose.

"I know," Louise said to Jeremiah, ignoring Ruby Rose again. "But I want to go. You've already given me your list, and I can get there faster than I can give you directions." Louise had made up her mind, and they all realized she wasn't going to change it.

On the drive to the Piggly Wiggly, Louise wondered what it was about Jeremiah that made him interesting and all she came up with was that he was young, handsome, and had a way about him that made her think he was open to adventure. Besides, having options with regard to boyfriends could be a good thing. One way of looking at it was that it was always better to be stuck in the middle than to be stuck with none. That way, she wouldn't become bored with just one man. Boredom didn't keep a schedule; it could arrive at any time. Since Medford was busy doing his own thing and there weren't any rules that said she couldn't be with someone else, she didn't see that she was doing anything wrong. Being with Jeremiah was just another way to pass the time.

Chapter Six

On the drive to the library, Medford wished he could remember something, anything, about his mother, but he couldn't. He parked his car in the lot and felt awkward walking into the building because it was Saturday, Louise's day off. The only time he came through was during the week when he was there to meet Louise after work. As he walked past her office, it reminded him of the way he was feeling inside: empty. He had been putting off this investigation long enough. It took Louise to provide the motivation for facing his lifelong question and give him the courage to receive the overdue answer. When he got into the elevator, he pushed the button for the second floor and headed to the periodical section. When he reached the reference help desk, he ordered the *Lemon City Chronicle* for the years 1929–1930 and began looking at the newspaper, reading everything about his sudden appearance on Clement's stoop that caught his attention: "Baby Found on Doorstep—Infant Unclaimed." "Missing Baby's Mother Still Gone." "Missing Baby's Mother Presumed Dead." "Missing Baby's Mother Thought to Be an Outsider." "Unknown Baby Believed to Have

Dropped from the Sky." "Mystery Baby Thought to Have Materialized from Mountain Drizzle and Fall Rain." "Unclaimed Baby Adopted by Local Man."

To avoid overlooking anything of importance, Medford read each article two or three times, but was frustrated because the stories lacked detail and seemed to say the same thing over and over again. *December 5, 1929—Clement Attaway, 18, unmarried, found a male baby in a basket on his doorstep. Attaway has gone public with his story and deciding to adopt the baby. The Ladies of Mt. Zion Baptist Church have promised to provide the citizen with any support, supplies, or baby-sitting he would need. If anyone has any information about this child or the whereabouts of its mother, please contact the* Lemon City Chronicle, *the Lemon City Child Welfare Bureau, or the Lemon City Sheriff's Office.*

There were no more references made to the mystery baby after the year 1929, and Medford concluded everyone had given up looking for answers and the search for the baby's identity had ended. There were no more clippings in the newspaper. Case closed.

Medford recalled that at the time of his arrival on Clement's doorstep, Granddaddy Dunlap was the Lemon City Sheriff. After spending all afternoon looking at microfilm and old newspapers and getting nowhere, Medford decided to check out his father's friend to see what he could learn.

He found Granddaddy sitting in his rocking chair reading *Jet* magazine, snacking on walnuts.

"Well now. How you doing today?" Granddaddy asked with his legs elevated, throwing the walnut shells into a bowl. "Have some," he said to Medford.

Medford took a handful of nuts and cracked them one by one, pulling out the meat.

"I came to ask you a question," said Medford. He felt slightly uncomfortable, not knowing the best way to start the conversation. So, getting impatient, Granddaddy took the initiative and did it for him.

"What's on your mind?" he asked, resting his reading material on his lap.

"Granddaddy," Medford started. "One day I'd like to marry Louise, that is, if it's alright with you."

"Is that a fact, now? You don't seem to be so sure 'bout it."

"I'm absolutely positive about that." Medford cracked a walnut with the nutcracker. "I know I need your permission first," he continued. "But there's something I have to do before I can start my own family."

"You don't say."

"I need to find my mother." Medford sighed. "And that's an area I know nothing about at all . . . who she is, where she is, if in fact she's still alive."

Granddaddy knew Medford wasn't finished so he waited, wondering what had taken him so long to bring up the subject.

"Can you please tell me all that you remember about my dad finding me on December 5, 1929?"

"I'm surprised you haven't asked before now," said Granddaddy. "I remember the police report as if it were yesterday, because I was the one who took down all the information.

"It was two weeks after the 1929 Annual County Fair when it seemed that fall was coming early. The northwesterly wind had started blowing, followed by the rain. Clement was tossing and turning in the middle of the night, couldn't sleep due to a pounding hangover that even aspirin couldn't cure, and the rain that sounded like stones rolling down from the mountain, crashing into his roof. When he finally got some shut-eye, what made him wake up again was the wailing sound of a baby crying. At first he thought he was dreaming, but the disturbance wouldn't go away. Stumbling out of bed, he got up to see where the noise was coming from, and it got louder as he got closer to the front door. Opening the door, he looked down at the source of the commotion and there was a little tiny baby, brown as a coffee bean inside a basket, inside a wooden box with some bottles of milk and diapers but no note attached and no explanation about how it got there. Clement sobered up quickly at the sight of the baby. And he brought it inside to get it out of the rain that had now dwindled to a drizzle. He thought about calling one of his lady friends, but decided against it since it was three o'clock in the morning and he couldn't think of anyone who wouldn't slap him in the face or cuss him out calling at that time of night. Clement decided to wait until morning, when his head would be clear and he could do his best thinking. He transferred the bottles of milk from the wooden box into the refrigerator and kept one to warm up in a skillet, because it was the first thing he grabbed when he opened the cabinet. When the bottle was ready, he tested the temperature of the milk on his hand. As he held the bottle, the little baby sucked the milk down quickly. The meal helped it quiet down and fall asleep. By the time morning came, Clement decided not to call any of the women he knew. It was a male child and he thought he would raise the infant by himself, because he noticed it was the first time he'd made an effort to stay sober. He went out to the garage and cut some clean rags into squares to use as bibs and extra diapers and found some masking tape to hold the cloth together. Inspired by his car, Clement decided to name the baby Medford, because he had a 1928 medium-sized Ford Model A open-cabin pickup truck and he liked the sound of combining the words *medium* and *Ford* together."

Granddaddy pointed his finger at Medford for reinforcement. "Medford, it was you who marked the beginning of Clement giving up hard liquor, because he had sense enough to know that he had to be in his right mind to take care of a baby.

"The next day, Clement called me to file a Missing Mother Report. He was surprised when I told him to keep the incident quiet, that maybe the real mother would show up and there would be no need for public embarrassment. Clement agreed, but after three months passed he was getting cabin fever and he wanted me—because as you know, I was sheriff at the time—to let the story out. Clement being out of sight and absent from town for three months wasn't so peculiar. No one even missed him not being about. Everyone just assumed he was drunk and on one of his long-term binges.

"On December fifth, exactly three months later to the day Clement found you, he asked me to put a mention in the *Lemon City Chronicle* and the *Jefferson County Times*. So the announcement in the newspaper became your birth date, and not that rainy day in September when Clement found you. Don't ask me why he told you you were born in the month of Christmas; maybe it was just more appealing to him that you were a gift and weren't born around the Annual County Fair or maybe he was just so drunk he couldn't remember. Anyway, me and the Ladies of Mt. Zion Baptist Church put up posters on telephone poles and bulletin boards, circulated flyers at Sunday-morning service, even blasted the news over the radio airwaves and on local TV. When no one claimed the baby after one year, I told Clement he should keep it. I saw it for myself: you as a baby had turned Clement into a new man. You made him stop drinking, shave every day, keep his hair combed nice and his clothes clean. His teeth changed from yellow to white and he had become an individual that was now well respected by men as well as women."

"Everyone except my mother, I gather," said Medford, feeling sorry for himself as he discovered he was actually born on September fifth and had been lied to all his life, celebrating his birthday three months late, and was probably a Virgo and not a Sagittarius like he'd originally thought. Now he knew why he had never asked the question before. It hurt. It hurt him to know that his mother didn't want him and that she gave him up and never turned around to look back. He didn't care much about who is real father was. He already had one of those, even though he wasn't blood-related. It didn't matter. Clement was a good father, and Medford felt he couldn't have dreamed up a better one.

"Sorry I can't be more helpful," said Granddaddy. "Sure you don't want something to eat besides nuts?" Knowing that food sometimes provided comfort, Granddaddy thought that something substantial in the stomach might prevent Medford from being so upset.

"I'll take a raincheck, Granddaddy. I'm not hungry anyway. Thanks for all your help." As he reached the gate, he remembered, "Tell Nana I said hello."

As Ruby Rose watched late-afternoon cartoons on TV and worked on her math homework during the commercials, she was thinking about how much she didn't like that woman Louise who ignored her while talking to her brother. She wasn't only beginning to think the woman Louise was rude, but she was greedy too, wanting to hog up two boyfriends at one time. She could tell by the way Louise looked at Jeremiah that she liked him. She knew it because a boy in her third-grade class was always sniffing around her like she was a honey bun glazed with sugar and grinning in that same way Louise and Jeremiah were grinning at each other. She'd had to tell the boy that if he wanted something sweet he should go down to the corner candy store and buy himself some chocolate or bubble gum and leave her alone. Ruby Rose had counted on Nana to stop her granddaughter from being pushy as a bulldozer trying to roll over a road. But when Nana did nothing, she started to get mad at Nana too. She was mad at both Nana and Louise for different reasons, but especially at Nana, who Ruby Rose felt could have done a better job sticking up for her in the kitchen, making sure she got the treatment and respect she deserved. She had bad luck with grown women, especially mamas who were supposed to protect little children. It seemed like she was always getting pushed around by them like a kick can that someone crushed and booted around the street. One of these days she vowed to get back at a grown-up, just like she'd always wanted to snatch the wig off Miss Molly Esther Reynolds' head and punch her in the face.

Ruby Rose folded her arms across her chest and huffed and swore she saw smoke coming out of her nose the more she thought about Louise. She stared at the TV as if it were the only thing worth paying attention to in the room.

Suddenly, there was a knock at the door.

"I'll get it." Ruby Rose jumped up from her seat, as if she had forgotten her attitude. When she opened the door, there stood one of the ladies she had seen at Nana Dunlap's house on Christmas.

"Is your brother here, young lady?" she asked.

The old lady looked tired, like she wasn't feeling very well, like the color had left her face and it wasn't pale just from the cold.

"Jeremiah!" Ruby Rose called. "Jeremiah!" she repeated loudly. "Someone is here to see you."

Jeremiah came to the door.

"Hello, Jeremiah." The lady stretched out a cold and bony hand. "We met at the Dunlaps, where I caught a whiff of your snakeroot."

"Are you familiar with snakeroot?" asked Jeremiah. His forehead wrinkled with curiosity about the old woman. Only healers were aware of the powers of snakeroot, and not all of them, at that.

"Let's just say in some ways we're kindred spirits and I respect your level of healing." She let go of his hand. "Let me reintroduce myself. My name is Lurleen Johnson."

Jeremiah asked Ole Miss Johnson to come inside and sit down. When they were seated at the kitchen table, he asked her how he could help. Ruby Rose pulled up a chair at the table as well, curious about what the lady had to say.

"About three months ago, shortly before Thanksgiving, there was a bad storm, like a tornado and a hurricane, all mixed into one. I passed out in my backyard and the next thing I knew I woke up and found myself underneath a branch of a white oak tree, then inside a speeding ambulance on my way to a hospital. I broke my shoulder bone right here." Ole Miss Johnson put her hand on her left shoulder to illustrate that part of the body. "And cracked a couple of ribs." She put her hands on either side of her ribs as if Jeremiah needed to be reminded where those bones were. "I was feeling better a couple weeks ago, but now I'm feeling worse." She frowned as if to allow a sharp pain to pass through her body. "I don't feel right at'all. My body aches with arthritis, my joints don't move, and my muscles are sore most of the time. I need to be able to use my hands. I got the Annual County Fair coming up and I have to be able to work in my garden. I can't tell you how important it is for me to put my hands in the earth and plant my tomatoes. I got the best tomatoes in the whole dern town, maybe even in all of Jefferson County. Everybody'll tell you that, if they're telling the truth, and everybody'll let you know I'll do whatever it takes to keep it that way. I ain't got no childrens, no husband, no animals. All I got is my tomatoes." Ole Miss Johnson thought she might cry when she started to let the loneliness that had engulfed her for most of her life get to her, but she wouldn't give in to that unpredictable creature that stalked her more often than death. " 'Sides, I got to beat Ernestine again this year to hold onto my crown. My tomatoes have always been bigger and better than hers and I got to do whatever I can to keep it that way."

Ruby Rose listened intently and watched Jeremiah. She wondered what he was going to do and how he was planning to help the lady.

"Ruby Rose, is your bed made up?"

"No," she said, embarrassed to make the admission in front of company.

"I need you to make it up right now. I need Mrs. Johnson to lie down on it for a little bit so I can work."

Ruby Rose ran into her room to make up her bed.

"I'll do whatever I can to make your pain go away," Jeremiah said to Ole Miss Johnson as he patted her hand. "I can't promise anything, but I'll do my best to help."

The first thing Jeremiah did was wash his hands, then he took his leather backpack out of the closet and pulled out his wooden box containing his "small bags of miracles." Inside the pouch were his healing herbs and crystals. He opened the box and located the green calcite, which was for treating arthritis, stiff muscles, and achy joints. He looked inside another pouch and pulled out yarrow root, willow bark, and dandelion leaves. He asked his sister to make herself useful and heat up a pot of boiling water. He walked Ole Miss Johnson into his sister's bedroom, took off her coat, and asked her to lie down.

"Relax and be still." He waited for the old lady to get comfortable. "Be filled with the light and the healing power of God to mend your bones and make your body strong." Jeremiah laid hands over Ole Miss Johnson, spacing them the appropriate distance from each other, moving them slowly, pausing over her ribs and joints, lingering longer over problem areas.

Ruby Rose came into the room just in time to see what she thought looked like heat waves leaving her brother's hands and entering the woman's body. She stayed where she was to observe from the doorway because she didn't want to get too close.

Ole Miss Johnson felt her body fill with heat, like her insides were being warmed by the rays of the sun, or the embers of kindling in a fireplace. As Jeremiah passed his hands over her, she could feel the warmth begin to soothe her aches and pains. He touched the fragile parts of her shoulder and visualized his fingers fusing the broken bones together. With healing hands, he gently massaged her elbows, sending heat to her skin. Massaging the inside of each wrist, both her kneecaps and anklebones, he prayed over her joints, including the ones in her fingers. He took the green calcite into both hands and held it above the crown of her head. As he took deep, slow breaths, Ole Miss Johnson could hear Jeremiah's breathing, like wind passing in and out of long, hollow reeds growing rampant in meadows. It seemed like her heart rate relaxed and adjusted to match his rhythm. After a while she felt something open up in her body that she couldn't explain, like a valve loosening in a pipe allowing a gush of water to flow through. The tightness all over her body was replaced by a pleasant stream of warmth that traveled through every inch of her, providing energy to the parts that needed it most. The force made her feel weightless, like she was hovering over the mattress.

Jeremiah asked her to lie still for a few more minutes while he made her some tea.

Afraid of what she'd witnessed, Ruby Rose tiptoed toward Ole Miss Johnson so she wouldn't disturb the old lady's peace. Curious about what just happened, she wanted to take a closer look.

"Chile, your brother is amazing." Ole Miss Johnson was lying on her back with her eyes closed, sensing Ruby Rose was upon her.

"What did he do to you?" Ruby Rose stammered, unsure of what she saw.

"He laid hands on me to lessen my pain. I need to get back into my backyard and start growing my tomatoes so I can compete with my neighbor. Timing is everything."

"Nana grows tomatoes too?"

"You darn tootin'. But I'm the one who's got a green thumb. She got a thumb that would wilt the side of a barn if she touched it."

Ruby Rose stood at the old lady's bedside, listening to her story, taking it all in.

"It's me who keeps winning the grand prize in the tomato competition at the Annual County Fair," Ole Miss Johnson said weakly as the thought of her annual rivalry started to get her all wound up. "I'm the one who always gets crowned Tomato Queen for a Day. But I don't take winning for granted and can't afford to take chances. With my hands as bad are they are, and my body broke, I need all the help I can get. That's why I think your brother is truly amazing. I'm feeling better already. I just need to lay here a little while longer and rest."

After a while, Ruby Rose and Ole Miss Johnson emerged from the bedroom. Ruby Rose looked up at the lady who'd been dragging her feet when she first came to the cottage, who now appeared to be more lively.

"Chile, your brother is something else." Ole Miss Johnson said it out loud this time so Jeremiah could hear. "You oughta be glad he found you, and I hope y'all never have to be split up again."

Jeremiah helped Ole Miss Johnson to a chair, and they sat at the kitchen table while he watched her drink her cup of tea.

"I made you two quarts," he said, placing two plastic containers in front of her. "You drink three cups a day, and let me know how you're feeling by the end of the week."

"Hot diggity," said Ole Miss Johnson. "I feel better already." She stuck her hand inside her coat pocket and handed Jeremiah two twenty-dollar bills. "Here's for your services, and a little leftover for you to get some more of them herbs 'cause I have a feeling I'm gonna need them."

Ruby Rose walked Ole Miss Johnson to the door and stared after her until she reached the end of the driveway.

Later that day there was another knock on the door, and Ruby Rose was beginning to think that this boring town was livelier than she'd first thought. When she opened it, this time it was Louise standing at the entrance, holding two bags of groceries.

"Jeremiah. It's Louise!" she yelled to her brother over her shoulder.

"Hello, Ruby Rose," said Louise. "What's happening, Li'l Sis?"

"I'm fine," Ruby Rose replied, looking at the floor. "You just missed Ole Miss Johnson," she blurted out to Louise. It was all she could think to say to the woman.

"Oh, yeah? And why was she here?" Louise stepped inside.

"Jeremiah fixed her arthritis. He fixed her shoulder and her broken ribs," said Ruby Rose, bragging about her brother's skills.

"That's enough, Ruby Rose," said Jeremiah, coming to the door. "I didn't fix anything. I only helped take away some of her pain." He took the grocery bags from Louise. "You work pretty fast."

"I've been told that before," said Louise, grinning.

"Come on in and make yourself at home. I mean, comfortable, since you're already at home, in a way."

"I want to hear more about what you did to Ole Miss Johnson." Louise sat down on the black crushed-velvet love seat. "It sounds interesting. I may have something that needs fixing one day."

"He's a healer," said Ruby Rose. "It's almost like being a doctor." She was anxious to see what was in the grocery bags.

"I have a gift as a healer," said Jeremiah, unpacking cereal, cookies, and pancake mix. "It comes in handy. Besides that, my training in Vietnam and the drugstore where I worked, it's how I make my living."

"If you're any good, the whole town oughta know about this," said Louise.

"Well, it's one way I can pay for these groceries," said Jeremiah. After looking at the receipt, he handed Louise a twenty-dollar bill that Ole Miss Johnson had given him to reimburse her for the food and for going out of her way. He unpacked a pot roast, a bag of sweet potatoes, fresh string beans, and a bottle of Mateus wine.

"By the way, that's for us," said Louise.

"Good thinking. I'll open it right now." He unscrewed the cap.

Ruby Rose sat at the kitchen table, doodling in her word puzzle book, not liking the way she was being excluded from the conversation and refreshments. She started humming the "Old MacDonald" song. When that didn't work to get their attention, Ruby Rose took her pencil and turned it upside down so the eraser hit the table in a steady beat. She did it slowly at first, then picked up the pace until the eraser started to accompany her loud hum.

Jeremiah took three wineglasses from the cabinet. He poured wine for himself and Louise, then he poured apple juice for his sister.

"I wish I had some music to play while we sit here and talk," said Jeremiah, taking a sip from his glass. "I would love to hear some Stevie Wonder, but I'm afraid I had to leave all my albums, my eight-tracks . . . all my music behind."

"No problem," said Louise. "Listening to the TV in the background is fine."

"Roberta Flack is good too. 'Killing Me Softly' is my favorite song," said Ruby Rose to let Louise know she wasn't stupid and that she and her brother shared common interests as well.

"I can turn on the radio instead," Jeremiah offered, getting up to approach the Philco on the kitchen counter. "Unfortunately I'm not set up for entertaining."

"Not a biggie," said Louise. "The wine and the great company is fine by me." She looked at Ruby Rose and sensed a hint of jealousy. "Cheers," she added to the girl, hoping to make peace.

"Cheers," Jeremiah and Ruby Rose said, and they all clinked their glasses.

"Ruby Rose, that looks like fun. What are you doing?" Louise asked, gesturing to the paper book she was doodling in.

"A puzzle. And I finished my math homework too that Elvira gave me. Want to see my math book?"

"Sure, Li'l Sis."

Ruby Rose ran into her bedroom as fast as she could to get her mathematics book, because she didn't want to miss anything that was being said. When she came back to the table, she didn't like what she heard.

"I've got music at my house," Louise said to Jeremiah. "And if you miss hearing it, I've got some powerful Panasonic speakers too. You've gotta come by and check them out."

Ruby Rose could feel the blood fill her cheeks like air being pumped into a balloon. Her fingers wrapped around the pencil she was carrying to the point where she thought it might snap. She glanced at Jeremiah to see how he would react to Louise's invitation, which had skipped over her like a rock skimming across water. Not only that, she didn't like the look that Jeremiah was giving Louise. It was the same look he'd given Louise at Nana's house.

"I'll be more than happy to," Jeremiah said.

"How 'bout this Saturday night?" Louise looked at Ruby Rose, then added, "I'm sure Nana would be willing to babysit, or child sit, as the case may be."

As Louise giggled, Ruby Rose didn't think the correction she'd made in her statement was funny.

"You can bring your math and puzzle books to Nana's house too," Louise continued.

"You've got a deal," jumped in Jeremiah. He teasingly tugged one of Ruby Rose's braids and she pulled away, reclaiming her head. She wasn't in the mood for playing. As Louise turned the pages of the math book reviewing the decimal numbers and fractions, the solid geometric objects and the measurement of volume, capacity, and time, Ruby Rose wanted to grab her property back. She no longer felt like sharing.

The blustering wind swept into Lemon City swirling around the houses, passing through the cracks of partially opened windows, spreading the smell of Outsiders around the town like a new scent that had just been added to the kitchen, and before long everyone knew the story of Jeremiah and Ruby Rose and that Jeremiah was a healer. As a result, the folks who couldn't find relief from traditional medicines or wanted to have the option of alternative treatments started to line up outside the cottage door.

As word spread through town about the strangers, Saturday couldn't come fast enough for Louise. She got up like she usually did, taking a birth-control pill with a glass of water followed by a cup of coffee. After finding her notepad, she reviewed her checklist. She knew what she was going to wear, the meal she was going to cook, the time she would start cleaning her house, and the music she would play while they chatted. The only thing she wasn't quite sure about and didn't explore completely was how far she might go with Jeremiah. Since "Make Love Not War" was the mantra of her day, she always leaned on the side of nonviolence.

As she made up her bed thinking about the countless number of times she and Medford had lain down in it, she found herself imagining what it would be like alongside Jeremiah. She liked Medford well enough, but didn't see why sleeping with him prevented her from enjoying someone else. She knew it wasn't how most women were raised, and she certainly wasn't brought up that way herself, to make love to more than one man at a time, but she didn't see the harm in it. Most of the pain she had either heard about or experienced firsthand with regard to relationships occurred when a woman was devoted to one man, not two. With that in mind, she felt two was a much safer number, like an awning over the heart, serving as an umbrella, always around when you needed it in case of rain. Since she never envisioned herself spending the rest of her life with one man anyway, she didn't see why she should set a precedent now.

Throughout the day Louise prepared for Jeremiah's arrival, and when it was time to take a break she began to read *The Correct Thing to Do, to Say, to Wear* by Charlotte Hawkins Brown because if she didn't open the book, she'd never hear the end of it from her grandmother. To be quite honest, she didn't know what to expect, but she thought the title spoke for itself. She started with the chapter on "Dress for Girls." *Girls should always dress for dinner, whether at home or school. And when there are invited guests, long dresses with sleeves are quite appropriate. If the dinner is formal, sleeveless evening dresses with appropriate slippers may be worn.* Louise hadn't heard of anything so ridiculous and old-fashioned in her life, but she continued to flip through the pages until she landed on the chapter "Boy and Girl Relationships": *A girl must be considerate, not overbearing or dictatorial. A girl must not do all the talking. It is the nature of man to dominate.* After reading that last line, she couldn't take it anymore and moved on to the "Earmarks of a Lady," thinking it had to get better than this. *A lady is polite when entering or leaving a room. Does not chew gum in public. Awaits her turn; never briskly pushes ahead. Does not make advances for acquaintance of young men or go out of her way to attract their attention.* At that, Louise burst out laughing and stomping her feet so loud that she thought Elvira and Billy would hear her through the floorboards even though they were carpet-covered, and she couldn't read another word because she couldn't keep the book still enough for her eyes to focus on the page. When she finally quieted down and wiped the tears from her eyes, she decided that next Christmas she would make life easier with Nana by just picking out what to wear beforehand, making sure it was a dress. She couldn't believe what caught her attention when she looked into the book again. It was a total coincidence: *The daily habit of setting aside what is going to be worn the next day, choosing the accessories, cleaning and polishing shoes, pressing out the wrinkles (and these instructions are applicable to boys as well), will facilitate the morning preparation for school or business and assure one of being well attired.*

Louise was sure that applied to holidays too. Now she and Charlotte had something in common because they were on the same wavelength. Coming to that conclusion, she seasoned the pot roast, peeled the potatoes, and chopped the carrots. After putting everything into the roasting pan, she put the pan into the oven and set the timer.

When Louise took her next break, she curled up on the sofa with a book that she was sure would be exciting and couldn't wait to open. *More Joy of Sex* had arrived at the library yesterday. She had already read the prequel, *Joy of Sex*, again and again, and the timing couldn't be more perfect. As she thumbed through the pages looking at the pictures, the various positions made her curious about what might occur tonight.

When she finished her break, Louise began to dust and vacuum. In the process of doing domestic work, she started to think about mothers. At least she'd known her mother and had twelve years of wonderful memories of the good times they spent together on earth. Jeremiah's was an addict and unfit altogether, and poor Medford didn't have anything—no memories, no hugs or kisses or clue, and Louise couldn't imagine what it would be like not having a mother at all. In that sense, she considered herself to be pretty lucky, and blessed with what little time she had with the woman who brought her into the world. Then the phone rang, interrupting her thoughts.

"Hello," Louise answered, sounding as if she'd been awakened from a nap.

"Hey, foxy mama," said Medford, trying his best to be cheerful.

"What's happening?" She turned off the vacuum cleaner.

"You, girl."

"Besides that."

There was a pause.

"So what are you doing this evening?"

"I . . . uh. I . . . uh. I have company coming over for dinner." Louise could have kicked herself for not sounding more confident.

"Oh?"

His voice went up, and Louise could tell he was wondering who the mystery guest could possibly be.

"Who's stopping by?" Medford hadn't known Louise to have dinner company other than him for the past couple of months. "Is it Elvira and Billy?"

Louise felt like she didn't have to answer to Medford and tell him all her business. It was her house, her food, and her time. On the other hand, she would never lie to him. "It's Jeremiah. I invited Jeremiah over for dinner."

"The Outsider?" He didn't think Louise would go this far. "Oh."

As Medford's voice dropped, Louise also thought his heart sank too.

"Well, I guess I'll be going now." Medford felt he had heard enough.

"Okay," she said, waiting for more, but it never came. "Are you alright?" Louise regretted asking that question. Medford was a grown man and could take care of himself.

"Yeah. I'm cool. Are you?"

"Yeah, I'm cool."

"Then catch you later." Medford hung up.

Louise stared at the phone as if there were something more to add, but there was nothing left to say.

If Medford could keep secrets, so could she. She continued to run the vacuum cleaner over the carpet and for a split second felt guilty about being stubborn, but the moment didn't last. Medford would have to come clean with her about what he was doing in his spare time and quit playing games. Just as clean as her shag carpet was going to become in a matter of minutes.

After that burst of energy, Louise took another break. This time she stared out her bedroom window and looked at the nest that was left empty by the wood thrush that had flown south for the winter. Then she looked beyond the mulberry tree, the black tupelos, red spruce, pitch, and Virginia pines to the mountains that were her backyard. The view was truly amazing, and although she never saw what was on the other side of the sprawling rock, curiosity wasn't enough to make her climb over. Staring at the mountains, she felt they had something in common. For one, the natural barrier that stretched along the west would never come down, nor would the man-made one that reached across her heart.

The last snowfall of winter filled the trails of the mountains from the soaring peaks to the rolling plateaus of open fields and meadows to the lowest valleys, adding a blanket of white to the brown hardwood forest floor. Snow-covered branches dangled toward the ground and icicles sparkled on hanging jagged rocks. Shadows cast from the trees stood tall against the dotted ground for as far as the eye could see, creating a contrast of darkness against the white. There was a stillness in winter surrounding Lemon City that remained uninterrupted until spring.

Jeremiah kicked the light snow off his boots, rang the doorbell, and waited.

Louise took one last look at herself in the mirror and headed downstairs to let the dinner guest in.

He was wearing a navy-blue turtleneck sweater with black flared pants and snow boots that seemed to contradict his outfit, but were appropriate for the current weather conditions. With a big smile spread across his face when she opened the door, he seemed genuinely happy to see her. It was the first time Louise had seen him without Ruby Rose.

Louise took Jeremiah's coat, then lit the dinner candles, and they sat down to eat. The first thing Louise noticed was his hands and how much softer and graceful they were than Medford's, whose hands seemed large enough to wrap around a great chestnut oak. She also had to admit that it was nice to see a man who wasn't wearing construction clothes for a change.

"So tell me about yourself," Louise said, taking her first bite of the pot roast, happy at the way it had turned out.

"Not much to say other than what I've already told everyone at Christmas dinner. I'm just trying to create a new life for my sister and me."

"Where do you plan on doing that?" asked Louise, hoping Jeremiah wouldn't think she was being too nosey.

"The thought occurred to me to go to Plymouth, Massachusetts, to find Dick Gregory and go into business with him, if he'll have me."

"Oh, my goodness. I absolutely love Dick Gregory. He's my favorite everything. Do you know him?"

"Not personally, but I really admire him—the fact that he's a comedian, a political activist, author, anti-drug crusader, nutritionist . . . and let's see, he even had the courage to run for the presidency in 1968 as a write-in candidate for the Freedom and Peace Party."

"I know all about that—the fact that he got over a million votes, and that some folks say he probably made Humphrey lose to Nixon."

"On the other hand, if Mr. Gregory is not interested in a business partnership with me that would combine using my healing herbs with his nutrition expertise, then Ruby Rose and I will just keep moving north." Jeremiah had a quizzical expression on his face, then added, "You know, I never considered moving out west."

"The Midwest is where Dick Gregory is from," added Louise, thinking it was nice to have an intellectual conversation for a change.

"I know . . . from Chicago."

"Speaking of Chicago." Louise laughed nervously. "There's a new sitcom on TV tonight called *Good Times* that takes place in Chicago."

"Oh yeah? What's it about?"

"I read it's about a family, and I guess the parents want their kids to have a better life. I think they live in the projects or something . . . you know, and they're trying to get out."

"That's all I want, is for Ruby Rose to have a better life. At least a better childhood than I had." He took a bite and waited until he finished chewing. "It's not been easy getting back on my feet after Vietnam. Not that I had it together before I was drafted three years ago, at age eighteen." Jeremiah reflected on his past. "But I dispensed medication to men who had lost limbs caused by land mines and booby traps, I treated men who were hit by mortars and gunfire, and tried to heal some emotional wounds as well." He picked up his napkin and dabbed the sides of his mouth. "Anyway, I know it's not proper dinner conversation, but that's how I became interested in medicine and healing." He cleared his throat. "The point I was making was, I hope the world will be a safer and better place for my sister when she grows up. Since the President just pulled out the troops last year, I'm sure it will be."

Louise hadn't given much thought to the war. Only a handful of young men from Lemon City had been drafted. As far as she knew they were distributed equally among the Army, Marines, Coast Guard, Navy, and Air Force, and were all sending letters home, except for one. He hadn't been overseas for three months before his parents received the visit that accompanied the dreadful news. It was the first time she recalled Military Outsiders being in Lemon City, and Louise hoped that kind of Outsiders would never come to town again.

She took a sip of wine before asking her next question. "What's going on in your life now?"

"What do you mean?"

"I'm just curious. Are there any other women in the picture besides Ruby Rose? Did you leave a girlfriend behind?"

"No. I don't have the time for that. I've always been kinda solo and on the move."

"That must be pretty lonely."

"Sometimes it is and sometimes being alone is just right." Jeremiah took a sip of wine. "How about you?"

"I have . . . uh . . . a friend. You've met him . . . Medford."

"Is he your boyfriend?"

"We've known each other all our lives. I'd call him a *good* friend," said Louise.

"He's not the kind of *good* friend who would come bustin' in here 'cause he minded me having a candlelit dinner with you, is he?"

"No." Louise laughed. "Don't worry about Medford. He's not that type of guy."

"Then he wouldn't mind me telling you that I find you extremely smart and fly and not necessarily in that order."

"Jeremiah, are you flirting with me?"

"Can't blame a brother for trying."

Louise felt herself blush. What little she knew about Jeremiah, she liked. His independence, youth, and courage made her feel she had more in common with him than with Medford. Jeremiah didn't have to be married or get bogged down in the detail of a commitment. He was free. Then she caught herself comparing the two men and realized that even though Jeremiah was sitting right in front of her, she was unable to get Medford out of her mind.

Louise put Stevie Wonder's *Innervisions* album on the turntable when they finished dessert. They moved from the kitchen into the living room to relax and get more comfortable.

"Can I help you with the dishes?" Jeremiah offered.

"No. Just make yourself at home." Louise gestured to the couch, but it seemed Jeremiah preferred to stand.

"Nice place you got here," Jeremiah said, looking around her apartment. "And it's so nice to listen to music coming from stereo speakers again."

"Thanks. Granddaddy built this house. He believes in keeping his family close."

"I hear that. Must be comforting to be based somewhere."

"I can't imagine living anywhere else."

"I mean, based in Lemon City in general," Jeremiah clarified. "Having a home base. I never stayed any one place long enough to call home."

"Oh, yeah. I love it here."

"Golden Lady" wasn't exactly a dance tune, but since Jeremiah was already standing, she extended her hand to him when it started to play and they began to move. Their bodies were slow and awkward at first trying to adjust to the beat, as it gave them the option of dancing apart to a faster tempo or getting close and dancing slow. Louise kept her distance at first, then the wine she had been drinking gave her the sudden urge to taste Jeremiah's mouth and feel his body against hers.

The next thing Louise knew, Jeremiah opened his arms and she stepped into his embrace. The moment they touched she got an electric shock from dancing on the shag carpet, but she preferred to think the sparks were from the chemistry flying between them instead. Heat seemed to generate from his limbs when he encircled her waist, making her feel they had been pulled together by an invisible force. He stepped one of his legs between hers and as they moved slowly to the music, she felt his joy begin to grow.

"I have to be honest with you." He looked into Louise's eyes. "I don't know how long I'm going to be in Lemon City."

"I know," said Louise, her breath growing heavy; she could feel it bounce off his skin and hit her in the face. "I've already thought about that."

"I'm not sure we should do this," he said, looking down at her.

"I don't have a problem with no strings attached."

"I can love you all night long, but I can't promise more than that."

"I'm not asking for anything."

He kissed her, and her mouth anxiously fell into his. He lifted her dashiki over her head at the same time she wrestled his turtleneck to the floor. Unlike Medford, who smelled like cocoa butter over the smoothness of his black skin, Jeremiah smelled of sweet aftershave that made her want to glide her nose along the nape of his neck to inhale the spicy scent even more. When Louise could no longer stand on her feet, she felt her knees buckle underneath her. The couple fell across the beanbag chair and slowly rolled onto the floor. At that moment, she knew she would miss the premiere of *Good Times*, but really didn't care because she was going to have her own good time just the same.

Back at Nana's house, Ruby Rose was determined not to have fun. She folded her arms across her chest and huffed a lot so Nana could see she was angry and disagreeable about being dropped off like soiled clothes at a Laundromat because Jeremiah had left her for Louise. Upon seeing the mood the girl was in, Granddaddy excused himself from the living room and went upstairs to watch TV to leave the two females to themselves. He'd had his share of being around moody women in his own family and he didn't feel obliged to inherit an Outsider problem, despite it coming in a small package.

In an effort to make her young guest feel at home, Nana offered Ruby Rose dinner, but the girl just sat at the table and picked at her food.

When it got to the point where Nana saw she was just playing, she had another idea. She offered Ruby Rose a tour of the basement to interest her in the fruits she had canned: the peaches, pears, and beefsteak tomatoes that would be ready for eating in the spring. Out of respect, Ruby Rose pretended to pay attention, but she couldn't stay focused. Not only that, she couldn't imagine eating shriveled-up food soaking in nasty liquid in a jar. Nana took Ruby Rose back upstairs, opened the drawer of her cherrywood china closet, and showed her the Virginia Dogwood patterned quilt that she and Sadie, Theola, and Vernelle were in the process of making. Against her will, Ruby Rose gave the quilt some attention because it was pretty and she had never known anyone in person who was in the process of making one before. There were pink flowers strung together on branches on top of squares that formed the green mountain background against a pale blue border. Ruby Rose patted the quilt and ran her fingers over the soft design and knew that if she looked outside Nana Dunlap's window in the spring, that would be exactly what she'd see—dogwoods, mountains, and a pale blue sky. Ruby Rose hoped she could stay in Lemon City long enough to wait for spring. She wasn't interested in finding Dick Gregory in Plymouth, Massachusetts. She liked where she was living right here.

Seeing that she'd piqued Ruby Rose's interest, Nana asked, "Would you like to sew a dogwood flower onto a block?"

Ruby Rose's eyes lit up and she began to let down her guard. "I don't know how to do it."

"I'll show you."

"Do you think I really can?"

"Sure you can." Nana was relieved to find an activity that would divert the child's attention away from whatever was causing her attitude, but she wanted to know what was on the girl's mind anyway.

"What's troubling you, chile?" Nana finally asked.

"That woman." Ruby Rose didn't move her head; she just raised her eyes up to Nana. She crinkled her forehead so much that she felt her eyebrows touch.

"What woman?"

Ruby Rose pointed her finger toward the house across the street.

"Why are you upset with Louise?"

"She didn't invite me to her party."

"They ain't having no party. She's just having dinner with your brother," Nana said, hoping that was all they were doing.

"I still don't like it."

"Well, there's no harm in grown folks eating." Nana patted Ruby Rose on her shoulder.

Ruby Rose didn't like Nana's reaction, didn't like her defending Louise one bit. It was as if Nana didn't care about her at all. She might be too young to do anything about how adults were treating her right now, but when she got older or got up the nerve, whichever came first, she would some day.

Nana pulled out the fabric from another drawer and cut a large square block. She pinned the dogwood appliqué onto the block and gave Ruby Rose a thimble and set her up with a needle and thread at the dining-room table. Nana showed Ruby Rose how to stitch by demonstrating how to run the needle in and out of the fabric, and the girl picked it up pretty fast. Ruby Rose tried to keep the stitches small, but she grew frustrated. All she could think about was her brother across the street, which made her angry all over again, and her stitches got big and her needle jabbed through the fabric. She thought she might prick herself, so she threw the block down.

"I don't want to do this anymore," declared Ruby Rose.

"That's alright, baby." Nana put her arm around Ruby Rose's shoulder. "We can do this another time . . . maybe you'd like to get together with Sadie, Theola, Vernelle, and me one day and do some quilting."

Ruby Rose shrugged her shoulders and sulked. Nana felt sorry for her and was upset with Louise for the way she was treating Ruby Rose, and especially for the way she was treating Medford. Her granddaughter was being irresponsible, inconsiderate, and reckless, and behavior like that usually had no reward.

"Oh, baby, look what time it is," Nana said, pointing at her watch, excited that it was almost eight o'clock. She looked at Ruby Rose, who rolled her eyes. "It's almost time for *Good Times*."

Ruby Rose didn't feel like having a good time and she certainly didn't want to see a show called *Good Times* either, but she felt she didn't have a choice. What else was she going to do? She decided to cooperate just to make Nana Dunlap happy and plopped down on the sofa in the living room as was expected. She saw the cat on the floor and called it to her lap, and was surprised when it responded to her as if it were a dog.

As it turned out, the man they called J.J. with the big mouth and the weird hat who kept yelling "Dy-no-mite" made her laugh, because he was silly and funny-looking. But when she remembered she wasn't supposed to be enjoying herself, she stopped laughing and put on her bored face again. Ruby Rose wanted Nana to know she was miserable and that it was her granddaughter who made her that way. Then she had an idea and hoped that after the show Nana would do her a favor.

"Nana."

"Yes, baby."

"Was that man who was here on Christmas Day Louise's boyfriend?"

Nana hesitated. "Why do you want to know?"

"I want to call him up and tell him his girlfriend is cheating on him."

"Around here, we stay out of folks' business, young lady."

"Please can I call him? Please can you give me his phone number? I'll call him from here. You can hear every word I say, and if I say something wrong you can push down the receiver and hang up. I won't talk long. I promise. I just think it's something he needs to know—that my brother is with his girlfriend, and he's the one who needs to be with his girlfriend. Don't you think so Nana? Don't you think I'm right?"

"It don't matter what I think. I ain't the one in the situation."

"Nana, you don't even have to tell me his number. You can just write it down. After I call him, I'll rip up the paper and throw it away. I swear. I promise. Please. Pretty please."

Nana thought about it long and hard. She didn't want Ruby Rose's brother to be with Louise either and she wanted to tell Medford about the intrusion that had sideswiped his relationship with Louise too, but she couldn't because of Rule Number Nine: MIND YOUR OWN BUSINESS PERSONALLY AND PROFESSIONALLY. If Ruby Rose was bold enough to send a message on both their behalves, she reckoned she could turn her back and cover her ears. "His name is Medford," she said, and she wrote down his home phone number on a piece of paper.

Ruby Rose dashed into the kitchen with Nana trailing behind. She picked up the phone and dialed the number.

"Medford?"

"Yes. Who's this?"

"This is Ruby Rose Wilkes. I came to Nana's house with my brother Jeremiah on Christmas Day?"

"Oh, hello, Ruby Rose. How are you?"

"I'm fine. I'm just calling to say that my brother is at your girlfriend's house right now and you should do something about it."

"Louise?" He paused, contemplating an answer. "Louise makes her own decisions."

"You ain't mad?" Ruby Rose waited for a response. When she didn't get one she shouted, "If I were you I'd be madder 'an a fire-fly trapped inside a jar, madder than a waterbug when the light came on."

"Ruby Rose," Medford said calmly. "You're the one who sounds angry."

"I ain't mad." She slammed down the phone. "There, Nana," Ruby Rose added, "I hung up for you."

Based on the one side of the conversation Nana had heard, she was surprised at Medford's response. She couldn't believe he didn't show any signs of jealousy or rage, and that he'd allow Louise to do whatever she wanted to do. At least now Medford knew there was someone else in the picture, and Nana felt better about him knowing the truth—even if he refused to accept it, or didn't want to see it, or plain ignored it.

Ruby Rose was beside herself. She put on her coat and wrapped it around her, not even taking the time to use the zipper. She said good-bye to Nana and stormed out the door, down the dark, moonlit road with bare sycamores on either side, looking like giant claws.

The word "dy-no-mite" was stuck in her head from that stupid TV show, and before she knew it she was saying it out loud so the words would keep her company and she wouldn't be too scared. "*Dy-no-mite . . . Dy-no-mite . . . Pick a fight . . . Pick a fight.*" The more she thought about it, the more she wanted to do something mean to get back at Louise. Then she became angry at Nana too, simply because they were related. Grown-ups were supposed to protect children, and she expected Nana to know that.

When Ruby Rose got to the cottage, she dragged a kitchen chair across the floor and positioned it right in front of the door. Still in her coat, she sat in the chair with her arms folded tight and the lights turned off. Ruby Rose waited. It was shortly after midnight when the door opened, and the cold air woke her up. The lights came on, and she and Jeremiah screamed at the sight of each other.

"What are you doing up so late, young lady?" Jeremiah asked. The way his sister had wrapped rigid arms around herself, he realized she had probably been upset all evening.

"Waiting for you."

"Well, put on your pajamas and go to bed. You need to get your rest. You're not going to be pretty with bags under your eyes in the morning. Come here. Give me a big bear hug and a kiss."

Ruby Rose moved toward Jeremiah, but when he hugged her, she was as stiff as a two-by-four plank of wood.

"What's the matter?" Jeremiah looked at Ruby Rose, trying to understand.

"I don't like that woman." Ruby Rose turned her bottom lip so low it looked like it was trying to reach the floor.

"Louise?"

"I don't like her." Ruby Rose put her hands on her hips.

"She's a nice lady. We're just friends. It's okay to spend time with friends, isn't it?"

"Not that much time." Ruby Rose stormed off to her room. "You wait until I get me some friends." She slammed the door.

Across town, Medford was also having trouble getting to sleep. He couldn't get the vision of his woman in the arms of another man out of his head. He had thought about going over to Louise's house and strangling the Outsider, but he knew it was her choice to be with him; she'd invited him in. Independence is what drove Louise and it never crossed his mind to take away her license to freedom. Since he also knew she was the kind of woman he couldn't confront with his anger, he couldn't risk turning her off; she might withdraw from him completely. He had no choice but to let her do her thing. If she was interested in someone else, he wasn't going to share what was in his heart about finding his mother. At this point in time, she didn't need to know. He leaned over to grab the first thing he laid his hand on and threw it. One of his work boots slammed against the wall and came crashing down on his dresser, breaking glass, shattering the picture frame with him and Louise.

Medford didn't care what broke. He grabbed the covers, yanking them over his head, and rolled over. Maybe Louise was having one last fling before they got married, he thought to make himself feel better, as if there were such a thing. If that was true, it was best she get it out of her system now. With that in mind, he remembered there was one thing that had always troubled him about Rule Number Five, CHEATING MAKES YOU LOWER THAN A DOG SCRATCHING UP A WORM IN THE DIRT. He was never quite sure if it applied to relationships or exclusively to marriage, or to both.

Flipping over onto his back, Medford reminded himself he had his own issues to occupy his time. Even though it was hard to watch what was going down with Louise without losing his temper, he had to stay focused and keep his cool. Besides, he wasn't going to act a fool for any woman. If Louise didn't know what was best for her, it wasn't his place to do the convincing. She had to make her own decision and if it led her down someone else's path, then they would just go their separate ways.

Medford got up, went into the kitchen, and slugged down a shot of Johnny Walker Red. Then he warmed up some milk. After drinking it, he climbed back into bed and tossed and turned some more. Then he threw off the blankets for the last time, got into his clothes and work boots, and went outside in the cold. He grabbed his axe and started chopping wood. With every swing of his arms, he felt some relief from his tension. He kept chopping until he worked up a sweat and became concerned that the water forming on his face might freeze.

Meanwhile, Clement, who was asleep on the other side of the house, was dreaming there was a mighty powerful red-bellied woodpecker in his backyard announcing the coming of spring.

Chapter Seven

The next day, when Ruby Rose woke up she looked out her window and saw that the local deer had brought along a friend to share the search for any evergreen rhododendron leaves caught protruding from the snow-covered ground. Watching the two deer, it dawned on her that although she had thrown away the piece of paper with Medford's phone number, she had memorized it, so she dialed him.

"Hello? How are you today?" Ruby Rose said nervously, rattling off her words rapidly as if they were one.

"Ruby Rose, is that you?" asked Medford, wiping the sleep from his eyes.

"Yes, it's me." She paused. "I'm not mad anymore." She thought that she and Medford should be friends since they were both in the same boat, abandoned by the ones they loved.

"That's good. What's happenin'?"

"I want to come by and talk, or do something. I'm bored." She began to feel more relaxed.

"Where's your brother today?"

"He's planning a date with your girlfriend," Ruby Rose said flatly.

"Don't say it like that."

"It's true. They're going in town to go bowling."

"They're just friends."

"Believe what you want to believe. I may have been born at night, but not last night."

Medford smirked. "Listen, I'm about to go to the church office before it closes. I've got to look through some old files. If you want to, you can come along with me while I do some research."

"What are you looking for?"

"I'm trying to locate someone." Medford wasn't sure how much he should reveal to her. "So I want to know what things were like around town in the late 1920s."

"Whew, boy. That's ancient history."

Medford smiled. "You know where the church is?"

"Who are you looking for?" Ruby Rose demanded.

"My mother." He decided it wouldn't hurt to tell the girl, and he could use an ally right about now. "I never knew her, and I'm trying to find out who she was." He didn't like the sound of the past tense in his sentence and changed his mind. "I'm trying to find out where she is."

"I'll come with you." To Ruby Rose, Medford's search sounded like an adventure.

"Okay. Make sure it's okay with your brother and I'll pick you up in thirty minutes."

When Medford rang the doorbell, he saw that Ruby Rose was dressed and ready to go. Jeremiah came to the door and extended his arm.

"What's happening, Blood? That's what we used to call each other in 'Nam." Jeremiah smiled.

"Are we fightin'?"

"Uh, no." Jeremiah was confused by the question. "Look, I don't have any beef with you."

Medford hesitated, but shook Jeremiah's hand anyway. He hadn't been this close to the Outsider since Christmas and was reluctant to touch the hand that he was sure was fondling his woman.

"I hear y'all are going to church today." Jeremiah decided it was best to change the subject, and hoped that Medford would elaborate on his schedule. "It's Saturday. Getting some religion a day early?" He tried to make light of the situation to give Medford a chance to respond.

"I got some family business to attend to." Medford wasn't in the mood for small talk.

"Sounds like it's personal."

"It is."

"I hope everything turns out okay." Jeremiah forced another smile.

"I'm not worried about it." Medford kept his eyes on the stranger standing before him. "I'm a patient man." He paused long enough, careful not to rush his words. "What I'm looking for is worth waiting for." He narrowed his eyes at the Outsider. "And I usually get what I want . . . eventually."

"Whatever it is, I wish you luck with it, brother."

"Won't need it," Medford snapped. "Just time, so the pieces will fall into place."

"Listen, bro, take care of my little sister." Jeremiah thought he'd get to the point. "She's all the family I got."

"She'll be safe with me." Medford looked over his shoulder at the sycamores in the woods, then turned back to the Outsider again. "I'd expect the same level of courtesy from you, if you know what I mean, Blood." Even though Medford made what he said sound like a threat, he extended his hand to Jeremiah, who thought it was best to slap him five.

"I hear that," Jeremiah replied, his jaw tightening.

"We'll be gone for most of the afternoon," Medford said, backing his way to the road. "I'll return your sister before dark."

Ruby Rose walked out the door. "Let's book," she said, grabbing Medford's hand. Then she added to her brother, "Medford is my friend." Climbing into the passenger side of the pickup truck, she yelled out the window, "I don't know how long I'll be. So don't stay up for me." She locked the door and looked straight ahead, waiting for Medford to start up the engine.

When Medford and Ruby Rose walked into the church, Sadie was at the organ rehearsing hymns for Sunday service.

"What brings y'all here a day early?" she asked, looking beyond the music stand, glancing over her glasses. "Y'all know service don't start until tomorrow morning. I wish all of our members were as anxious as you." She chuckled at her own little joke.

"Miss Sadie," said Medford. "I'm doing some research on trying to find out who my mama is or was, and I want to look through the church records to see if there's anything in the files to give me a clue."

Sadie didn't answer at first. She looked like she was deep in thought as her mind flashed back through the calendar years.

"That happened a long time ago when you arrived at your Daddy's front door. Why you want to open up Pandora's box?" Sadie pushed her glasses farther up on the bridge of her nose, giving her a look of concern.

"I've put it off long enough."

"Sometimes, it's good to leave well enough alone." Sadie waited patiently for Medford's response and when she didn't get one, she added, "Does your Daddy know about this?" She felt a ripple of warm heat rise within her, and she picked up her fan and started waving.

"No, Ma'am. I haven't bothered him with it. Besides, I don't need his permission," Medford said, sounding more defensive than intended.

"He done raised you all by himself. He might think you weren't happy with the job he did."

"That ain't the point, Miss Sadie. You know I love Clement."

"You may be stirring up more trouble than it's worth, and you know what you might find when you get to the bottom of the pot? Residue; something you cain't use 'cause it's crusty and burnt. Sometimes it ain't worth raising the dead. You might not like looking at what's left over."

"Miss Sadie, you've known me all my life and you've known my father for a very long time too. What do you remember about that night?"

"I don't remember squat. All I know was that he was a drunk. Then you showed up." She took a deep breath, then looked Medford in the eyes. "We all knew Clement wasn't past doing something crazy, but kidnapping a little baby was beyond anyone's thinking and no one believed that's how it happened. Back in those days, if Clement was gonna go out and steal something, you could be sure it wasn't gonna be somebody's baby, it was gonna be another bottle of Old Crow. So when he showed us he had a little baby, we had no idea how it got there. Everybody explored every angle of possibility and came up empty-handed. After a while we just forgot about it, and you became Clement's son, plain and simple. There were no more questions asked, and you was just a natural part of Lemon City as if Clement had delivered you himself."

Having finished her little speech, Sadie started playing the organ again. But when she realized Medford wasn't going to move until she did, she reluctantly stood up to grant his request. "Come on. I'll take y'all to the church office, but I doubt you'll find anything useful." She pulled on the back of the skirt that clung to her round behind, which resembled two cantaloupes stuck together on top of thin legs that looked like twigs of asparagus. "You're just wasting your time." She led the way, with Medford and Ruby Rose following her through the sanctuary.

Medford winked and lowered his hand to Ruby Rose, who slapped him five, then he flipped over his hand and she slapped him five on the black hand side.

Sadie showed Medford the file cabinets and pointed to the one that chronicled church history. "How far back you wanna go?"

"Nineteen twenty-eight to 1929, if you have the file."

"Here's 1920 to 1930." She grouped the folders with the dates he requested. "Good luck. Hope you find what you're looking for. If you need anything, I'll be downstairs . . . minding my own business . . . staying outta trouble . . . not bothering nobody."

Medford sifted through the folders until he spotted the one labeled 1929. Looking through various newspaper articles on church functions and events and numerous photographs taken by church members for the monthly newsletter was fascinating. He thought the material should be archived in a library where the history could be copied, stored, and properly maintained. Louise would make sure of it. Then a disturbing image of Louise and Jeremiah came into his head and he tried to replace it with the fantasy of finding his mother.

As Medford glanced over at Ruby Rose to change the course of his thinking, he could see she was sitting patiently, anxious for what he might discover, and he resumed his mission of searching the files until something grabbed his attention.

" 'December 5, 1929. Baby found,' " Medford read aloud from

the article he was holding in his hand. Then he unfolded the old newspaper clipping from the *Lemon City Chronicle* and turned to face Ruby Rose. "In the *Chronicle*, it says, 'Male baby found on Clement Attaway's doorstep, December fifth. Dropped off by accident, or delivered to wrong address. Rightful owner, please come forward and claim.' "

"No one came to claim you, so it was case closed," Sadie said, waving her church fan across her face, startling Medford and Ruby Rose. Neither one of them had heard her walk up the creaky church steps, and they wondered if she had been standing outside the door all along. She snatched the file from Medford's hand, put it back where it belonged, and closed the cabinet drawer until she heard the click that meant it was locked.

"Wait. I didn't finish 1929, and I need to check out 1930." Medford put his hand on the drawer handle and Sadie reluctantly moved out of his way.

"Be my guest," she said. She reopened the drawer, still waving her fan despite the comfortable room temperature.

As Medford continued turning page after page in the folder, Sadie kept an eye on him while striking up a conversation with Ruby Rose.

"Look at how long and beautiful your fingers are, young lady." She walked over to where Ruby Rose was sitting and touched her hand. "I was admiring them at Christmas. You should learn how to play the piano one day. I could teach you."

"I already know how to play." Ruby Rose looked at her fingers, examining them as if she were seeing them for the very first time. "I'm up to *John Thompson's Modern Course for the Piano Fifth Grade Book*."

"You are? Well, why didn't you say so? I'd be happy to have another student. I could teach you how to play the classics and gospel music." Sadie started singing "Go Tell It On the Mountain." Her fingers pounced on the air as if she were playing actual keys. Her voice was loud, sounding like a cross between opera and gospel, and Ruby Rose was starting to get a headache. Medford had a hard time concentrating on what he was doing. Ruby Rose tried to be polite and not interrupt the private performance, but she couldn't help herself and shouted over the woman's voice.

"What about radio music?" Ruby Rose asked, forcing a smile on her face.

"I don't know much about radio music," said Sadie, stopping in the middle of her phrase.

"I want to learn how to play Roberta Flack . . . 'Killing Me Softly With His Song' is my favorite. Can you teach me how to play that?"

"Oh." Sadie gasped and clutched her chest. "Killing me what? We can't play 'killing' songs in church."

Ruby Rose wanted to laugh, but she didn't. "It's not about killing. It's a nice song." She stood up from her chair to make a more formal request so Sadie could see that she was serious. "I'd like to take piano lessons again. Will you teach me? Please. Nana said she was going to call you about it, anyway."

"Lord, chile. We can start on Monday. Just check with your brother to make sure it's alright."

Ruby Rose was beside herself. She couldn't believe her luck. She had a nice place to live, she had a new friend, and now she had piano lessons.

Medford started looking through the folder labeled 1930. To his surprise, there was no mention of the mysterious baby, but what he found instead were familiar faces in old black-and-white photographs that had yellowed with age. One of the pictures showed Nana and Granddaddy holding hands with a little girl, who was younger than Ruby Rose, and Ole Miss Johnson and Easely standing beside them. It made sense that the little girl was

Louise's mother and although he had never seen a picture of Easely before, the way Ole Miss Johnson was cozied up to the handsome man, it must have been her husband. There was another picture of Nana. This time she was with Theola, Vernelle, Sadie, and Ole Miss Johnson with their arms over each other's shoulders and their legs at an angle as if they were in a chorus line. Then there was a smaller photo in a newsletter of Sadie with her arm around Ole Miss Johnson with the caption reading, "First-Runner Up and Grand Prize Winner at This Year's Annual County Fair." Behind that picture was another one stuck to it. It was Ole Miss Johnson standing on her front porch with a hoe in her hand and Sadie beside her in a white nurse's uniform with a stethoscope around her neck. Medford had no idea that Sadie and Ole Miss Johnson had been friends. He wondered why the two weren't close today, but he knew that Ole Miss Johnson had the kind of personality that could make cast iron run from a skillet and would eventually push everyone away. Nor did he realize that Sadie used to be a nurse, and he wondered why she'd given up saving lives in exchange for saving souls. These pictures had a lot of stories to tell, but none that led him to the information he was looking for.

"Thanks," Medford said to Sadie. "You were right. There's nothing here."

"Not a problem, young man," said Sadie with a look of satisfaction on her face. "Y'all come back here tomorrow, for Sunday service, ya hear? Where you'll find Jesus and won't have a need to look for nothing else ever again."

Medford nodded in politeness. As he and Ruby Rose started walking out the door, Sadie called after them.

"And by the way, Ruby Rose," she said. "I'm usually in the church in the afternoons, so come back for your first lesson on Monday. All it takes is practice, practice, practice . . . until you're perfect." Each time she said the word "practice," she clapped the back of one hand against the palm of the other as if she were a metronome. Ruby Rose didn't know if she did it to show that she had rhythm or to demonstrate she smacked her students if they hit a wrong note.

"And if you're good at it, and if you're still in Lemon City, there's a big recital around the time of the Annual County Fair," Sadie added before her visitors were gone.

As Medford drove Ruby Rose down the road to the cottage, the little girl turned to him and said, "Having a mother you didn't know is better than having one who didn't care, like me. At least you can pretend that she was nice and had to give you away for a good reason."

Medford smiled at Ruby Rose, appreciating her effort at consolation.

After dropping her off at the cottage, he reflected on the day, and something Miss Sadie said that kept coming back to him like a gnat circling his ear. He didn't want Clement to think that he wasn't a decent father.

Later that night Medford found him sitting in his favorite chair that faced the bay window overlooking the mountains, smoking his pipe. The room smelled of cherry tobacco and the way the moonlight illuminated Clement, it made him appear to be a silhouette surrounded by a fog. Medford wanted to chat with Clement to make sure he wasn't upset by his search for his mother. Between puffs, Clement began to speak.

"First of all, I ain't offended by your curiosity. I been curious about who left you here many times myself. But that was only every now and then, mostly in the beginning. After a while, I didn't worry about how you got here. I just enjoyed your company. You was a good boy, weren't no trouble at'all. Still ain't no trouble. And I was just happy to have someone to teach everything I know. You were good at skinnin' opossum with a pelting knife, holding a Winchester .44 and bringin' down a deer with a single shot at less than a hundred yards. Not scared of stalkin' and takin' aim at a big ole black bear, dern lucky at long-lining a trout using a single pole and one bait, and you still is good at all of that. You were only just okay in school, barely got through, just like me . . . having more interest in going outside to see what you could do with your hands rather than staying inside feeling awkward with words. I knew you was gonna be a builder just like me, and since you had growed up to be just like me, I stopped caring about who left you on the porch. It didn't seem to matter as you got older. I just considered you was mine and treated you as such." He took a hit off his pipe and the smoke hovered in a haze. "I feel bad because I ain't got nothing else to tell you, other than what I been saying for all these years." To make sure he was clear, Clement added, "In other words, do what you got to do. It's okay by me."

Medford got down on his knees beside the chair and looked Clement in the eyes. "Pops, I'm so grateful that the good fairy dropped me off on your doorstep instead of someone else's." He leaned over and hugged Clement's small frame, which looked like it was in the middle of a cloud. "You know, finding my mother has nothing to do with the love that you gave me. It's all about *me* trying to get answers to questions."

"I know that, son. I hope you find what you're looking for. If you don't, just remember you've been living without knowing for this long. Sometimes having new information don't make a difference."

Ruby Rose didn't like the idea of Jeremiah seeing Louise, and the feeling stayed with her like a bad rash on her skin. After weeks went by and she couldn't figure out a practical joke to play on Louise, she finally came up with a prank to play on her grandmother. It was a mischievous way to show her dissatisfaction, but she felt if other people didn't have a problem being mean, she could take advantage of an opportunity to find out the benefits of evil for herself.

While Jeremiah was in the shower, Ruby Rose rummaged around the top shelf of the closet and finally found what she was looking for. Once she put her hands on it, she became afraid she might get caught and scurried back into the living room, pretending to watch *Soul Train* on TV. But now was the perfect time, she decided, to follow through with her plan.

She ran back to the closet, unzipped Jeremiah's backpack, and opened the box with the "small bags of miracles." It was a good thing she remembered the herb jumbo bush. If there were ever a time that Ruby Rose needed something to grow, it was now. She lifted each pouch to her nose until she found the one that smelled like stale swamp and black licorice. Unsure of how much of the herb was needed, she took the whole thing, then wrapped the pouch in aluminum foil and shoved it inside her pants pocket. Pleased with herself, she smirked at the fact she'd be around to see her little prank play out between the tomato-planting season and the Annual County Fair. Darting back to the living room, she sat down in front of the TV before Jeremiah came out of the shower so she'd look like she hadn't budged.

"What are you doing today?" Jeremiah asked, emerging from the shower a few minutes later fully dressed, picking his wet hair. "Do you want to hang out with Louise and me? We may take a walk in the park, if it's not too chilly." He glanced out the window. "It looks pretty nice out today. Or we may play cards, backgammon, board games, or listen to music." He grabbed an apple from the fruit bowl. "Want to come?"

"No thanks," she said to Jeremiah. "I've got other things to do."

"Like what?" He took a bite of the apple. "Your homework? You shouldn't be inside watching TV all day."

"I finished it. I'm going out soon." Ruby Rose shrugged her shoulders, like she was bored. "I may take a walk along the creek in back of the cottage, or somethin'."

"You be careful in those woods, you hear? If parts of the creek are frozen, it doesn't mean the ice is safe," Jeremiah warned. He slipped into his coat. "And don't walk too far." He put on his hat. "For all we know that creek could empty into the James." He opened the door. "I won't be out too late," he added. "And if you get lonely, go up to Nana's."

"I will," Ruby Rose said as Jeremiah turned his back, and she placed her finger in her mouth over her tongue like she was going to gag. But the truth was that wasn't the destination she had in mind. She was planning to pay a visit to Ole Miss Johnson.

"Later," Jeremiah said, as he closed the door.

Ruby Rose stared out the window after him until the GTO was completely out of sight. She took another look at the jumbo bush that she'd stuffed inside her pocket to make sure it was all there, then walked up Tuckahoe Road to Ole Miss Johnson's house.

Ole Miss Johnson was surprised and happy to see the little girl standing at her door.

"Come on in, chile. Have a seat. Can I get you some chamomile tea or hot chocolate? How about a slice of blackberry walnut cake?"

"No, thanks, Ma'am. I'm fine." Ruby Rose sat in the Queen Anne chair in a room that smelled like lemons, looking around the old lady's house that was dark with old furniture.

Ole Miss Johnson sat down on the sofa across from Ruby Rose, not bothering with small talk, knowing the girl had a purpose for her visit and waiting for her to speak.

"I brought you something from my brother that I think you might find helpful," Ruby Rose finally said, reaching into her pocket.

"He's already helped my arthritis, and I'm eternally grateful to him. I'm getting back to being myself every day." Ole Miss Johnson circled her wrists to show her new flexibility and mobility and squeezed her fingers together to make a gnarly fist.

"It's not for your arthritis," said Ruby Rose. She paused to make sure her host understood. "It's for your garden and your tomatoes." She handed the aluminum foil to the old lady.

"What's this?" The smell was so overwhelming that before the girl even answered, she knew immediately what it was.

"Jumbo bush," said Ruby Rose, pleased with herself.

"*Grobus benzoin?*" Ole Miss Johnson called out its Latin name as she carefully pulled back the foil and smelled the foul herb. "Black licorice, how sweet!"

"Jeremiah says it makes things grow, like a hormone. If it stimulates hair and nail growth; maybe it could make your tomatoes bigger too."

Ruby Rose could see the thoughts begin to connect in the old lady's head. "And you could win the competition at the Annual County Fair."

"Yes indeed." Ole Miss Johnson's face brightened. "Make my tomatoes grow like they were incubating in super-duper fertilizer," she said as if she were talking to herself, then she imagined wearing the red robe and leafy green crown that she would don when she became Tomato Queen for a Day. After seeing that image, her expression changed to suspicion as her daydream came to an end and she transitioned back to reality. "Why are you doing this, chile?"

"Because I like you . . . because you came to visit us," Ruby Rose stammered.

"Are you sure that's the reason?" Ole Miss Johnson gave the eagle eye that made Ruby Rose wiggle in her seat.

"Okay," she blurted out. "Nana Dunlap isn't doing anything about Louise seeing my brother and I don't like that."

"Louise is fine by me. She's a good girl, but I understand your ambivalence about the other. Her grandmother is least desirable and undeserving of the title 'Queen Tomato.' That crown always has and always will belong to me as long as my fingers keep moving and my legs continue to take me where I need to go." She stood up, clutching the aluminum foil to her sagging bosom as if she were hanging onto black gold. She beckoned the girl to follow her. "Come into the kitchen," she invited. "I'll make you a ham sandwich. I smoked a Taylor hickory last night. Have a cup of tea to refresh yourself, and a slice of blackberry walnut cake too."

Ruby Rose reluctantly followed Ole Miss Johnson into the kitchen.

On her way back down Tuckahoe Road, before she even reached the cottage, Ruby Rose was feeling guilty about what she had done. She actually liked Nana Dunlap; she was just mad at Louise and felt like getting back at someone in the family. Thinking it would make her feel better to give the old lady an unfair advantage, Ruby Rose soon realized that it didn't. In fact, she felt slightly worse. She didn't think being mean suited her at all. Besides, Jeremiah was the one she should be mad at for leaving her alone, but she couldn't be too upset with him, as he was all she had.

Ruby Rose would be returning to the cottage soon, and Jeremiah was rushing, trying to finish cooking dinner while listening to the six o'clock news. That's when he heard the anniversary story of how a year ago to the day, March 28, 1973, the President had withdrawn the last of the troops from Vietnam. Jeremiah was glad the country could put that war behind it. His mind flashed back to the unbearable jungle heat, the mosquitoes carrying malaria, the mortars lighting up the midnight sky, and the stench of death that his sense of smell would always hold onto like a deer tick grabbing onto skin. While the country was involved in the war abroad, there were struggles with the Civil Rights movement at home. Combat fatalities were staggering in 'Nam, but there were also casualties for freedom fighters here. Seeing the battle-scene reminders from Cambodia and the protest marchers from Washington, D.C., got him stirred up all over again. He began to think about the returning vets and the tough transitions they underwent back to civilian life after all the sacrifices they had made. And that got him to reflect on his own future. Now that spring was just around the corner, he imagined the property in Plymouth would be ripe for the plowing and Dick Gregory would be settling into one of the houses on his four hundred acres of rich, fertile farmland—far away from any battlefield. He was excited about moving on and starting over, but with Louise in the picture and Ruby Rose enjoying Lemon City, things were becoming a bit more complex.

After lowering the heat underneath his pots, he returned to his seat to watch the rest of the news. He grabbed a Winston from his shirt pocket and lit it with a wooden match, then stared at the tip of burning ash as if it would help him put things in perspective.

Chapter Eight

The weather's temperament began to change as the days got warmer and longer. Snowmelt turning into water cascading into trout-filled streams was the welcome sign of early spring. The warming of the mountains made way for blossoms to grow on trees like spuds sprouting on a potato. Hummingbirds, warblers, wrens, and yellow-bellied sapsuckers took over the air as wildflowers like bloodroot and chickweed emerged slowly from the waking soil. Spring began to spread over the barren range as trees became full, creating their canopy in lush shades of green depending on where the sun's shadows fell and its rays struck the earth. Winter's bareness was now being covered by a coat of color as a blanket of geraniums, catawba rhododendrons, flame azaleas, dogwoods, and mountain laurels began to reappear. The subtle sweetness that lingered was a signal to the Lemonites that the downpouring of the rains would soon come. When the sky finished its disruption and quieted down and the clouds got over their temper tantrums, the townspeople would break ground to begin planting for the Annual County Fair.

Everyone was bursting with anticipation, and in keeping with tradition, Nana and Ole Miss Johnson approached the competition like two chickens fighting for the same space in a henhouse.

Planting was the preoccupation of many Lemonites during this season. Tomatoes in particular were of interest to Nana and Ole Miss Johnson. Last year, Nana had planted Big Boys, Mountain Prides, and Jubilees, but now decided to change her strategy and add Champions to the list. The reason was obvious, her motive simple. If a Champion was what she wanted to be, then that's what she needed to plant. Although she wasn't a superstitious person, Nana wasn't above cultivating all the luck she could get.

Nana went outside wearing a heavy knit cardigan and her brand-new garden tool belt strapped around her waist, with Saint trailing behind. Sitting on her stool, she sharpened her tools, then began using her rotary tiller to soften the earth. When that was done, she plunged her spade six to eight inches into the ground to begin the planting process. In between rows, she stood up to rest and wipe the sweat from her forehead. Sensing she had company in her yard besides Saint, she turned around to catch sight of her neighbor staring back at her over the picket fence.

"Morning, Lurleen," said Nana.

"Morning, yourself," replied Ole Miss Johnson, being careful how she moved her body so her ribs wouldn't hurt and would continue to heal. "Whatcha doing there?"

"Don't concern you," said Nana to the dirt.

"Humph." Ole Miss Johnson became indignant.

Saint poked her head through the picket fence and instinctively Ole Miss Johnson picked up a broom. Nana swore her neighbor straddled that broom at night and rode it across the moon against a black-lit sky. When she'd extended the courtesy to invite her to Christmas dinner several months ago they were civilized. But that was a while back, and now they were outside and the circumstances were different. Everything they'd do between April and September would be about scrutinizing the other's moves in order to win the crown at the Annual County Fair.

"Don't you think about hurting my cat either, like you tried to do last year," yelled Nana. "Unless you want me to come take a swat at you." Remembering how badly Ole Miss Johnson treated Saint last summer, Nana wanted to get that off her chest early on to set her neighbor straight.

"Who you talking to, Ernestine?"

"Just want to make sure we have an understanding, that's all . . . you old hag," Nana mumbled under her breath.

"Who you calling a hag? I heard you." Ole Miss Johnson sucked her teeth.

"I don't want to start nothing, Lurleen."

"Too late for that. You just wait and see. I ain't gonna say nothin' else. Let my tomatoes do all the talkin' when they start speakin' the language of 'bigger and better than ever before.' You'll see that you're just wasting your time."

Nana picked up Saint and put her inside the house as if she wanted to spare the animal from the nasty confrontation. Then she returned to her garden in silence and continued working the rest of the afternoon.

By nightfall, Nana was exhausted and her back was aching. She ran a bath with Epsom salts and could have soaked for hours if Granddaddy hadn't called her into the living room to see history in the making. After twenty minutes of winding down and giving her muscles a rest, she got out of the tub, dried off, put on her bathrobe, and went downstairs. She got there just in time to see Cicely Tyson receive a Best Actress award for her performance in the movie *The Autobiography of Miss Jane Pittman*. Last year, when Nana first heard it was coming on TV, she'd invited everyone over to her house to see it. The movie was so spectacular that it left them all practically in tears, including Billy, although even to this day he would never admit it. Now Nana was watching Cicely win the Emmy Award for Best Actress, and the movie itself win for Best Drama. That was the good news. The bad news was that it made her think about the oppressive slave images, the struggle for freedom, and the hardships of plantation life that her ancestors experienced. Those were times that she wanted to push aside and the movie made her sad, thinking about that period of history all over again.

That night when she and Granddaddy went to bed, Nana prayed the gardening she'd done that day wouldn't make her body ache with pains, or worse, throw out her back so she'd be unable to move in the morning. As she closed her eyes and finally sank into a comfortable sleep, the last thing she remembered hearing was barking. In her dream, there were the sounds of bloodhounds in the distance. She saw a young woman with twisted braids in a dirty white dress who looked to be about six months pregnant. Running through a tobacco field, then into a forest, the young woman holding her belly kept looking behind her as she continued her journey through the wetlands. Panting and out of breath, she stepped over rocks and fallen branches, trying to get herself and her unborn child out of harm's way. Then the slave woman stopped long enough to feel the baby move in her stomach and seemed to be relieved. But the sound of bloodhounds grew louder and she began to panic.

Nana's eyes popped wide open. Her body was shaking, waking up from her disturbing dream. Trembling in bed, her breathing was quick, and she put her hand across her chest to see if she was having a heart attack. She looked over to Granddaddy, who was sound asleep, and when her breath became steady and she didn't die, she decided not to wake him up. She stared out the window until her ears captured the sound of the great-horned owl chanting "hooo-hooo" and wondered who the woman was in her dream. It was almost dawn when she ventured downstairs to make some coffee. As she watched the liquid bubble inside the percolator, she decided to blame her dream on Cicely Tyson and *The Autobiography of Miss Jane Pittman* and swore off watching awards shows on television before bedtime ever again.

"I had the strangest dream last night," Nana said to Sadie, Theola, and Vernelle as they sat on her front porch, working on their Dogwood quilt that was draped over the round white wicker table.

"What about?" asked Vernelle, chewing Chiclet gum with her white purse at her side. She carried the same white purse with her wherever she went, making it a permanent part of her wardrobe. It got to the point where some folks thought the purse held secrets that she wanted to guard inside, that she didn't want to let out of her sight.

"It was about this slave woman," said Nana, making a backstitch on fabric cut into the shape of a green leaf.

"Did you watch that TV awards show last night?" asked Theola, putting her needle through the three layers of quilt. "That Cicely Tyson was something else in that Jane Pittman movie, wasn't she?"

"Yes," admitted Nana, looking at Theola. The white streak that blazed through her friend's hair reminded her of a snow trail on a mountain. Almost every time she looked at Theola's hair, it made her picture an image in black and white.

"Maybe that triggered it," said Sadie, fanning herself with her free hand, in the middle of one of her hot flashes.

"That's what I thought," continued Nana. "But the young woman in my dream was obviously pregnant. She was running away from a plantation and dogs were chasing after her. Poor thing kept rubbing her stomach." Nana put both hands to her ears. "And those hound dogs were justa howlin'," she complained. "Woke me up in a cold sweat."

"That musta been truly awful, Ernestine. I imagine you must be exhausted, not getting any sleep," said Vernelle, changing her hoop's position while she swiped her nose with the back of her hand. Her allergies were acting up and her nose was itching. "Pollen is out today," she added, looking at the air as if she could actually see the particles and prepare a defense against their next attack.

"It's obvious to me," said Theola. "That dream means that someone you know is pregnant."

"Maybe it's Elvira," offered Sadie. "Wouldn't that be good news?"

"Could be that someone's chasing you," added Vernelle. She dropped the hoop and sneezed into a tissue.

"I like Sadie's idea," said Nana. "Elvira being pregnant. I can't wait to become a great-grandmother. You're the midwife," she said to Vernelle. "What do you know about pregnant-women dreams?"

"Well, I'm no expert. I only know how to deliver real babies." Vernelle put the used tissue in her white purse and closed it, then screwed her hoop back into place. "I think it has to do with that show you saw on TV. The whole thing may be as simple as that."

"Who else we know have anything to do with being a mama?" asked Sadie, looking up from her glasses.

"Y'all know Louise's boyfriend is searching for his mama."

They all looked from the quilt to Theola.

"Somebody said something 'bout that at the church, 'cause they seen the ad in the *Chronicle* a while ago." Theola leaned over to Nana and whispered loudly. "At least I know Medford *used* to be her boyfriend," she added. "Lately, I've been seeing Louise and the Outsider out and about. Ain't no secret they've been together."

"I know. I seen 'em too. Guess I have to take the blame for that. It's 'cause of that little girl that I encouraged them to stay." Nana shook her head. "I thought I done right, but maybe I done wrong."

Sadie patted Nana's hand and added, "Medford ain't had a mama since he was born. What that grown man look like lookin' for a mama now? It just makes me think of Psalm 127, 'Sons are a heritage from the Lord. Children a reward from him.' Medford should just settle for that."

"What I heard was he just wants to know his family," said Vernelle. "Can't blame him for takin' an interest. You know what they say, 'better late than never.' "

"Unless he's using it as an excuse." Theola examined her stitches closely to make sure they were even and in line.

"An excuse for what?" asked Nana.

"Not to get married," declared Theola.

The Ladies looked at Theola, who sometimes said too much. This was one of those times when they wished they could wrap her white streak around her mouth to keep it shut.

"He's in love with Louise," defended Nana.

"Judging by what I seen lately, she ain't in love with him," retorted Theola as if she were an expert on the subject.

"Don't be so harsh now, jumping to conclusions," said Nana. "How you know what's inside someone's heart?"

"I don't," said Theola. "I'm just judging by what's in they pants."

"Theola, you are fresh!" said Sadie. "No wonder Clement keeps as far away from you as possible. He can see you got less sense than no money in the bank."

"Aw. I just like to have fun, that's all," said Theola, throwing a hand at Sadie. "Sex keeps you young and if you ain't having it, trying to get it is the next best thing, and if that don't work, talking about it at least makes you feel good."

"Now what about this boy's mama?" asked Vernelle in between sneezes, getting the conversation back on track.

"All I know is that he showed up in a basket on Clement's doorstep one day. He thought about naming the baby Moses, but later thought better about it," reflected Nana. "It's a good thing he did."

"Didn't your husband investigate the incident?" asked Sadie, pushing her glasses back onto the bridge of her nose.

"Sure did," replied Nana. "But it weren't no lengthy investigation and since no one was harmed, they dropped it."

"I remember when that happened," proclaimed Theola, holding her hoop firmly into place.

"Folks just thought it was a blessing that a baby was heaven sent." Vernelle took out another tissue and let out a sneeze that sounded like it came from a tuba.

"But the truth is, babies do got mamas," said Theola, holding her hoop to her face to scrutinize her stitches. As the only member of the group who didn't wear glasses, she was determined to keep it that way, despite the fact that she was farsighted and couldn't see anything close. "I just think the poor fella is walking down a dead-end road."

"Ernestine, how long you gonna keep the Outsider in town?" Sadie asked, switching topics again. "You know that ain't right," she added.

"Because of the girl . . . Ruby Rose, I said they could stay until the Annual County Fair," Nana answered.

"How she doin'?" asked Vernelle.

"Ain't seen the chile in over a month. Poor thing is having a bit of a hard time with her brother being with Louise," said Nana. "I am too, to tell you the truth, but I think it's making the girl hateful." Nana shook her head in disgust.

" '. . . for man's anger does not bring about the righteous life that God desires,' " said Vernelle, ending her Scripture quote with a sniffle.

"I can't imagine," said Theola, feeling sympathetic. "Growing up without a mother. Now the only family she's got is off galavantin' with some hussy."

Sadie and Vernelle turned to each other and gasped.

"Excuse me," Nana said. "That 'hussy' is my granddaughter." This time when Nana looked at Theola, the white part in the middle of her hair looked like it had been painted on with a brush.

"Nothing personal intended, Ernestine," Theola said apologetically. "No reflection on you, of course."

"I know you been preoccupied with your tomatoes," Vernelle said to Nana. She took a pack of Chiclets from her purse and passed it around the table. "And I know it's not foremost on your mind, but don't let them hang around like clothes in a closet or age spots on your skin. Girl or no girl, they are Outsiders and they can't stay permanent."

"All I can say is, while he's here he can keep making me hawthorne root tea. It helps keep my blood pressure down. It's cheaper than going to a doctor and it works," stated Sadie. "I just hope he gives me the recipe before he leaves."

"I hate to say it, but the slippery elm bark tea he gave me for my heartburn did the trick," added Vernelle. "But I may have to schedule some laying-on-of-hands time to help my hip. I must confess, I'm glad you're not getting rid of him too soon."

"Now that's what I'm talkin' 'bout," giggled Theola, turning her head to Nana. "And don't kick him out before I get Clement in there to see him, Ernestine. 'Cause maybe he's got something in that bag of his to make opposites attract."

"You're as twisted as a branch on a dogwood." Sadie shook her head. "There's absolutely no help for you."

Theola laughed so hard, she made the whole table shake.

"Y'all hear the gas shortage is finally over?" asked Vernelle to get the conversation going again.

"Hallelujah!" sang Nana, checking the back of the quilt to look for a wrinkle or a tuck.

"No more sitting in lines. No high prices. No odd-or-even days," said Theola.

"I don't know why you care, Theola. You ride your bike most days."

"I know. I'm just tired of y'all complaining."

They all laughed.

"You smell that?" asked Sadie, sniffing the air with her glasses at the tip of her nose.

Vernelle tried to sniff, but her sinuses were clogged as if the pollen had turned to cotton that someone had shoved up her nose.

"Ummhmm . . . sure smells good," said Theola. "Smells like it might be coming from the cottage. Don't tell me that boy can cook too . . . oooh weee!"

"Cool your jets, Theola," Sadie said, waving her hand because she felt another hot flash coming.

"Ernestine, you might have another kind of problem on your hands," said Vernelle, cutting her eyes in Theola's direction.

"Never mind me," Theola declared. "I ain't thinking about that boy, but I know who is." She locked eyes with Nana. "The problem Ernestine might have is another granddaughter, namely Louise, in violation of Rule Number One: 'Never Marry an Outsider. If You Do, the Boll Weevil Will Bite You Back.'"

Chapter Nine

Theola's comment scared Nana half to death, and she had to call Louise for her own peace of mind.

"Did you read that book, *The Correct Thing to Do, to Say, to Wear*?" Nana blurted out, bypassing "hello."

"I read parts of it," confessed Louise, hearing the agitation in Nana's voice.

"Well, you better read all the parts so you get the whole picture," Nana snapped.

Knowing Nana the way she did, Louise could tell her grandmother was upset about something, and she wanted to know what. "Nana, how was your day?"

"I spent most of my time quilting with The Ladies. Why?"

"What were y'all talking about?"

"You ain't gonna do nothing foolish, are you?" Nana asked, finally getting to the heart of the matter.

"What do you mean?"

"You know what I mean. Keep your distance from the Outsider. Medford is a good man."

"I know, Nana," said Louise.

"He's looking for his mama. That's what he's doing. That's why he ain't been 'round here and I ain't seen him in a while. You better finish readin' that book so you can be ready if he comes looking for you when he's done, is all I have to say. Ain't nothing like being prepared for when the time comes."

"Nana, are you talking about marriage again? That why you're pushing Medford on me?"

"I ain't doing nothing of the sort. Stop trying to accuse me of something that's your fault."

"Nana, what's my fault?"

"I'm done talking right now. I trust you'll know what's best for you and stop dilly-dallying around." Nana hung up the phone just as Louise began to open her mouth.

Nana was getting riled up over nothing, Louise thought. But what did she mean about Medford looking for his mother? Was she the "other woman" who was the source of his preoccupation? If that were the case, she'd feel really stupid, but in a way it was already too late. She had become fond of Jeremiah, and the back-and-forth between the two men was making her tired. Even though she spent more time with Jeremiah than Medford, the combination of exerting physical energy with the former and expending mental energy on the latter made her feel like she was spiraling downward toward a serious vitamin deficiency. It was beyond exhausting. Yet despite that, she noticed something interesting was beginning to happen that she couldn't ignore. It was as if she couldn't go anywhere with Jeremiah without feeling the obvious were missing, like taking a walk in the park and one day noticing the grass had disappeared.

While Louise and Jeremiah always enjoyed their time together, the thought of Medford kept intruding on her fun. There was a change taking place that she couldn't explain—like an overlap, having some kind of crossover effect. When she and Jeremiah had gone to a matinee to see the new movie *Uptown Saturday Night*, a strange thing occurred. Every now and then, she'd see Medford's face on the giant screen instead of Sidney Poitier's. She had to squeeze her eyes and rub them with her hands to try to make the illusion go away, but Medford's image was stubborn, and sometimes it just stayed in a scene with Bill Cosby longer than she'd like. The movie was roll-over, belly-aching funny, and she couldn't remember the last time she'd laughed that hard, probably not since Elvira accidentally washed Billy's police uniform instead of taking it to the dry cleaners and he put it on and split his pants.

Even after the movie, when Louise and Jeremiah went back to her house and tried several new positions from the *More Joy of Sex* book and made love like long-eared jackrabbits half the night, Louise could feel Medford's presence in the room. It was as if another set of eyes were watching her in the dark and it was creepy, making her feel as if she were being caught in an act of betrayal. It didn't use to be that way, and she wished she could blow away the mirage as easily as she could hold the stem and force air to release the white cottony seeds of a dandelion in spring.

When Medford finally made time to take Louise out on a date, they went to see the new movie *Claudine*. A single mother raising six kids with a boyfriend in the picture who was trying to help out was more serious than fun. She loved Diahann Carroll and James Earl Jones, but thought the movie was slow-moving and methodical, which was a little like being with Medford. Regardless, she enjoyed the time with him and realized she missed him dearly.

That night when she and Medford went back to her house after the movie and made love, the sex was much different than it was with Jeremiah. Sex with Medford was also slow and methodical, which worked in his favor. There was a long interlude of fore-play and a leisurely stroll up to climax. Satisfaction ran high with Medford. With him, there was no need for a second round.

When his hand took control of her body, it was the only time she considered surrender. The way it spread her legs wide open and fondled the source of her pleasure made her melt into a place that was frozen in time, suspended in space, surrounded by four walls attached to a floor, and beyond was no outside world, only nebulous clouds floating by.

When their breathing got back to normal, Louise kissed his birthmark as if it were a sweet spot demanding her to caress it with her tongue over and over again until he moaned like a baby. Then she held him in her arms until he collapsed, his full weight upon her body, and fell asleep. It was getting to the point where Louise was beginning to realize she could no more control her feelings for Medford than she could hold back an avalanche with a shovel.

Louise woke up to the smell of coffee and when she opened her eyes, Medford's clothes were gone. When she sat up, she heard him stirring in the kitchen. "What are you doing up so early?" she asked, rearranging her cornrows to make herself presentable.

"Good morning." He smiled, walking into the bedroom, carrying two cups of coffee. "Want some?"

Louise nodded.

Medford knew just how she liked it—coffee with a little milk to match her cocoa-colored skin, with one teaspoon of sugar to take off the bitter edge. He handed her the Huey Newton mug while he drank his coffee with the Angela Davis silkscreen across the ceramic. The Black Panther line of mugs were collector's items that Louise had special-ordered last year; they included the like-nesses of H. Rap Brown, Bobby Seale, Stokely Carmichael, and Eldridge Cleaver.

"I'm going to the Town Hall, to the Municipal Offices," Medford finally said, sitting on the edge of her bed. "I'm going to the Child Welfare Bureau, Office of Family Assistance, Missing Person's Department, and anyplace else where I can get some information on my mother." Medford took one big swallow and looked squarely at Louise. "I'm in the process of looking for her. That's what I've been doing with my time. I know you've been occupied with other things, but when and if I find her, I'd like to ask you to marry me. I know how you get nervous and all about making commitments, but I'm just taking your fling with the Outsider as being temporary, as a last chance to sow your wild oats. Do it now, 'cause when you decide to be with me, your sowing classes will be over."

Louise listened to Medford's words, which was all she could do because she wasn't prepared to give him a response.

"Now when I find my mother . . . *if* I find her . . . and at least I have to try . . . at that time, I'll feel my life is complete. Then I can be ready to ask you for your hand in marriage. Of course, I'll have to ask Granddaddy first."

Having her suspicions overturned by Medford after wrongfully accusing him of seeing another woman made Louise want to go underground and voluntarily disappear, much like Huey Newton exiled himself to Cuba this year.

"Meanwhile, I need you to wait for me and consider my offer." Medford, sensing he had stepped into a lion's den, was hopeful his scent was nonthreatening.

Louise could hardly return his gaze, feeling like she'd been put on the spot. Even though he had made up his mind, she hadn't given their relationship any overall thought. "Medford, it's too early to talk about this," she complained. "I haven't even finished my coffee."

Medford stood up abruptly, annoyed that she'd returned his affections with selfish disregard. "Well, I have." His smile disappeared as he took his last swallow, walked into the kitchen, and placed Angela Davis in the sink. "I'll catch up with you later," he said, trying to conceal his anger as he closed the door.

Louise put her Huey Newton mug on the night table, then pulled the covers over her head to block out the daylight and escape her own insensitivity. If Medford wanted to look for his mama, that was *his* issue, not hers. If Medford wanted to get married, that was *his* issue, not hers. She couldn't make his issues her own. She only wanted to have fun and didn't see anything wrong with that. She would no more take on anyone else's problems than she would walk barefoot on broken glass. Besides, as much as she hated to admit it, she thought she might be falling in love with Jeremiah. The notion made her think about Rule Number Five: CHEATING MAKES YOU LOWER THAN A DOG SCRATCHING UP A WORM IN THE DIRT, but she didn't feel that applied to her because she wasn't married. However, in doubt and needing confirmation, she called Elvira for support.

"Hey, Vi."

"Watch you doing up there?" Elvira was washing breakfast dishes. "Why don't you come downstairs and talk?"

"I'm still in bed," Louise yawned, pretending to be sleepy. "Anyway, I'll make it quick. Tell me what you think about this . . ." Louise took a breath before she proceeded, like holding her nose before going underwater because it might be some time before she resurfaced. "I'm starting to really dig Jeremiah," she fired off rapidly, then threw the phone on the bed, covered her ears, and still heard Elvira's shrill response through the receiver.

"*What?*"

Now that she'd got that part over with, Louise reached for the phone. "I've seen him a few times and I think he's nice."

"You mean, that's not Medford I hear upstairs?"

"Not all the time."

"You little hussy! Louise, what are you doing?" Elvira took the liberty of yelling because she was in the house by herself.

"Just havin' fun . . . I think." Louise could hear Elvira shouting through the floorboards and wondered if she even needed to use the telephone service for this conversation.

"You have to stop seeing him right now, Louise Dunlap," Elvira scolded, turning off the water.

"I just found out that Medford is not seeing another woman."

"I already told you that."

"Vi, what am I gonna do?"

"You know what you're gonna do. Why are you asking me? You have the answer to that question. You're a take-charge woman. Control yourself. Stop having feelings for that Outsider—cut 'em off like chopping vegetables with a knife. If you're bored, get a hobby, not another man. You just gone crazy out your mind. Think, girl. Think nothing but trouble, 'cause it's only gonna lead to no good." Elvira hesitated, starting to worry. "Do you need some help out the situation? 'Cause I'll get Billy. I've never known you to be sensitive about hurtin' nobody's feelings. Tell him don't come up the road no more. Do you need Billy to have a talk with him to make him stay his behind at the cottage? I'm sure it can be arranged. It's no sweat for me to do it."

"Vi, Vi. It's me who's keeping this thing going, not Jeremiah," Louise interrupted, trying to get a word in. "And I appreciate the thought, but keep Billy out of this. There's no need to get him involved, and don't tell him I called you about this either." When Louise hung up, she looked at the phone and said to no one, "Thank you for your advice. It was really helpful."

It was a good thing Billy had left for work not too long ago. Elvira thought about calling him at the Sheriff's Office or on his

CB radio, but she tried to hold back and honor Louise's request. Instead, she dried her last pot, grabbed a bag of Cheez Doodles, and started eating. She also found a pad and pencil and started jotting down details of the conversation in case she forgot pieces of the story because she might have to share them with her husband later. She didn't necessarily want to make it part of their dinner conversation, but if they discussed something that was related, at least she'd have the option to pull out the pad with her news.

Medford didn't have time to be tripping over Louise if she was going to have an attitude. He had to use the day to stay focused. With more important things to do in his life right now, if she didn't want to be included in his plans, that was her problem and her loss.

Turning on the radio in the pickup truck, Medford heard Marvin Gaye's "Trouble Man" and thought about how women *make you want to holler and throw up both your hands*. Then he turned down the road to the cottage and thought that even little women could sometimes make you want to do the same.

Ruby Rose had two textbooks and a notebook under her arm while she waited for Medford at the cottage door. When she saw him, she ran to the truck and hopped into the front seat.

"Where are we heading this time?" She closed the car door.

"Town Hall, here we come," Medford said as they drove off, noticing her science and social studies books.

After sitting quietly for a while, Ruby Rose could no longer contain herself. "Jeremiah was just on the phone with her, if you want to know."

"No. I don't want to know," said Medford, annoyed at the news. "I'm not interested in hearing about Jeremiah and Louise, and if we're going to be friends, you have to remember Rule Num-

ber Nine: 'Mind Your Own Business Personally and Professionally.'"

"Hmmph," replied Ruby Rose. "I'm just saying what I saw. It's
not like I was listening. And I don't blame you for not spending
time with her today, 'cause mamas are way more important than
girlfriends, especially two-timing ones."

Medford shook his head as he parked the pickup truck, and he
and Ruby Rose went inside the Town Hall building and looked at
the directory. He spent the first part of the day covering the main
floor for information, examining files as closely as a prison guard
combing a new inmate for ticks. He scoured the Lemon City
Health and Human Services Department and the Domestic Rela-
tions Court Clerk Office, looking through documents, asking as
many questions as he could that would forward his investigation.
So far, he'd found nothing useful; it was as if he had dunked his
cup into a water well and come up with dry sand. At the Office of
Family Assistance, where the gentleman behind the counter wasn't
of any help, Medford suggested he modify the sign on the door to
read "Office of Family Assistance, *Depending*." *Depending* on what
year you were researching, *depending* on how much information
people wanted to reveal, *depending* on which files were selected
way back when to be kept, *depending* on the case. He and Ruby
Rose spent the whole afternoon on the second floor at the Department of Birth Records and Death Certificates, the Missing Persons
Department, and the Office of Referral Services and Clearing-
house. He looked through information as far back as the 1900s
until his eyes felt like they were about to cross and his head hurt
from reading so much material. Everyone who was old enough recalled the incident of baby Medford in a basket on the front
porch, like Moses in a basket on the Nile, but that was about it.
Memories stopped as if they'd reached a dead end after a certain

period of time. It seemed the only thing the Lemonites cared about was that the baby was safe. Since the mama never revealed herself, it was as though she'd never even existed.

Disappointment weighed heavily on Medford like an anvil resting on his chest, but then he remembered he hadn't gone to the Child Welfare Bureau. Spotting the arrow pointing to the other end of the hallway, he grabbed Ruby Rose's hand and followed the sign.

Chester Goody was biting the last remaining nail on his finger while reading the *Lemon City Chronicle*. He was sitting at his desk, peering at the clock every now and then as he usually did when it was an hour before quitting time. The Child Welfare Bureau was hardly ever busy, and today the phone had rung only four times, so when the two people came walking through the door, he was looking forward to having direct human contact and conversation.

"What can I do for you two today?" Chester offered getting up from his desk, trying not to appear too anxious to help. He looked the tall, dark-skinned man up and down, lingering a bit longer on his face. "Medford, is that you?"

"You know me?" Medford asked the man, who looked to be about the same age as Clement and Granddaddy.

"I know your father, Clement. I see you two together in town. Figured you were his son." He glanced down at Ruby Rose. "That your daughter?"

"No. Sorry. This here is my friend, Ruby Rose." The way Chester looked at him, Medford thought he'd rephrase the statement. "Ruby Rose is a family friend. As a matter of fact, that's why I'm here . . . because of family."

"Pray, tell," said Chester, becoming more interested.

Tired of hearing the same story over and over again, Ruby Rose found a chair and began to read her social studies book while Medford explained about his mama.

"If you know my father, then you're probably familiar with the story." Medford made sure that Chester understood.

"Sure am." Chester nodded, looking at the clock, determining he still had time to chat. "Never forget it. Seemed like every other week there was a headline about it in the *Chronicle*, or a story in the news. Let's see, that was back there in the late twenties . . ."

"Nineteen twenty-nine, to be exact. In fact, the reason I'm here is because I'm investigating how I got to Lemon City. What exactly happened? Why did it happen? Somebody must know something."

"We was all together," started Chester.

"Who?" asked Medford.

"Back in high school, we were all in the same class—Clement, Willie, Ernestine, Lurleen, Easley, Theola, Sadie, and Vernelle. They used to be in a group. All of 'em as tight as a metal cap on a bottle of root beer." Chester laughed at his own little joke. "But I also knew Earthalee Tisdale."

"Earthalee?"

"Yes. Earthalee wasn't in that group. But I knew her too."

"The woman who owns and manages Do Drop In Stay As Long As You Like?" Do Drop In was an apothecary, on Mansahutten and Main, on the other side of town.

"That would be the same."

"What about her?"

Chester looked at the clock. He had about a half-hour left before closing, enough time to tell his story.

"Earthalee Tisdale. Everyone used to call her Dizzy-Tizzy, but she wasn't nobody's fool. She was ambitious and ruddy-looking; a woman whose name suited her, because she was as brown as the earth with her feet planted firmly on the ground because it seemed no one could uproot her from her opinions, least of all me, but I'll get to that later. She was a woman who knew what she wanted and would stop at nothing to get it. When Earthalee decided to expand on the apothecary her great-great-great-grandfather Solomon Butler built, she knocked down and renovated the original structure, made it more modern, and turned it into a coffee shop so folks could have a casual place to eat and relax. Then she built a large addition off the coffee shop for the drugstore part of her business. In the middle of her project, something terrible happened. Her husband Horace died when he was crushed by fallen scaffolding that broke his back. But that didn't strop Earthalee. She wanted to stay on schedule, and that's when she found herself a new husband named Profitt to finish what she started, and things have been going smooth for her ever since. Of course, Earthalee had it in her mind since high school that she was gonna be successful, and that's when we dated, but she left me for Horace."

Chester lowered his eyes to the counter, shaking his head, remembering the day he was dumped like old clothes into the Goodwill bin like it was yesterday. Medford wondered what this story had to do with him.

"Now here's the part I think you'll find interesting." Chester began to perk back up. "Next thing I know, I see Earthalee walking down the street and she's bigger than I've ever seen her before. Looked to be round in a family kind of way to me. Then the next thing I know is I don't see her for almost a year and when I do, she's back to being herself again. Now I always had been suspicious about that—women skinny and then fat and then skinny again—weight going up and down like a yo-yo, disappearing for an extended period of time. Maybe she told her first husband,

Horace, she didn't want any kids and she got pregnant and went away somewhere and had you. Now that you're standing here telling me that you're looking for you mama, I'm thinking Earthalee might be the one. She's probably the right age to have given birth to a man like you. She's a big woman now and you're kinda big-boned yourself. Don't hold me to it, but I'm sure you're familiar with Rule Number Six: 'What Goes Around Will Always Come Back Around and Hit You in the Head.'" Chester leaned over the counter, closer to Medford, so Ruby Rose couldn't hear. "All I know is, sooner or later, you were bound to show up and come a-lookin' for her." Chester took a deep breath, then glanced at the clock. "If I were you, I'd have a talk with Earthalee. But remember Rule Number Four: 'Don't Let the Mojo Lady Know You Got Troubles. If You Do, She'll Give You More.'" Chester leaned closer to Medford and said in a whisper, "If I were you, I'd also keep this to myself." He made a head gesture toward Ruby Rose. "I'd suggest you go to Do Drop In Stay As Long As You Like, but you probably won't make it there before closing time. The doors lock at five o'clock on Thursdays."

Ruby Rose gasped at how late it was. "Medford, I have to be at Elvira's by five-thirty."

"What's your name again?" Medford thought that was an amazing story.

"Chester . . . Chester Goody . . . that's with a 'y.' Some people think it's spelled with an 'ing,' but that's not me. That's someone else."

"Chester, brother. Thanks a million." Medford shook his hand.

"My pleasure." As Medford and Ruby Rose walked out the door, Chester added, "I thought Earthalee was coming back to me after Horace died, but she got attached to Profitt instead."

Medford closed the door.

"I wished things had turned out different," Chester continued, talking to himself. "Don't get me wrong, I'm really happy for her. Honestly I am," he said to no one. He searched his fingernails for something left to chew and found a piece of skin to satisfy his hunger, then he turned out the lights and locked the door.

When Medford got into his pickup, he hoped it would be the last time he'd have to see Town Hall. He had a smile on his face and was happy for the lead. He was excited to learn about Earthalee. However, since Do Drop In Stay As Long As You Like was on the other side of town and he had only been there on a few occasions, he had a hard time attaching a face to the name. Now that he had his first piece of concrete information—had finally encountered someone who had some thoughts on the matter, despite the fact that the old guy was a little weird—Medford thought he'd follow up first thing in the morning. At that moment, his stomach began to feel queasy, and he pulled over to the side of the road and vomited.

Ruby Rose watched in horror until she realized Medford's stomach was probably having a hard time digesting everything that had happened today.

"I'll go with you in the morning," she offered, while reaching over to pat his shoulder. "Don't worry. I'm your friend."

Medford looked at the little girl who was becoming such a gem in his life.

Ruby Rose was trying to read her social studies book, but every time Medford hit a bump in the road her eyes jumped off the page. So far she had just learned about the Civil War, which was the chapter preceding Lemon City history. She'd read about the Founding Fathers, the five men who established Lemon City: Benjamin T. Washington, who was responsible for Religion; Shadrach Mosby Dunlap, who was responsible for Law and Government; Tobias Crawford, whose area was Education; Eli Johnson, whose job was Agriculture; and Solomon Butler, who was responsible for Medicine and Health.

Based on her new knowledge, she determined that if Medford was related to Earthalee Tisdale, whose great-great-grandfather was Solomon Butler, then he would be descended from one of the Founding Fathers of Lemon City, and she thought that would be pretty cool. If that were the case, she also thought it would be pretty neat that his ancestor's name was Jeremiah. More than a coincidence, it would be something else they had in common.

Medford pulled up outside the two-family house and Ruby Rose jumped out of the truck.

"Don't forget to pick me up in the morning."

"Okay. I'll call first."

"Okay." Ruby Rose trotted up the walkway and rang Elvira's doorbell.

Medford looked upstairs to see if there was any movement in Louise's top half of the house. The curtains were pulled back and the windows were cracked open, but it didn't look like anyone was home.

When Elvira came to the door, she and Medford waved to each other. Then he pressed the clutch down to the floor, put the truck in gear, and pulled off.

As soon as Ruby Rose walked through the door, she was excited to tell Elvira everything she had learned about the Civil War, leading up to Lemon City history. Then she said hello to Billy and gave him a big hug. Then she turned around suddenly, having heard unexpected footsteps coming from the kitchen. The sight of Louise made her jaw drop and her feet stop dead in her tracks as if they had their own brakes.

"Hello, Ruby Rose," said Louise, coming out of the kitchen. "Elvira tells me you're a pretty good student." When Ruby Rose didn't respond, Louise continued. "Because you work really hard, and I hear you're doing so well, I thought you deserved a little reward. I was hoping after your lesson today, the three of us could make some lemon cookies."

Ruby Rose looked at Elvira, who nodded her head and smiled. Then she looked at Louise and was at a loss for words. She didn't want to respond with the truth, but she didn't want to tell a lie.

"What do you say to that?" asked Elvira, prodding for a favorable response.

"I guess it's okay." Ruby Rose looked at her shoes.

"Okay?" asked Billy, who couldn't help overhearing. "Is that all you have to say? All that sugar you just gave me, I know you must like sweets."

Ruby Rose giggled when she looked at Billy, but her mouth straightened when she returned to Louise. "I like cookies."

"Good." Louise smiled. "Just come on back in the kitchen when you're done. We'll have fun." Then she disappeared behind the door.

Ruby Rose took a test that Elvira gave her based on her social studies homework. After that it was time for science, and Elvira gave an introduction to the biology of plants. Botany, she called it, and spoke specifically about the growth process, using tomatoes as an example. By the time the lesson ended, Ruby Rose knew a lot about tomatoes—the classification of seeds, tomato reproduction, how to plant a tomato garden, the different tomato varieties, pests and diseases. The more she learned about tomatoes, the more respect she had for Nana and the more guilty she felt about giving Ole Miss Johnson the jumbo bush. She wished she could get it back from the old lady, but she already knew it was too late.

Now that Louise was making an effort to be nice to her, Ruby Rose was starting to feel guilty about that too. Maybe she was wrong about Louise. It was probably way too early to tell, since baking a batch of cookies wasn't enough evidence to remove her doubt.

When Ruby Rose's home schooling ended, she dragged her feet to the kitchen. Elvira and Louise were waiting for her so they could begin to prepare the cookie dough. They tried to get Billy to join them, but he complained there were too many women in the kitchen and he went to visit Granddaddy across the street.

While Ruby Rose was measuring the flour, she kept looking up at Louise as if she were waiting for a two-headed monster to appear, but it never did. When they finished making the batter and dropping the round shapes onto the cookie sheet, they listened to music. Elvira had an eight-track tape that played all the songs Ruby Rose heard on the radio, and they danced while they waited for the cookies to bake.

They talked about the last episode of *Good Times*, in which J.J. sold the family TV set in exchange for rent money, and how awful that was. When they started feeling sad, they cheered themselves up by talking about all the rides, games, and various performances and the amazing animals in the petting zoo at the Annual County Fair. With only four months left to go until the big event, the sisters promised Ruby Rose she'd have the time of her life.

When the cookies finished baking and cooling, they ate them along with a cold glass of milk.

"Let's not care about spoiling our appetites, just for one day," exclaimed Elvira. "I'm starving."

"Yeah. Let's have cookies for dinner," agreed Ruby Rose, toasting the sisters.

"I'll drink to that." Louise winked at Ruby Rose.

Ruby Rose half-smiled at Louise, which was more of a reflex reaction than a show of kindness. She also chose not to reciprocate the wink.

When they were all stuffed, Elvira put some cookies away for Billy. She also set aside a couple dozen for her fourth-grade class at school, and while she was saving cookies for other people, she ate a few more herself.

It was getting late and Ruby Rose decided it was time to go home. She put on her sweater and grabbed her books.

"Ruby Rose, would you like me to walk you to the cottage?" Louise was cheerful, feeling good about their time together.

Ruby Rose bristled like a porcupine, feeling the goose bumps rise on her neck. "No thank you. I know the way," she said coldly.

"I know you do." Louise maintained her composure so her words wouldn't snap. "Since we were having fun, I just thought you might like company."

"No thank you," Ruby Rose repeated. "I can walk on my own. I'm used to it," she responded flatly. Ruby Rose looked at Elvira and said, "Thanks, Elvira. See you in a couple days." Then she turned to Louise and added, "Good night."

On her way back to the cottage, Ruby Rose discovered a smooth rock in the middle of the road and started kicking it like she was playing soccer. She kicked it once pretending it was Louise, then kicked it again imagining it was Jeremiah. Finally she just launched it like a rocket with her foot into a cluster of black-eyed Susans and purple foxgloves along the side of the road. The last thing she wanted was for Louise to walk her home and then try to come inside when it was her turn to spend time with Jeremiah.

Jeremiah had dinner waiting on the table.

"How was your lesson today?" He put the pot of lima beans back on the stove.

"Fine." She put her books on the kitchen table next to her plate.

"That's no place for books."

"I need a desk."

"Okay. We'll get one." Jeremiah saw that his sister had an attitude and he eyed her suspiciously. "How's everything going with Medford?"

"Fine." Ruby Rose sat down at the table in front of a plate of food, but was too filled with cookies to eat. Then she had an idea. "Medford thinks he found his mama today."

"He does? Who is she?"

"She owns Do Drop In Stay As Long As You Like apothecary and coffee shop on the other side of town."

"That's close to Jefferson County, isn't it?"

"Yep."

"Does he know for sure that's her?"

"We're going to ask her tomorrow. Then when he finds out she's his mama, he'll ask Louise to marry him." She looked at her brother's face for a reaction, but she got nothing, so she added, "What do you think about that?"

"I think that's up to Louise."

"Do you want to marry her?"

"No. I don't want to marry her."

"Then why are you messin' around with her?"

"Ruby Rose, you know our plan is to head up north."

"But I like it here."

"But we got cops on our trail and we can't stay. We can't wait for another school year to come and go. We've got to leave sometime after the Annual County Fair." Jeremiah started pacing. "So far we've been lucky, and I don't want our luck to run out anytime soon. Plus, I'm scared someone will start talking to the wrong person about there being this great healer in town, and the next thing I know I'll have Outsiders lined up at my door, or worse, Jefferson County Sheriff Beauregard Taylor, knocking." Jeremiah caught himself making a reference to Outsiders as if he wasn't one himself. He had been in Lemon City for almost six months now and was surprised by his own comment.

"But *we're* Outsiders," Ruby Rose reminded him.

"That's exactly why we've got to go." Jeremiah sat down at the table so he could be at Ruby Rose's level. "I know it's spring and we haven't been doing a lot of things together and I'm sorry about that. Don't take it personally. That's because they're looking for a man with a young girl that fit our description and it's probably safer for us if we do things apart, at least for now. I know it's hard, but it won't last forever. The more time we put between us and Miss Molly Esther Reynolds and the more space we put between us and Mattoxville, the better off we'll be."

Ruby Rose didn't like it when Jeremiah talked of leaving Lemon City. She liked it there.

That night Ruby Rose tossed and turned. She wanted Medford to find his mama, but in a way, she hoped he didn't so that everything could stay the same. Lately, she felt she was getting along fine without her brother, but now she had a new fear and was concerned about losing a friend.

In the morning, Ruby Rose heard the horn blow outside and ran to the pickup truck to greet it.

It took fifteen minutes to get from one side of town to the other. When they arrived at Do Drop In Stay As Long As You Like, Medford put a nickel in the parking meter and they walked in.

It was crowded for a Thursday morning, but there were two stools left empty at the counter that appeared to be waiting for Medford and Ruby Rose. Scanning the coffee shop, Medford recognized a few faces, shook hands, and said hello. He and Ruby Rose sat at the counter, and when the waitress came over they ordered breakfast. When she left, Medford leaned back to check out the rear section of the store that must have been the new addition Chester had referred to. As he peered around the coffee shop and glanced down as many aisles in the apothecary section as he could, he was trying to spot someone who looked like she might be named Earthalee.

"What are you gonna say?" asked Ruby Rose, drinking her orange juice.

"I'm gonna ask for Earthalee."

"Then what are you gonna say? You gonna ask her if she's your mama?"

"It's not as simple as that." Medford scratched the space between his neck and chin. "I'm just gonna have a conversation with the woman." The truth was, he hadn't figured that part out yet. All he knew was that he had to be tactful. "Don't worry. I'll handle it."

After a while, the waitress came back with their food.

"Excuse me," Medford said to the woman. "Is Earthalee Tisdale here today?"

"She's upstairs in the office and doesn't come down until noon."

Medford looked at his watch, which indicated ten-thirty. "I'm not usually on this side of town, and I believe her to be an old friend of my dad's and I'd like to say hello. Would it be possible for her to come downstairs?"

"I'll ask if she's available." The waitress left carrying a half-filled pot of coffee.

"Are you ready for this?" asked Ruby Rose

"Right on, little sistah." Medford pointed a Black Power fist to the air and made his arm shake on purpose. "I'm not nervous." He and Ruby Rose laughed.

Earthalee Tisdale was a big, tall, brown-skinned woman in her early to mid-sixties who looked strong enough to lift the kind of lumber needed to build a house if she had to. Attempting to be inconspicuous, Medford glanced her up and down for any sign of resemblance. Her height, weight, and muscular build were familiar and her hands were big. Her face was stern and her eyes were narrow and he could tell they liked to get straight to the point; she was a woman who had no time for tomfoolery, who didn't take any nonsense. Despite her rigid appearance of sixty-something years, she was still beautiful and looked like she could spread on charm like butter melting between two slabs of warm toast.

"What can I do for y'all today?" Earthalee asked in a drawl that was even Southern for Lemon City. She started wiping the counter with a damp cloth even though it was already clean.

"Good morning," said Medford, trying to swallow a forkful of grits. "My name is Medford Attaway, and this here is Ruby Rose Wilkes."

Medford and Earthalee shook hands.

"Nice to meet y'all." Earthalee showed off a smile that displayed sturdy teeth that looked as strong as stainless steel.

"Do you know a Chester Goody at the Child Welfare Bureau in town?" Medford asked.

"I know Chester, but I don't know nothing about him and child welfare. According to my memory, he could hardly take care of himself." Earthalee let out a hearty laugh that started somewhere in the middle of her stomach and circulated throughout her body to make it rumble and shake.

Medford and Ruby Rose exchanged glances.

"Umm," said Medford, not sure where to go from there.

"Chester said he went to high school with you," piped up Ruby Rose.

"Yes, he did," admitted Earthalee. "What's this all about, anyway? Been a long time since I was in high school and almost as long since I last seen Chester."

"Ma'am, this is kind of awkward for me, and I don't know quite how to put this," stumbled Medford. "But does the name Medford Attaway mean anything to you?" Medford could see Earthalee thinking. "I was adopted, and I was wondering if you might remember anything about it."

"Oh . . . I see . . . uh-huh. So you're Clement's boy. You're that baby that showed up on his doorstep. I recall when that happened. At first, we were all shocked and stunned by the incident, but we all recovered quickly and things just got back to normal. Just another day, just another baby being brought into the world." Earthalee lifted Medford's chin to examine him more closely. "My, my. Look how nice you turned out. All good-looking and I bet you're smart too." Earthalee nodded her head in approval. "Clement did a good job with you. Didn't think he had it in him with his drinking an' all. Nobody knew how that story was gonna turn out, but it looks like he fooled every single one of us. Looks like he did alright."

"Are you his mama?" Ruby Rose blurted out, getting impatient.

Earthalee raised her damp cloth and shook it in front of Ruby Rose's face. "No, I ain't this boy's mama, young lady. Who do you think you are asking me a question like that?" she snapped.

"She didn't mean any harm, Miss Tisdale," defended Medford.

"I ain't nobody's mama," confirmed Earthalee. "I rebuilt this apothecary and built this coffee shop from the ground up. I ain't got time to be nobody's mama."

"That's what Chester Goody says," replied Medford.

"What does Chester know? He's just a spurned lover. Been torn up about us breaking up for over forty years. That's almost half a century, man still hasn't gotten over it. He just hangs onto stuff worse than old gum stuck to the bottom of your shoe," said Earthalee as she walked behind the counter. "If that's what you

came over here to talk to me about, you're just wasting your time."
She made her way back up the stairs, climbing each step as if it
were part of a military drill.

Medford paid the check, and he and Ruby Rose took to the
street.

By the way Earthalee had turned on them, Medford wasn't
completely convinced she was innocent of the charge. Her overre-
action to the question made him even more suspicious. He understood the fact that a mother who gave away her baby forty-four
years ago might deny the unthinkable had occurred and be unpre-
pared to make a confession. The memory was probably as painful
for her as it was for him. Besides, springing news on someone like
that and taking her by surprise didn't seem to be a good thing.
Putting people on the spot appeared to be a recurring habit with
him lately, and he'd have to get better at handling confrontation.
Whatever he was doing wasn't working. It wasn't getting him the
results he needed. His goal wasn't to make people recoil and re-
treat.

As soon as he'd regrouped, Medford thought he'd revisit
Chester Goody and ask to go through his files to see if he could
make any sense of the pieces and put them all together. He'd also
inquire about Earthalee's first husband, Horace. Although Horace
was dead, maybe there were clues that connected him to Medford's past. Ignoring any possibility would be negligence on his
part. Perhaps he'd have a chat with Earthalee's new husband, Profitt, as well.

"What are we gonna do now?" Ruby Rose asked, craning her
neck to look out the back window as if she was half-expecting
Earthalee to come out of nowhere and chase them down the road
like a German shepherd coming after trespassers long after they
had gone.

"I'm gonna take you to piano lessons," Medford responded. As much as he appreciated Ruby Rose's company, he would be glad to be by himself so he could think.

"No," she said. "I mean about Earthalee."

"I'm gonna look into her background a bit more, check out the story and try to figure things out."

"I'm sorry about shouting out the question about her being your mama," apologized Ruby Rose.

"No sweat. Next time just let me do all the talking."

Medford let Ruby Rose out in front of the church. They waved good-bye and he drove off, thinking about Earthalee Tisdale, trying to understand how she got the nickname Dizzy-Tizzy because, like Chester said, the woman was nobody's fool.

Sadie was inside the sanctuary, pouring all her emotion into singing and playing "Blessed Assurance" on the piano. When she saw Ruby Rose coming toward her, she changed her tune to something more cheery: "When the Saints Go Marching In."

After they exchanged pleasantries, Ruby Rose sat down on the bench next to Sadie and warmed up her fingers over the keys, playing scales. Then, reading the sheet music, she played the melody for "When the Saints Go Marching In" while Sadie looked on. When Ruby Rose got the hang of it, Sadie stood up to give her more room to play the entire song, this time adding her left hand and foot pedals. In an effort to be perfect, Ruby Rose stopped whenever she made a mistake and started from the beginning. Overall, she thought she sounded pretty good, and by the contentment on Sadie's face she could tell she was getting better.

"Have you been practicing at Ernestine's house too?"

"No, Ma'am. I've just been practicing here a few days a week."

"Is that right? I guess you're what they call 'a natural.'" Sadie smiled, looking at the ceiling. "I hear you when I'm upstairs working in the office, and you sound just like an angel." She paused.

"Okay. Let's try it again. Slow down the tempo this time." Sadie clapped her hands to help Ruby Rose keep the rhythm. But it was when Sadie started singing in her high-pitched signature style that was a cross between opera and gospel and amounted to a howling sound that Ruby Rose got all mixed up.

"Miss Sadie," Ruby Rose said as she continued playing.

"Yes, darlin'." Sadie didn't like being interrupted.

"I don't mean to hurt your feelings or anything, Miss Sadie, but I think I can play better when you don't sing."

"Okay, darlin'. No trouble at all."

When Sadie stopped singing she was sitting so close to Ruby Rose that Ruby Rose could feel the old lady's breath hitting against her face, creating a different kind of annoyance.

"Just play it one more time, dear. Then we'll practice the song you're going to perform in the recital."

Ruby Rose found herself in a tug of war with Sadie over which song to play in the recital that would take place the weekend after the Annual County Fair. Ruby Rose wanted to play a song from the radio, but Sadie wanted her to play a gospel tune. If Ruby Rose wanted to play "You've Got a Friend" by James Taylor, Sadie would strongly recommend she play "Go Tell It On the Mountain." If Ruby Rose wanted to play "Lean on Me" by Bill Withers, Sadie would encourage her to play "If You See My Savior." After a while, Ruby Rose talked her way out of performing gospel music, saying other students were already playing it and she could make the recital more interesting by adding variety. She clinched the argument by convincing Sadie that modern music would be a good way to attract young people to the church. Although Miss Sadie looked at her with a squinty eye, after thinking about it, she saw Ruby Rose's point of view and let her have her way.

Now that Ruby Rose had talked Miss Sadie into letting her play her original song, "Killing Me Softly With His Song" by

Roberta Flack, she was reminded there were only a few months left before the Annual County Fair. While she had plenty of time to practice her solo, and was looking forward to her first public performance, she also knew the Fair benchmarked when she and Jeremiah would be leaving Lemon City for good. There was a bittersweet taste in her mouth as if her saliva had turned to acid, forming the knot that resulted in her stomach. She loved her new Lemon City family. It was the best family she'd ever had, and she thought Jeremiah couldn't have picked a better place to make their home.

Chapter Ten

A blue haze hovered over the mountains like a halo. The craggy ridges, giant boulders, and high peaks appeared to form a steep staircase that reached from the ground to the sky. The flowers in late May created a colorful mix. It was the only time of year when it seemed the rainbows left the sky and spread themselves across the earth.

Nana looked up from her wide-brimmed straw hat, happy that the thin layer of clouds protected her from the sun. The weather conditions made working in her garden all afternoon more bearable, and she listened to the news on the National Black Network radio station to keep her company. Pruning her plants, inspecting them for bugs, adding fertilizer, and watering her prized possessions took hours. As a result of her labor, her back began to hurt. She stood up for a while to work out the pain that made her feel like an old accordion being stretched beyond its reach. The men were playing chess on the porch and every now and then, Nana would hear them raising their voices, bragging about who made the best move and teasing the one who made the worse. Granddaddy, Clement, and Bootsie were listening to the National Black Network radio station too, which made the front and backyards at the Dunlap house sound like stereo.

In contrast, Ole Miss Johnson was listening to the blues. And the two different radios playing in such close proximity blended like plaids combined with bold prints in the same outfit. The noise was hard on the ears, and Nana wished her neighbor would turn down the music. Big Mama Thornton was belting out "Hound Dog," a tune that she originated long before Elvis knew what a hound dog was, which was competing with the National Black Network trying to tell people about Hank Aaron tying Babe Ruth's record. As much as Nana loved Big Mama, it was Hank who deserved to take center stage now. Nana increased the sound on her radio to hear the details of how Aaron, on his first swing in the first inning of the first game of his twenty-first big-league season, had just made baseball history by beating Babe Ruth's thirty-eight-year-old home-run record. Granddaddy, Clement, and Bootsie, in the middle of their chess game, started hootin' and hollerin' and carryin' on at the much anticipated sports history– making news. Ole Miss Johnson turned up her blues station even more to drown out their joyous outbursts, which prevented Nana from hearing any further elaboration on Hank Aaron's tie-breaking game and what it meant for the Atlanta Braves.

Angered by her neighbor's meanness, Nana put down her watering hose and started heading toward the fence. Just as she was about to give the woman a piece of what was on her mind, another special news bulletin came across the airwaves and removed all her hostility. Because she was hearing the emergency report coming from both backyards, it seemed as if it were being broadcast over a public address system and she and Ole Miss Johnson were forced to listen to the same information at the same time. As the ladies had their radio programs interrupted for a local news flash, they stopped what they were doing to pay close attention. The announcer delivered the heartbreaking news that the great Duke Ellington, leader of the big-band swing era, had died. Both ladies stood frozen in place, staring at their radio as if it had told them a lie. They were truly numbed by the news, in a state of shock. In an instant, the one thing they had in common—the memory of their youth—flashed across their minds simultaneously as they went back in time to formal dances with their husbands, wild house and rent parties, loud juke joints, jumping jamborees, and swing. Dancing all night with finger-popping, showboating daddies until the crack of dawn and sleeping half the day on Saturday and still getting up fresh and going to church Sunday morning. Having shared all those images as if they were adjoined to the same memory, for that brief moment, the unimaginable and unthinkable occurred and the ladies temporarily put their differences aside and wrapped their arms around each other to console one another over the death of the good times. After weeping considerably over their mutual loss, Nana was the first to stop sobbing and speak.

"Sophisticated Lady," she said, with tears in her eyes, arms still wrapped around her neighbor.

" 'A' Train," said Ole Miss Johnson, sobbing into Nana's shoulder.

"Satin Doll," said Nana, wiping away a tear.

"Mood Indigo," said Ole Miss Johnson, raising her eyebrow, peeking up from Nana's shoulder with suspicion, wondering if her neighbor was trying to compete in a version of "Name That Tune" with the titles of the Duke Ellington's songs.

"Black, Brown and Beige," said Nana.

"Solitude!" shouted Ole Miss Johnson, and the temporary friendship spell was broken.

Nana quickly withdrew from the clutches of her neighbor

when something red and round the size of a softball caught her eye. Suddenly, clusters of the large red objects appeared in her neighbor's garden in full focus and clear view. Nana was absolutely appalled at the sight.

"Lurleen, how'd you get those tomatoes to grow that big so fast?" she asked. "You started plantin' the same time as me."

"Never you mind."

"There's something wrong here."

"I didn't break any guidelines or any rules," said Ole Miss Johnson in her defense.

"That's alright," said Nana. "The bigger they get, the faster they'll fall off and die and won't none of them giant behemoths be able to roll their way to the fair."

"This is just a test." Ole Miss Johnson had a sheepish grin. "Besides, that's my business. I know what I'm doing is all. I got the talent. I got the touch."

"Touch, schmuch. You cheated. That ain't right. You're up to something and it ain't anything good." Nana stared at her neighbor's gigantic tomatoes. Then she put it all together and came up with a theory. "You used that root doctor, didn't ya?" she asked, not expecting to get back the truth.

"You better back out of my yard the same way you came in." Ole Miss Johnson threatened Nana with her fist.

Nana went to her side of the fence and mumbled words underneath her breath because it was against her religion to say them out loud. She'd have to talk to someone at the Town Council about this freakish incident to get that dishonest wench disqualified from the competition. But at the moment, Nana couldn't think of how she could prove her neighbor's wrongdoing. Then her anger turned toward the Outsider. How could Jeremiah have given Ole Miss Johnson such an unfair advantage with those gargantuan tomatoes? After all she had done for him and his sister, how could he return her gratitude with a stab in the back? If she had any sense, she'd make the Outsider leave before the Annual County Fair. The only thing that stopped her was plain and simple, like a base stitch on a Butterick dress pattern—the fact that she really liked Ruby Rose.

Nana was so furious over what had happened that day that at night when she tried to sleep, she couldn't. She was so upset about her neighbor's humongous tomatoes that she felt like a valve with a cap that needed to open to release the steam and take off the pressure. After tossing and turning for about an hour, waiting for the discomfort to go away, she finally began to drift into slumber. The next thing she knew she was hearing the barking sounds of bloodhounds in the distance. As the paisley-print wallpaper in her bedroom faded and was replaced with an open, cold steel-gray sky, she saw the pregnant slave woman return to her dream.

The woman's stomach had grown with child, and she was giving birth in the underbrush alongside a river. She pushed and pushed and screamed a silent scream, and the baby slid out onto the soft mud. She held it up and saw that it was a boy and wrapped him in her old tattered jacket. Then, holding him close, she waded across the river. The water was cold and the currents were rough. She lifted him over her head so he wouldn't get wet. As she pushed her legs through the density, her son suddenly became heavy. When she looked up, she found that he had grown. She was carrying a boy-child in her hands and it startled her, and she let go of him and dropped him in the river. Realizing what she had done, she frantically pushed back the currents until she found his hand. He didn't choke or gag; no water appeared to have gotten into his lungs. She was surprised by how untouched he was by the rushing water, and it frightened her. As soon as they reached the other side of the river and collapsed on the riverbank, she looked at her son to make sure he was okay and she saw that he had grown again. This time, he had turned into a teen, and she stared at him, terrified and confused. The howls of the bloodhounds were getting louder as they closed in, and she reached for her son's hand to run. As she turned her head to look down the river, she saw it coming, but it was too late. It was something more frightening than any hound. A giant tidal wave was heading their way, about to sweep over them. Stretching out her arm to her son, she desperately tried to save him, but by now he had changed into a grown man and didn't want her help; he could save himself, and he waved good-bye. The slave woman who had crossed the river and was now free and her born-free son were separated. They both vanished into the engulfing waters.

Nana sat up in bed gagging and choking and Granddaddy woke up, turned on the light, and patted her hard on the back. She grabbed the glass that she usually kept on her night table, but when she recognized the water, she put the glass back down and began to cry.

"Woman, what's wrong with you?" Granddaddy sat up in bed, annoyed that his sleep had been disturbed. "I thought you told me you were done with all your life changes."

"I had a dream. It was awful. It seemed so real. There was this slave woman and her baby." Nana pulled a tissue from the box on her night table and dabbed the beads of sweat from her forehead.

"Please don't tell me about it now. It's three o'clock in the morning."

"And the hounds were chasing her." Nana moved the tissue to her neck to pat it dry.

"I don't need the details right this minute," Granddaddy reassured her. "You can wait until daylight to tell me the story."

"And then the baby turned into a man." Nana seemed more upset by this part than anything else.

"Calm down, now."

"Oh, it was terrible," Nana added.

"Go back to sleep." Granddaddy turned off the light.

"I can't," Nana said in the dark. "I'm going downstairs to get something to eat." She turned the light back on.

"Don't eat at this hour. You'll get heartburn and indigestion. Your stomach will back up on you, and you'll wind up having nightmares all over again." Granddaddy turned the light off. "Come on, now. Lay down here with me." He saw that his wife didn't know what to do, so he made the decision for her. He gently pulled her to him and she leaned back into his arms, rolling slowly like a giant tree falling to the ground. He tucked her head into the fold of his shoulder and massaged her temples and stroked the top of her head until her breathing became heavy and deep and she made little snoring sounds and he knew she was asleep.

The next day, Nana was still disturbed by her dream. While she was happy to be with friends and have the distraction of working on her quilt to help her to forget, her head became heavy and her eyes began to close.

"Ernestine. Wake up," said Vernelle, sitting next to her white purse. "Didn't you get a good night's sleep last night?"

"I had that pregnant dream again," said Nana, catching herself dozing. She tugged on the backing to make sure it was straight. "It woke me up in the middle of the night and I had a hard time getting my rest."

"Why you keep dreaming about pregnant women?" asked Sadie, pushing her glasses to the top of her nose.

"It was the same one as before," said Nana.

Sadie looked down at the fabric. "Are you sure Elvira's not pregnant? 'As you do not know the path of the wind or how the body is formed in a mother's womb, so you cannot understand the work of God the maker of all things.' Ecclesiastes," she added.

"If Elvira were pregnant, I'd be the second person to know," replied Nana.

" 'Blessed are you among women and blessed is the child you will bear.' That's Luke," added Vernelle.

"I assure you, I'm not the one pregnant. I don't care how old Sarah was when she was carrying Isaac."

"Maybe there's something wrong with Ernestine's stomach, like an ulcer," Sadie said to Theola about Nana.

"Could be her appendix," chimed in Vernelle. "Are you having any abdominal pains?"

"Maybe it's nothing more than indigestion and gas," added Sadie.

"Since she pretends Jeremiah and Louise don't bother her during the day, maybe that stress is sneaking in there, taking its toll at night," offered Theola. "If my granddaughter were with an Outsider, I'd have a big knot coming out my stomach too."

"Just ignore Theola," Vernelle advised Nana. "Tell us. What happened in the dream this time?"

"She had the baby," Nana confirmed, adjusting the new patch of fabric to fit into her hoop. "But when it popped out between her legs, it turned into a man."

"Ain't nothing wrong with a man between your legs," snickered Theola. "Are you sure you weren't awake and it wasn't your husband?"

"Theola!" reprimanded Vernelle, moving her hoop. "You startin' to remind me of Ole Miss Johnson back when we used to call her by her first name, Lurleen, and she was always talkin' trash and actin' like a floozy."

"Well, I don't want no parts of that." Theola became more interested in the facts. "All right, Ernestine. What happened in your pregnant dream?"

"It was the strangest thing." Nana looked at Theola's hair and thought of a white strip of frosting on top a chocolate cake. She pulled the thread through the square and then continued her story. "They had to cross this river and then the baby turned into a man and then this big ole tidal wave comes and swallows them both. The other odd thing is, the dream picked up where it left off two months ago. And to think it all began with Cicely Tyson winning that TV award . . . um . . . um . . . um." Nana shook her head and looked down at her hand as if she were talking to her needle and thread.

"Don't blame Cicely for this. She ain't got nothing to do with your obsession," said Theola.

"Well, ain't none of us pregnant, that's for sure. As long as that's the case, I wouldn't worry about it," said Vernelle. She took a pack of Chiclet gum from her purse and offered it to everyone at the table.

After a few minutes of concentrating on their quilting, the conversation resumed.

"How are things going with you and lover boy, Clement?" Sadie gave Theola a playful nudge.

"Very funny. I ain't seen him," Theola said curtly.

"Why don't you bake him a cake or some cookies, make up an excuse to pay him a visit," suggested Sadie, looking at Nana for a sign of approval.

Theola shrugged her shoulders. "I'll see him soon enough at the Annual County Fair."

"That's months away," teased Nana, looking at Theola's hair, thinking what her black shirt would look like if she poured a streak of bleach down the middle.

"I can wait," Theola said with a straight face, lowering her eyes to the quilt, pretending she was having a hard time getting the needle through the fabric.

Nana, Sadie, and Vernelle all looked at their friend, knowing that patience to Theola was far worse than enduring torture and pain.

"How's Ruby Rose doing with her piano lessons?" Nana asked Sadie, happy to change the subject to get an update on the little girl.

"Oh, she's catching on fast," Sadie beamed with pride. "She already plays pretty well and I'm happy to announce that she recently graduated to the *John Thompson's Modern Course for the Piano Sixth Grade Book*." Sadie's smile showed she was happy about Ruby Rose's progress. "She comes to the church to practice just about every day now. She'll be in the recital this fall. She's a natural, that one is." Sadie was starting to sweat, and pulled her blouse away from her skin to generate whatever breeze there might be in the air.

"Her brother seems like a 'natural' too," said Theola, choosing to examine the fabric to make sure her stitches were consistent rather than make eye contact with her friends.

"What's that supposed to mean?" Nana asked, looking over her glasses at her friend.

"All I'm saying is he's quite the charmer," Theola said, using a defensive tone.

"Hush, Theola," said Sadie. "She's gotta be careful how she gets herself involved with young folks' mess."

"I'm hoping Jeremiah'll step aside so Medford can open the door and step back in," said Nana, trying to be optimistic. "I'm praying on it."

"Ernestine knows better than to go bustin' in on their dating,"

Vernelle said to Theola. "She don't want Louise to think she's meddling. If she does, she may take the steering wheel and drive off in the opposite direction."

"You got that right," said Sadie in agreement.

"Besides," said Nana. "I ain't about to break Rule Number Nine either: 'Mind Your Own Business Personally and Professionally.' So all I'm gonna say is, this whole thing is just terrible, and I wish she'd go back to Medford full time."

"That boy find his mama yet?" asked Theola, smoothing down her hair.

It looked to Nana as if Theola had just rubbed a line of white flour down the middle, from the crown to the nape of her head.

"Nope," said Sadie, pulling the backing of the fabric to make sure it was straight. "Not as far as I know, and I doubt he ever will."

The day turned out to be uneventful with Chester Goody at the Child Welfare Bureau, and Medford was starting to lose hope. Chester didn't provide any new information and there wasn't anything worthwhile in the files. It was as if the years had produced layers of dust that covered the tracks of his birth and time had wiped all memories clean. Even the hope he'd held out for Earthalee Tisdale came to nothing.

Earthalee had left town that one year to care for her poor dying aunt in Lynchburg. As it turned out, the aunt was really poor, having less money than she cared to admit, and Earthalee, who had a mind for construction but lacked the skills to put together a meal, almost starved to death. The aunt's weight nearly dropped to under a hundred pounds until the neighbors finally stepped in and took over and sent Earthalee back home. When they first laid eyes on their daughter, Earthalee's parents were delighted that she'd used the visit as an opportunity to lose unwanted weight. They never knew that the diet was unintended.

Happy to return to Lemon City, Earthalee married Horace and took over as manager at the Do Drop In Stay As Long As You Like full-time. All that information was reported in the Marriage Announcement section of the *Lemon City Chronicle*. The year was 1929, the same year Medford was born. It was easy to see how Chester could have made that connection, but he could have discovered the truth about Earthalee himself if he'd cared to look at the details.

Since Medford had eliminated Earthalee as a prospect and Horace was dead, he asked Chester about Profitt, only to learn that the man just had heart surgery and was at home convalescing and wouldn't be available to have visitors for weeks.

Feeling down on his luck, Medford stopped to pick up some groceries from the Piggly Wiggly. As he was driving back from the supermarket, he was starting to think he might have to look outside Lemon City for his mother. Although he didn't want to, the notion of his mother being an Outsider was a possibility he had to consider.

Making all this effort without much progress frustrated Medford and he pounded the steering wheel with his fist. He was angry about being abandoned, angry about not getting any answers and coming up empty-handed. Despite all the love he had in his life, he couldn't help but feel alone. He wished he could psyche himself into thinking that finding his mother wasn't important to him, but it was. It would be worse if he pretended she didn't matter, because she did. Living a lie wasn't an option. He turned his attention to the birthmark on his shoulder and touched it through the neck of his T-shirt. The older he got, the more the kidney-bean-shaped mark began to feel raised against his skin and take on the characteristics of a large mole. He rubbed the spot until it became irritated and started to hurt. The irony was that his birthmark was throbbing, just like the ache in his heart.

As Medford parked his pickup truck in the driveway and turned off the ignition, he sat and watched Clement sawing plywood in the yard, making the most of what little sun was left in the day. Sitting in the truck, Medford gazed at the mountains, mesmerized by one of the most amazing sunsets he had ever seen. Layers of yellows, oranges, lavenders, and reds draped the earth like a ruffled curtain falling over a window. The backdrop of streaming light over the rolling hills and valleys sunk into dark shadows, which was where Medford felt he was heading—to a dark place, like an underground limestone cavern. There were hundreds of those caves tucked away in the Blue Ridge. Looking for his mother was beginning to feel like being stuck in one of the chambers surrounded by rows of giant stalagmites and stalactites hanging from the floors and ceilings, like enormous white columns forming a confusing maze that refused to reveal what he was looking for.

Medford's focus returned to Clement, who was still sawing plywood, wearing plastic goggles to protect his eyes from the wood shavings. With the eyewear and the loud noise the electric saw made, Medford knew his father probably wouldn't see or hear him approach. He didn't want to tap him on the shoulder and startle him with the jagged-tooth weapon in his hand, so he picked up a rock and threw it in his father's direction, hoping it would get his attention. Clement looked up at his son and turned off his saw.

"How's it going, Pops?" Medford asked, carrying a bag of groceries, looking at all the plywood panels and two-by-fours his father had cut.

"See for yourself," said Clement, raising his goggles over his head. "I did all this work with no help from you," he teased his son. "On the other hand, I ain't complaining. I didn't need your assistance nohow," Clement added. "Just because I'm old, don't think I'm not as strong as you. And don't let these skinny arms fool you." He put down his saw and threw a couple of punches in the air, pretending to spar with his son to prove his point. "And I can do for myself. Don't you forget it. That's how life is. You got to do for yourself."

"I know, Pops," said Medford, pretending to block. "Maybe *you* don't need my help, but I need something from you. There's something I can't do for myself because I was too young to remember."

"What's going on now?" Clement asked. "You need my advice on how to win that gal back? Let me tell you something about women, son . . ."

Medford interrupted his father. "No, I don't need your advice. I just need you to think if there's anything else you can tell me about the first night I appeared at your doorstep."

"Gracious, man! Ain't you over that yet? Why you wanna go upsettin' yourself about something that happened a long time ago? Besides, I done told you everything I know."

"Maybe there's one more thing. One little thing you forgot. One piece of detail. Something you haven't thought about in years. Something that may seem so insignificant that it's easy to overlook."

Clement took a deep breath and squeezed his eyes shut, as if the inside of his eyelids would give him a better glimpse of the past. He remembered back to the night when he was drunk and couldn't go to sleep and the cries of a baby made him get up. He retraced his footsteps from his bedroom to the front door. Barefoot, he walked toward the direction of the sounds. His head was lowered, making sure to put one foot in front of the next to reach the source of the tiny wails. When he opened the door, he was already looking down. There was a baby, inside a basket, inside a wooden crate. "Oh, yeah," he said.

"Oh yeah, what?" repeated Medford, anxiously.

"I did tell you about the wooden crate, didn't I?"

"Yes."

"Did I tell you that I kept that old thing?"

"Where is it?" asked Clement, already in motion.

"In the basement. Somewhere in the basement, in a corner. On my old worktable, in the back near my old tools. That was ages ago, son." Clement scratched his head underneath his houndstooth newsboy cap. "I can't remember everything."

Medford didn't hear the last part of what Clement said. He was already running, on his way inside the house, with his bag of groceries trailing behind.

Medford couldn't remember the last time he was in the basement. It was used mostly for storage, and had been packed with so many memories over the years that it became almost impossible to squeeze through the debris and decipher the valuables from the clutter. It was dark and damp and moldy-smelling, and Medford was forced to remind himself of how much bigger he was than the water bugs that might be lurking in the shadows. He turned on the light at the top of the stairs and listened for any critters, thankful he didn't hear any scampering. As he descended the creaky steps, he felt he was walking on eggshells and prayed the wood was strong enough to hold his weight. The bulb at the bottom of the steps had a chain and when he pulled it, he scanned the concrete room and got a good look at the cobwebs and dust, old appliances, cardboard boxes stuffed with forgotten treasures, discarded furniture, and who-knew-what-else left from the remains of time. Shoving things aside, Medford made his way to one side of the room, looking for his father's worktable, but he didn't see any table at all. Boxes were stacked from the floor to the ceiling along with dressers, odds and ends, broken tables and chairs. Then Medford moved across the room, pushing things aside as if he were wading through an ocean of rubble, and finally found what looked to be the only worktable in the basement. Judging by the layers of dust, everything that was underground had been untouched for years. He had wondered where his Schwinn bicycle had gone with its banged-up fender, twisted handlebar, and crushed rim after he had left it in the driveway and Clement accidentally ran over it with his truck. His dad had told him he took the bike to the junk-yard, but there it was right in front of him, leaning against the table with the rear end angled on the wall. Medford remembered crying nonstop for seven days when Clement told him his bike couldn't be fixed and that he had to be careful where he left things and that it wouldn't be replaced for a long, long while because money didn't grow on trees. But the following week, Medford had a brand-new shiny bike and from that day on, he never left it any-where but beside the house standing upright on its kickstand.

Cardboard boxes were stacked on top of the worktable, and Medford took them off one by one in search of the wooden crate. Setting them down on what little space he could create on the floor, he noticed a box filled with old dusty photo albums. Blow-ing off the dust made him sneeze and he opened the first one care-fully, peeling apart the pages that were stuck together from age. Inside the plastic sleeves were newspaper clippings highlighting his father's track-and-field achievements in high school. Medford never knew his dad was a gold medalist in several major events over the three-year period. Based on the number of articles, his fa-ther must have been the fastest man in Lemon City back in the late 1920s. Medford felt something on the back side of the photo album and turned it over to find two more photos stuck together. He carefully separated the black-and-white pictures and looked at them one at a time. Squinting to identify the happy faces that had yellowed with age, a smile slowly grew across his own face when he saw familiarity. It was a group shot of Willie, Clement, Bootsie, Easely Johnson, and a man whose face he didn't recognize at all, then Ernestine, Lurleen, Sadie, Vernelle, and Theola. The men were standing in the back row and the women were squatting down in the front. The men were dressed in square-shouldered, double-breasted suits wearing stylish felt derby or porkpie hats, and the women were in their finest with fur-collared jackets, flaunting fox heads and feet, or mink stoles draped around their shoulders and short white gloves. Only Nana and Vernelle were wearing hats with high crowns and short brims, tilted to the side. The other ladies were hatless, showing off their fashionable Roaring Twenties finger-wave hairdos. They all looked happy, like they were just going to a dance and life was carefree and perfect. The sight of Miss Theola tickled him now that he knew his father was a track star, thinking Clement might have been lightning-quick back then, but that he was no match for getting away from fast Miss Theola now. Exploring their individual faces over again, tracing them with his finger, comparing them to the way they looked today, it suddenly became obvious to Medford the longevity they had between them. They had been close for many more years than he had realized, with the exception of the one man whose face he didn't know. Besides the stranger, the other thing that bothered him was the person behind the camera. Who had organized the subjects and snapped the picture? Maybe it was Rufus, Vernelle's soon-to-be husband, or Dugga Junior Dowdy, Sadie's former husband, or Theola's former husband whose name he could never recall—or even Chester, for that matter, or Horace, for all he knew.

When he finished looking at the memory, Medford tucked the picture inside his breast pocket and put the album away. Curiosity made him pick up the book underneath. It was Clement's high school yearbook—the class of 1929, the year Medford was born and Clement was only eighteen. Such a major undertaking for Clement, who was a young man at the time, to be committed to becoming a parent, especially when he didn't have to, thought Medford, browsing through the pages.

Thumbing through the yearbook, Medford came upon another group photo. This time the same group was posed on the Lemon City High School steps, alternating boy-girl, boy-girl. Lurleen and Sadie had their arms around his dad, who was standing between them. Willie was holding Ernestine's hand, Theola was cuddled next to the same unidentified man, and Vernelle was hugging tight onto Bootsie like she wouldn't let him go. It was funny how they all basically looked the same today except that their features had softened and sagged over time, becoming more rounded, a little less defined, leaving enough evidence that they were still themselves. He slid the photo beside the other one in his breast pocket.

Medford put away the books and moved all the boxes to the floor. And there it was, hiding behind an old medicine cabinet: a wooden crate. It was the only wooden crate on the table, and Medford was excited that it must be the one that originally belonged to him. It was an ordinary, plain crate with nothing unusual about it. It could have come from anywhere, but to him, the wood was worth more than gold and it was the most special crate in the world. Blowing off the dust and cobwebs, Medford found an old rag and wiped off whatever dirt was willing to part from the wood's crevices. Carrying the crate to the bottom of the steps where he could take full advantage of the direct light, he examined the slats closely, looking for any clues of origins or previous ownership. Just when he was about to give up, a marking on the wood inside the crate caught his attention and he flipped the crate over.

There it was, in fine print that he could barely make out. He rubbed his thumb over the raised stamp and lettering to smooth away any additional dirt and dust to take a better look. He made out the letters S-R-B-C. Then he sounded out the words underneath the letters out loud. "Southern . . . Regional . . . Box . . . Company," he said slowly, pronouncing each word with distinct clarity. He said it out loud again, thinking it might ring a bell. It didn't register that there was any company in Lemon City with that name, or for that matter, in Jefferson County—maybe not even in the state of Virginia. Southern Regional Box Company could be anywhere in the world. Obviously, whoever had imported the crate wasn't able to get the job done locally, and deferred to Rule Number Eight: DO BUSINESS AT HOME FIRST, THEN WITH OUTSIDERS YOU CAN INVITE INTO YOUR HOME, AS A LAST RESORT. Apparently, whoever ordered the crate couldn't do business at home and had decided not to invite an Outsider in, but rather to deal with one from a distance.

Medford knew it was a long shot, but he wasn't going to rule out anything. Tomorrow he'd go to the reference section of the library to do some research and look up the SRBC Outsider business. Once he found the location of the company—and he hoped it was still in operation—he'd send a letter to the customer service department. With any luck he'd get a response and be one step closer to tracking down his mother—or not. Either way, he had nothing to lose.

When he walked into his bedroom, he removed the pictures from his breast pocket and carefully placed them inside his dresser drawer. He was so excited about his discovery that he immediately found a notebook and a pen and began his correspondence. There was so much to think about while he waited for Clement to finish his wood project and come inside for the night. There were a lot of questions about the pictures he wanted to ask and he knew there'd be just as many stories, perhaps as many secrets, too.

It was no surprise to anyone in Lemon City that Nana had her heart set on winning the tomato competition at the Annual County Fair. A hot day in July sent her walking through her garden down the first row of tomatoes, inspecting stems and turning over leaves. She was pleased to find everything just fine. However, walking down the second row she saw something she didn't like. She spotted a patch of white, then touched the plant and the moving cloud spread its wings and took off like airplanes on a runway. Whiteflies! She couldn't believe she had those tiny white airborne plant-sucking little pests. Frantically, Nana walked through the remaining rows of her garden, turning over leaves, spotting more clusters of clouds like tiny snowflakes flying up through the air. She ran into the house to fill her bucket with soapy water, grabbed a handful of cotton, and began rubbing the underside of the leaves as best she could, because that was where the bad bugs usually congregated. Then she got out the can of pesticide and sprayed the plants just to be sure she had destroyed all the adult whiteflies. To kill the larvae, before they demolished the rest of her tomato plants, Nana would have to spray the pesticide at least eight times a day for almost a week in order to get rid of them for good.

With as much attention as she'd given her tomatoes and as often as she stood guard protecting them, she didn't understand how they could be vulnerable to this kind of attack. However, if whiteflies had flown into her garden, she became curious to see if they had made a landing on her neighbor's property as well. She sneaked over into Ole Miss Johnson's yard and was astonished to see the tomatoes that had grown to the size of grapefruits, with stalks that drooped like curved umbrella handles due to their weight. She turned over a few of the leaves, but they all looked clean, perfectly green and not spotted with white at all. Immediately she was furious. The most she could hope for was that the giant tomatoes detach from their stems and drop to the ground like bombs, imploding to the earth to be consumed by crawling land bugs.

"Ernestine, last summer I had your cat sneaking over here. Now I got you," Ole Miss Johnson said, standing with a broom in her hand. "Ain't you got no shame?"

"I'm just checking," said Nana, embarrassed. "I thought you might have what I have. And I was coming over to warn you."

"What you got?" asked Ole Miss Johnson in a voice more grating than a jackhammer drilling into a brick.

"I got whiteflies," Nana said, easing her way out of her neighbor's yard. "Now I hope I got dead ones."

"You better not bring any of them bugs over here dead or alive!" Ole Miss Johnson yelled. "And don't bring yourself over here anymore either."

Nana went back home, and as a matter of precaution asked her husband to take her to the gardening store to get yellow sticky strips. Whiteflies were attracted to yellow, and the glue on the strips would put an end to their reign of terror. Meanwhile, her only saving grace, the only light that came out of the situation, was that she still had enough healthy tomatoes left to compete.

It was late August, a week before the Annual County Fair, when the rains came down like floods of fury. When the clouds retreated, the sun emerged to dry out the earth and soak up the moisture like a sponge. Counting down the days, Nana went out into her yard for one of the last times this summer. After careful inspection she was relieved to find that her whiteflies were gone, but was shocked to discover that the skin on some of her tomatoes had started to crack. Now that a few of her tomatoes had radial scars, she felt she was about to lose it herself and finally crack up too. She threw her hands up in the air and asked, "Why?" Anger made her pluck off one of the damaged tomatoes and throw it across the fence into her neighbor's yard, hoping Ole Miss Johnson's tomatoes might also become cursed. It wasn't like her to lose her temper, but the exercise in pitching made her feel good. Frustrated and exhausted, Nana plopped down on her stool and decided all the cracked tomatoes shouldn't go to waste. Saint was by her side and already feasting on the wounded. Nana removed a damaged tomato from its stem, shined it against her smock, and bit into it. There was something soft and squishy inside her mouth that tasted like more than just a juicy cavity. When Nana looked down at what she was eating, she noticed half its body squirming in place. She screamed and gagged and spit out the other half. Saint, terrified by his master's bloodcurdling reaction, ran clear to the other side of the yard. Nana was so totally disgusted by the worm and by the odds against her winning in this year's Annual County Fair that she threw another tomato over the fence. After that last setback, she couldn't take it anymore and needed to separate herself from the thought that whatever could go wrong, would. With only a week left to go, she speculated there were enough healthy tomatoes left in her garden to make her chances of winning from halfway decent to fairly good. She had to be optimistic, if only because things couldn't get much worse.

Chapter Eleven

Summer took its time to get to Lemon City, but when it finally arrived, it flew by faster than a red-crested cardinal flitting from one dogwood tree branch to the next. The long-awaited Annual County Fair was here and the day couldn't be more perfect. The sky was pastel blue streaked with white clouds. The warblers and sparrows seemed to flap their wings to the bass while the hawks soared to the melody that the ragtime band played at the front gate at Founder's Park, where the looming statue of the five Founding Fathers stood above the crowd. Sounds of laughter, chatter, and joy from all ages came together to blend with the music to create one long, muffled rumble of fun. Lemonites were bustling about in all directions, taking advantage of everything the fair had to offer from amusements to food to entertainment. The town was 109 years old today, and there were still two or three folks who were around when Lemon City was first born.

The first thing Ruby Rose saw when she got inside Founder's Park was the first thing she wanted. Jeremiah handed her the cotton candy and gave the vendor five cents. When she finished putting her face into the pink puff that disintegrated into her mouth, she asked her brother for a candy apple. That's when the sugar kicked in and she wanted to bounce from ride to ride. Jeremiah stopped at the booth and bought a roll of tickets, and Ruby Rose grabbed his hand and dragged him to a sign out front that read "The Whip."

Ruby Rose screamed the whole time she was on the ride until her voice felt like it belonged to a frog. When the ride stopped, her legs were wobbly and she felt like she was walking on rubber bands and leaned on Jeremiah for support. The Ferris wheel across the way looked safe enough, and Ruby Rose pushed Jeremiah with her body until he moved in that direction. The problem was, the Ferris wheel didn't go around fast enough for Ruby Rose and when it stopped at the top and her feet were dangling in midair, she was bored. While she was hovering over the ground, she got a good view of the roller coaster clanging its way up the track and descending with such speed that the people's heads snapped back and their mouths stayed in a steady scream position until the ride stopped. Ruby Rose wanted to go on the roller coaster next, and when the Ferris wheel let them down she had to convince Jeremiah to go with her and not to be a chicken. Flapping her arms and clucking, she poked her neck in and out, pretending to be poultry, and Jeremiah chased her all the way to the back of the roller-coaster line.

Louise and Elvira were at their usual bake-sale booth collecting money for cakes, cookies, and pies. This year their table displayed carrot cake, black walnut pound cake, apple cake, pineapple upside-down cake, lemon pound cake, and Mississippi mud cake. As for the pies, there were apple, green tomato, lemon meringue, blackberry, sweet potato, and pecan.

Every time Elvira cut a slice from a pie or cake for a customer, Louise noticed that she didn't waste any crumbs and ate them off the table or picked them off the plate. Whenever Elvira served someone, she served herself. It was the fact that she was consuming leftovers at the rate of every three customers that was giving Louise cause for concern. Ever since Elvira had eaten those extra lemon cookies they made a while back, Louise could see the pounds adding on and swear her sister-in-law's sweet tooth and craving for junk food was getting worse.

Billy was patrolling the perimeter of the park from his car and then decided to get out on foot. He was reflecting on how the winter had blown the Outsiders onto his grandparents' front porch nine months ago and how the story checked out that Jeremiah kidnapped his sister. It was all in print on the front page of the *Richmond Review*, almost word for word the way the Outsider had told everyone after dinner. It was true that Jeremiah was a "wanted" man; however, back then Billy hadn't seen any harm in taking what was rightfully yours. Lately, however, he did see the harm in Jeremiah spending too much time with his sister, and he thought the Outsider should lighten up on his visits. As Billy was heading over to the bake-sale booth, he thought that perhaps the Outsider had even overstayed his welcome in general.

Sitting at a picnic table in the shade of a sycamore tree, Granddaddy and Clement were engaged in a close game of chess.

"Ain't that something about the President quittin' his job last month?" Clement said with his eyes on the board, tilting up the brim of his straw Panama hat so he could see which piece to move.

"When you deal with bugs, you got problems," Granddaddy replied, waiting patiently.

"They got bugs in the White House?"

"Found 'em in a hotel. There was bugging in some hotel with the Democrats . . . where you been?"

"The Republicans were bugging the Democrats? About what?" Clement moved his rook across the board.

"That's the whole reason the guy quit." Granddaddy found it hard to believe that Clement didn't know the details of the story. "Something about a cover-up. Tapes that got the President tellin' tales in the White House and the FBI and the CIA and who knows who else was involved—it's a mess—seems like more folks is coming out the woodwork every day with something new to say. The man had to quit before they sent him home a'packin', just like I'm about to send you to steppin' off the board." Granddaddy removed Clement's pawn and added it to his pile of the captured. "If the truth be told," Granddaddy added, watching Clement accept defeat, then start the process of concentrating all over again, "the President ain't quit, he resigned before they got rid of him."

"Let's just hope with the new President that the oil prices don't go back up," said Clement. "That's what I care about." He moved closer to Granddaddy's queen.

"Ain't that something about that young feller, Moses Malone, becoming the first high school kid in the country to join a pro basketball team and become a millionaire overnight?" asked Granddaddy, thinking about the best way to relocate his rook.

"They say that boy's from around the way in Petersburg."

"The Utah Stars got all six feet, eleven inches of him, I hear."

"If I was that tall I'd be averaging thirty-nine points, twenty-six rebounds, and blocking twelve shots per game too."

"If you were that tall and running down the court you'd be done tripped over your feet and died of a broken leg and a head injury," said Granddaddy, claiming his second piece on the board.

"Doggone it . . . got' blast it . . . dern it . . . shoot," said Clement as he moved his queen a square to track down Granddaddy's knight.

"You got your lady chasing after me," said Granddaddy. "Just like Theola coming after you full speed ahead." He pointed from the queen to the knight.

"I can't be with no woman who's on my tail all the time," said Clement, eyes fixed on the board, planning his next strategy. "Besides, I like mean women who have a kick to 'em like a good glass of whiskey; something that goes down slow and makes you go, ahhhh." He took off his Panama hat and started waving away the heat.

Granddaddy moved a pawn that was protecting his rook one square forward. "The truth is, you don't like women chasing after you 'cause your knees are starting to go, and you're too old to run."

Meanwhile, Medford was at the hamburger stand, sipping a chocolate milk shake, waiting for his two cheeseburgers and large order of fries to arrive. He caught a glimpse of Ruby Rose and Jeremiah heading in his direction, but before he had a chance to turn his back and look away, the child raised her arm in the air, waving it to get his attention. He waved back, wishing she wasn't with her brother. Ruby Rose let go of her brother's hand and ran to Medford. As soon as his fries came, she slid one out from the pile and popped it into her mouth without asking.

"Are you hungry?" asked Medford.

Ruby Rose nodded her head.

"What would you like?" asked Medford. He and Jeremiah simultaneously reached into their pockets for their wallets.

Without thinking, Ruby Rose turned to Medford and said she wanted a hamburger and fries and a strawberry shake. Since it was his sister, Medford looked at Jeremiah for approval, and he seemed to be okay with Medford treating Ruby Rose to lunch.

Knowing that Ruby Rose was in good company with Medford, Jeremiah told his sister that he would catch up with her later. It gave him a welcome break, and he went off to search for Louise.

Medford and Ruby Rose ate their lunch and then set off to enjoy some of the carnival games while they gave their food a chance to digest. After that, Ruby Rose and Medford rode through the haunted house to have a scary adventure.

On the other side of the fairgrounds at the bake-sale booth, Elvira had eaten so many sweets that she covered her mouth, turned her head to the side, and vomited in the trash can. Louise was able to pull her away from the table just in time to avoid any embarrassment and prevent any witnesses to the event. When Louise asked her what was wrong, Elvira said she thought she was coming down with the flu. But Louise knew better. It wasn't a virus that was attacking her sister-in-law; it was her appetite that was causing her stomach to be upset. She made Elvira sit down in a folding chair and rest while she went back to business selling desserts and trying to raise a record-breaking amount of money for the church.

A year's worth of excitement and anticipation was coming to a peak like a rock climber's struggle to reach the summit. Nana's hard work to be a contender in the tomato competition had paid off well enough to gain her recognition as one of the top five finalists. Now she was counting down, through process of elimination, hoping the judges would pluck off her competition one by one like petals on a dandelion in a child's game of "she loves me, she loves me not." Only this wasn't a game. It was way more serious than that.

The wind swept its way through the spectators, making the wide-brimmed hats of hundreds of ladies, gathered in front of the raised platform, look like a sea of wheat waving in a field. The five finalists with their tomato offspring placed in front of them were like mothers doting over children in a school play, secretly hoping that theirs would be picked for the lead.

With all her bad luck this summer, Nana hadn't expected to get this far in the running and she still felt she had a fair shot at the crown. Nana was at one end of the platform and Ole Miss

Johnson was at the other. Ole Miss Johnson leaned over the table, faced her opponent, and snarled.

All the contestants had their tomatoes lined up for inspection by the judges. By now, they had passed the beauty test, the texture test, and the color test. The judges jotted down their notes. All that was left were the flavor and the juicy tests. The judges strolled by the finalists with their sharp knives and cut the tomatoes in half. When the knives came down on the table, Nana thought it was her breath that was being cut short. She looked down at her perfect Champion and beamed because the skin didn't tear from the force of the blade and the seeds slipped off the edge as smooth as butter, revealing a cavity that was well formed. She smiled at the judges and they smiled back, and the crowd that was gathered around the platform clapped for the underdog. As Ole Miss Johnson looked at the happy faces rooting for Nana, she rolled her eyes and sucked her teeth.

One more test, Nana thought, and she'd be home free; since everything else was going well, the taste test should be a breeze. Each judge stood in front of one of the contestants. Ole Miss Johnson's judge took a bite into her Bragger, savored the taste, and jotted something down in her notebook. Ole Miss Johnson's smile spread as wide as the low branches on a white spruce. One by one the other judges tasted the tomatoes from the finalists until it was Nana's turn. Nana took a deep breath, held it in, and waited. The judge bit into the tomato, then spit it out.

"Yuck, bug spray!" the judge declared, wiping the nastiness from her mouth.

Nana let out a gasp. She knew she was in deep trouble. She glanced down the table at her neighbor, who gave her a knowing smirk, and all Nana could think of was her whitefly invasion, that she hadn't wiped out all the stages of larvae before it affected the tomato's flavor, or perhaps the insecticide had even permeated the skin and made the fruit taste bitter. Either way, she was mad at herself for being a magnet for pests for a second year in a row and mad at Jeremiah for giving Ole Miss Johnson that hoodoo herb to make her tomatoes grow. Now she couldn't wait to get her hands on the Outsider. Even though she didn't have any concrete proof that he'd aided and abetted her neighbor in this act of crime, she was sure he must be guilty. A life of criminal activity didn't stop with abducting his sister; he was probably just launching his law-breaking career. After all she had done for the Outsider! Now she was so furious that she couldn't wait to find Billy. In the meantime, taking her anger out on her competitor would just have to do.

"She cheated!" Nana pointed a finger at her neighbor, who stood at the end of the table looking innocent. "She put some-thing in those tomatoes to make 'em win!" she shouted with her hands on her hips.

"Ernestine, don't be such a sore loser!" Ole Miss Johnson yelled back at her.

Nana saw several folks in the crowd nodding their heads in agreement. To keep from being accused of acting childish, Nana kept her mouth shut as the judges added up their scores, draped the red cape around her neighbor, and restored her emerald gold-plated crown. Nana had no choice but to graciously yield to pub-lic defeat. The judges handed out the runner-up ribbons and like a good sport, Nana accepted. As the crowd cheered and clapped for the Tomato Queen, Nana reluctantly put her hands together twice. No matter how many times she lost this competition, she never got used to it. She didn't want to be known as a loser or a quitter, but perhaps she could settle for being a retiree.

Billy stopped by the bake-sale booth and discovered his wife sitting in a folding chair, clutching her stomach, sick as a dog.

"I told her to go home," Louise said to Billy. "She's not help-ing us sell anything looking as pale and as pitiful as she is."

"What's the matter, baby?" Billy asked his wife, lifting her crouching body by the shoulders to see her face.

"I'm pregnant," she said.

"What?" he asked, making sure he heard correctly.

Louise turned around to make sure her ears weren't mistaken too.

"I'm four months pregnant," Elvira repeated.

Billy let out a yahoo that seemed to reverberate through the mountains. Elvira managed a weak smile, and Louise hugged them both.

"Why are you just now telling me?" Billy asked, looking at his wife, holding her shoulders to keep her steady to prevent her from falling over.

"I wanted to be sure," Elvira said. "I wanted to get past the first trimester before I told you. I was so happy, I didn't want it to be another false alarm."

"We have to tell Nana. We have to tell Nana," Billy repeated, just in case no one heard him the first time.

"I have a feeling she'll need some good news," said Louise. "I hear folks murmuring about how she lost again."

They shook their heads as if they weren't surprised, but they knew the good news about the baby would cheer her up.

Billy grabbed the first two people that stopped by the booth and got them to take over the selling of desserts. As the three of them began searching for Nana, Billy was so happy and light on his feet that he felt like he was skipping on air.

Five years ago, the Sadie Hawkins dance was replaced by the Soul Mate Auction. The Ladies of Mt. Zion Baptist Church thought it would be the perfect fund-raiser, because individuals could auction off their services to the highest bidder and raise money for the town's community chest. At the last fair, Louise had bought Medford's services. The year before that, he had bought hers. This year, Louise was on the auction block again.

Louise stood on the stage with her hair in beaded cornrows. She wore a V-neck halter top held together by thick braided yarn, exposing her back, and a pair of denim bell-bottom jeans. The fact that both men in her life might show up at the auction made her uncomfortable, and her nervousness caused her to rock back and forth in her Earth Shoes. Regardless, nothing prepared Louise for when Medford and Jeremiah's faces seemed to pop out of the crowd like the unexpected in a horror movie. On the heels of her shoes, Louise felt she might tip over and fall.

Medford was standing, peering over people's heads on one side of the crowd to get a clear view of the stage, and Jeremiah was on the other side trying to get her attention. As Medford looked down, he started talking to his feet and Louise could see that the little person he was communicating with was Ruby Rose. Louise smiled at Medford when he finally looked in her direction, but it was her eyes that welcomed Jeremiah when he glanced her way.

The sun was beating down on the top of Louise's head and she hoped that her scalp wouldn't turn into a tic-tac-toe board, created by the lines of her cornrows. She wished she had thought to wear a hat, and now she was thinking that she should have brought a pair of large sunglasses as well to hide some of her embarrassment.

The auctioneer opened the bidding on two other people before getting to Louise, giving her a chance to catch her breath. Then it was her turn. Through the microphone, the auctioneer described her as one of God's most beautiful creatures; young, strong, and hard-working, an excellent cook, baker, and housekeeper, who could clean dust barely visible to the human eye out of corners. She was extremely well read, he added, and whoever bought her services would have the added benefit of good conversation and perhaps a free magazine subscription or a publication or two from the public library thrown in with the deal because she was the town's head librarian. Having provided that introduction, the auctioneer reminded bidders that the proceeds would go to a worthy cause and opened the bid at thirty dollars. Jeremiah was quick to enter the bid at thirty-five, and Medford immediately countered at fifty.

When Ruby Rose recognized her brother's voice, her confusion bordered on panic. She jumped up and down to see if she could spot him in the crowd, but there were too many tall and wide bodies pressed against each other blocking her view. She glanced up at Medford as he shouted out another dollar amount and detected an intense look on his face that she'd never seen before. Then she heard her brother's voice again as Jeremiah and Medford started shouting numbers like they were hurling rocks at each other. Torn between the two men, Ruby Rose didn't know where to stand, which one to be with, or whose side to be on, and she hadn't felt such chaos since growing up in Livingston and moving to Mattoxville. What she did know was that Louise was at the center of all this activity. Ruby Rose felt she should migrate over to her brother because he was family, but she didn't know if that was a good enough reason. And she didn't think she should stay with Medford, either, since his mind seemed to be tangled up somewhere between his wallet and the stage. Upset with the two grown men in her life, she decided to duck them both in exchange for Nana and Granddaddy, where she'd be guaranteed to find peace of mind and comfort.

The bid went as high as two hundred dollars, and Medford topped it with two hundred and fifty. After a pause, the gavel hit the table and Louise was sold.

Louise couldn't let Medford see the disappointment in her face. She watched Jeremiah turn his back to the stage and leave the area as Medford made his way through the crowd to hand his money to the auctioneer and collect his prize.

Medford could see the care Louise held in her eyes as she looked after Jeremiah, but he refused to allow his face to show any pain. He knew that women sometimes became overwhelmed with emotion, which tended to clutter their logic. He took her by the hand and they walked to the parking lot, neither of them speaking, neither of them looking at the other, but Medford didn't mind because he was determined the silence wouldn't last long. Once they got to his house, he would put her to work.

Nana went from being furious about losing the tomato competition to feeling like she was royalty in her own right, floating on top of the world, riding high on a rocket in the sky when Billy and Elvira brought her the news. Her heart overflowed with joy and she shouted out to everyone within the sound of her voice that she was going to be a great-grandmother. All were thrilled to hear Nana's wonderful news, and shuttled like cattle to gather around her instead of Ole Miss Johnson in her emerald gold-plated crown and red robe, who was left standing by herself like a queen abandoned by her subjects.

This was the happiest day of Nana's life. So when Ruby Rose came to her distraught, crying for forgiveness and apologizing about giving Ole Miss Johnson jumbo root to grow her giant tomatoes, Nana could care less about the girl's deceit, but accepted her regrets just the same. She was also relieved that she didn't have to ask Billy to go after Jeremiah. She was too happy now to work herself up to seeking retribution. Putting her arm around Ruby Rose, Nana tried to quiet her down, wondering if there might be something else more important bothering her. She took Ruby Rose by the hand, and along with Elvira and Billy went off to find Granddaddy to share the great news.

Medford and Clement lived in a brick ranch-style two-family house on Rappahannock Road. Each side of the house was identical, with one adjoining door and a shared front and back porch. When Medford pulled into the driveway, the first thing he did was walk Louise to the kitchen. She was hoping to find some warmth behind the hint of coldness in his eyes, but what she received instead was an apron, a mop, a bucket, a broom, and a dustpan. He reminded her that this wasn't her first time in his house and that she knew where everything was and that he had paid a lot of money for her services. He pointed to the pot roast that was marinating inside the refrigerator, the potatoes that needed peeling, and the mustard greens that needed to be cleaned, seasoned, and cooked. On the counter, there were all the ingredients she needed to bake his favorite pineapple upside-down cake. Medford added that he had been preoccupied over the past several months on his mission to find his mama, and as she could see hadn't had a chance to do any housekeeping in a while. The rooms needed a good dusting and cleaning, he said, and the wood floors and bathroom tiles needed to be wiped down. His face was stern, not showing any signs of kindness after he dictated his instruction. Then he walked off to the TV room, leaving Louise by herself in the middle of the kitchen floor.

The only thing that prevented Louise from storming out the front door was that she was making a contribution to the Town Council Community Chest and the money Medford had donated for her services would go to a good cause. She looked around the room trying to figure out where to begin. After setting the oven temperature, Louise started sweeping the floor.

All afternoon Louise was cleaning until sweat began pouring down her face and she had to laugh at how silly she must look, the 'seventies feminist slaving away like a 'fifties housewife. The only thing that kept her going was the fact that her domestic duties weren't personal. What she was doing was about business only.

Hours passed and she cleaned from room to room, rearranging items in the medicine cabinet, moving around shaving cream, razors, and cologne, straightening up Medford's guest room, putting away socks, cuff links, belts, and pants left on the floor. The next thing she knew, she heard a thud and turned around to discover that Medford had thrown a pair of work boots on the floor on purpose.

"Hey. What are you doing?"

"Pick it up," Medford ordered. "You're here to do a job."

"I'm not here to do extra work!" Louise shouted at him, bending over, picking up the boots. The next thing she knew, a shirt landed on her head.

"Now, wait a doggoned minute."

"Money is going to charity, baby. Don't forget it. You don't want the Town Council to think you're not holding up to your part of the deal." After saying his piece, Medford returned to the TV room.

Louise grabbed the shirt off her head and followed him.

"No more clothes," she scolded. "Don't throw anything else on the floor," she said to the back of his head.

"Oops," said Medford, deliberately knocking his glass of water onto the carpet.

"That does it," said Louise. "I'm done." She took off her apron and threw it near the spilled water.

"No, you're not." Medford turned to face Louise in his chair. "I know you don't give up that easily, just like I'm not a quitter."

Louise stopped walking and looked at Medford.

"I've waited a whole year for this day to happen and I want you to stay here as long as possible," he continued. "If it takes moving all the clothes out of my closets, out of my dresser, and tossing them on the floor, removing the dishes from the cabinets and throwing them into the sink. Whatever it takes, then that's what I'll do." Medford faced the TV to give it his full attention again.

Louise stared at him as if he were crazy before realizing he was dead serious and the threat was coming from his heart.

"Now, I'd appreciate it if you'd get back to work. I paid for your time today. I have the receipt." Medford waved the piece of paper in his hand as he relaxed into his chair and continued watching TV.

Louise grabbed a roll of paper towels and a mop from the kitchen to absorb the water that Medford had spilled on the floor. She put her apron back on, staring at him, hoping he would catch a glimpse of the mutual care in her eyes, but he wouldn't break his gaze from the console.

Reluctantly, Louise went back to the spare room to finish cleaning. While dusting Medford's childhood photographs in the frames on the night tables, she gazed at his face longer than she should have. She wasn't even born when he was in third grade; it wasn't until he was high school age that she remembered him, and there on the dresser was his high-school graduation picture. Looking at his young face made her recall the first time she had seen it. The fact their families had been together for a very long time and had a shared history, combined with the sweetness he had given her over the years, brought tears to her eyes and she wondered why she treated him the way she did. It occurred to her how much she must have hurt Medford, which made her sad, and she wiped her cheek with his crumpled shirt until she realized what it was, then hung it up and continued patting her skin with her apron, holding back tears. Medford was a good man who had enough sadness in his life and she felt worse for adding to it. Being in his house was comfortable, and it was making her reconsider reconciliation. As she blew her nose into a tissue, she hoped that Medford would think it was a reaction from the dust.

When Louise had pulled herself together, she began opening and closing doors to all the rooms she had cleaned, making sure they passed her inspection. The only room left to clean was Medford's bedroom.

"Don't go into my bedroom," Medford warned from the TV room.

"How come?" Louise shouted back at him, standing in the hallway with a dustpan and broom.

"Don't go in there unless you mean it."

Since Medford knew better than to tell her what to do, he also was aware she couldn't resist challenging authority. Not knowing what to expect, she quietly turned the knob and opened the door. There were scented candles burning all over the immaculate room decorated with bouquets of colorful wildflowers. Taken by surprise, it reminded her of a sanctuary, a special place that required her to remove her shoes before entering, separate from the rest of the house. Looking around the room, everything was in perfect order until her eyes focused on the dresser and she noticed the broken glass. Moving closer to the debris, she discovered it was a picture of her and Medford that was taken at their first Soul Mate Auction years ago. She stared at the mess, the only place in the room that had been neglected, and it didn't sit right with her that the glass was shattered, the frame was in pieces, and the photograph was torn, and she picked up the image to try to put it back together. It was ripped in half, but it wasn't a clean tear and the paper was bent as if a big foot had gone through it. Tape would help to restore the picture, though it would never be the same.

However, there was no way to salvage the frame; it would have to be replaced. She began sweeping the glass into her dustpan. After that, she tried to match the edges of the frayed paper together. As she looked at how happy she and Medford were that day, she remembered that time in their lives, the spark of chemistry between them, how they couldn't keep their hands off each other. Now that she was standing in his wonderful room, distinguishing his scent from the candle fragrance, she thought about what it might be like to revisit that feeling. At that moment she felt Medford ease his way behind her, gently press his warm body against her back and buttocks, his arms slowly encircling her, his sweet breath blowing a subtle breeze in her ear. She wasn't startled, but rather his touch made her relax, and she sank into his arms almost as if she were expecting him. She was glad he had waited.

"Because you're in here, I'm assuming you mean it," Medford said.

Louise turned around and looked into his eyes, which had lost any signs of coldness. She touched his handsome face and felt herself lean into his strong chest as if her body had made the decision for her mind. She could tell he was waiting for her to make the first move, to give him a sign that the love they were about to make was consensual and not because of obligation or pressure. She kissed him, and then her mouth opened wide over his as if she couldn't get enough of his familiar taste. They fell back on the bed and stayed there for several hours until the house smelled like something was burning and they both knew it was time to get up. The pot roast was inedible, but they didn't care. They had already satisfied their insatiable appetites.

That night they had bologna sandwiches for dinner. They ate their pineapple upside-down cake on the back porch, feeding each other with their forks, watching the fireflies blink their lights on and off. Only after the mosquitoes became unbearable did they venture back inside the house. When they did, they took a slow shower together and made love all over again. Having read the *More Joy of Sex* book, Louise couldn't wait to show off a few things she had learned. But in the middle of a new position, Medford got suspicious and stopped what he was doing. When she revealed the source of her new knowledge, he made her swear on a stack of Bibles that she hadn't used these techniques before.

The whole time Louise was with Medford she never once thought about Jeremiah.

Nana couldn't wait to show Billy the baby wardrobe she had made that she kept inside the hope-chest collection at the foot of her bed. She opened up the trunk to reveal the sweaters, pants, dresses, booties, blankets, hats, mittens, and scarves she had knitted over the years, and laid the pieces on her bed so Billy could take a better look. The colors ranged from white to blue, pink, lavender, yellow, and green. Nana was proud of all the baby clothes and the fact that she had all the bases covered no matter if it turned out to be a boy or a girl. While in her bedroom, she suddenly remembered her pregnant dream and she put her hand to her bosom. The dream must have been about Elvira, she thought, but still the story of the pregnant slave woman dream didn't make any sense. Maybe it wasn't supposed to. But now that her daughter-in-law had revealed she was pregnant, she was hoping the dream had served its purpose and wouldn't haunt her again.

Monday morning, Louise was in her office at the library, cataloging new materials that had just arrived—*Sula* by Toni Morrison, *If Beale Street Could Talk* by James Baldwin, *The Good Fight* by Shirley Chisholm, and *Faith and the Good Thing* by Charles Johnson—trying to focus on her work and not the time she had spent with Medford over the weekend. What was distracting her was that she was beginning to see that she really loved Medford and how making a life with one man was a possibility—maybe.

Louise took the next publication off the pile on her desk and read the title: *The Papers of Charlotte Hawkins Brown, 1900–1961*. She wondered why the name sounded familiar, then remembered the book that Nana had given her, *The Correct Thing to Do, to Say, to Wear*. As she read through Charlotte's speeches, she began to realize the lady who had written about etiquette and proper behavior was actually a pioneer for racial, civic, and social equality, a recognized educator who traveled around the country and abroad addressing important issues. One of her papers read, "My success is due to the fact, I believe, that I deal in concrete things that everybody understands and not in generalities. I have main subjects that I use: 'Manners and Culture, the Basis of Education,' 'The Negro, an American Asset,' 'Iron Chariots,' 'The Role of the Negro Woman in American Life,' 'What America Means to Me,' 'Getting Acquainted With Oneself.' " As Louise continued flipping through the pages, she was captivated by the speeches: "My friends, the future of the Negro womanhood in America depends upon the application of the four freedoms to the lowliest of her race as much as to the highest. Negroes living in any section of this country cannot experience real freedom until all are free." "As with the nation, so with the race." "No people can exist half slave and half free." Louise couldn't believe it! Charlotte Hawkins Brown, the woman who wrote the corny book on how to dress and how to act, was down with the struggle, a radical like herself. The more she read, the more she learned about this lady who was born in Henderson, North Carolina, and founded Palmer Memorial Institute. What especially impressed Louise was that Charlotte was an advocate for children and a champion for women's rights. In her eyes, Charlotte was a true feminist, and in addition to her independence she still managed to have a husband, which made Louise think perhaps she could remain a feminist and be attached to one man too. Reading through pages and pages of speeches, newspaper articles, and letters to people like Booker T. Washington, W.E.B. Dubois, and Mary McLeod Bethune, Louise discovered a newfound respect for the woman Nana had been trying to shove down her throat like a spoonful of cod-liver oil. Suddenly Charlotte Hawkins Brown wasn't so old-fashioned anymore. If Sly Stone could get married in June in front of 23,000 people in Madison Square Garden in New York City, then perhaps she could seriously consider Medford's proposal and get married in Nana's tomato garden with a handful of folks from Lemon City. Maybe, maybe not. She was still conflicted, but just happy to know she had options.

Jeremiah was in the yard at the cottage, clenching the butt of a Winston between his teeth while sponging down the white GTO. The smoke blowing up his nose, into thin air, made him think about how quickly time evaporated before his very eyes. It was already September. He couldn't believe he had been in Lemon City for nine months when all he'd been looking for was a place to spend the night to get out of the cold, never expecting to stay this long, never thinking he would meet someone as special as Louise. He didn't feel guilty about leaving town, because he had warned her not to get too close. Even though she'd heard him, he didn't think she had paid attention. He'd never meant to hurt Louise, but what he had in his favor was that he'd made it clear that he never intended to stay. The person he had to worry about most was Ruby Rose, who would probably take their leaving Lemon City as if a rug were being snatched from underneath her feet.

Jeremiah picked up the hose and washed off the soapy water

on the car. He dried and waxed it, feeling relief from the cool breeze as the sun was beginning to set and summer was transitioning to fall.

When the car was clean and he could see his reflection in the chrome, Jeremiah went inside to call Louise. He told her that they needed to talk and that he would come by after he took a shower.

Louise didn't know what Jeremiah had to say, but she bet it had something to do with her going home with Medford. One thing she hated was a jealous man, especially one trying to force her to make a decision. But the truth was, it was too late. She had chosen, and she wanted to be with Medford. If she had been honest with herself from the beginning, she would have admitted that it wouldn't have worked with Jeremiah all along. She never meant to hurt his feelings; she only wanted to have a little fun. She didn't know how Jeremiah would take the news about her and Medford, but she hoped he would respect the truth and they could remain on friendly terms.

When Jeremiah arrived at her house, Louise gave him the courtesy of allowing him to talk first. Sitting across from her at the kitchen table, Jeremiah looked uncomfortable, shifting from one side of the chair to the other, but finally he was able to tell her the reason for his visit. He told her he was leaving Lemon City, that he'd stopped by Do Drop In Stay As Long As You Like for coffee, which she knew borders Jefferson County. After overhearing some talk about the County Sheriff's Office about to begin a search for a man and a girl, he was convinced the reference was about him and Ruby Rose. Being a "wanted man," he didn't think he should continue to put her family in jeopardy and that it was time for him to move on. He said that he and Ruby Rose were blessed to have met the Dunlaps, and that their hospitality meant a lot to him and his sister. Then he reached across the table and took Louise's hand into his.

"You know, fear is like crossing a bridge. Some people will never get to the other side. Others will take their time, even stroll to get over it. While others will run—looking forward to whatever will greet them." He leaned in closer, making sure to have eye contact. "Just get to the point where you know there is a bridge because believe it or not, some people refuse to see it; they won't even acknowledge it exists—pretend it isn't there." Jeremiah paused to take a breath. "There are times when we need to do things that scare us most. But when we finally take the leap and get to the other side of fear, we can't remember what it was that frightened us in the first place." Then he added, "Medford is a good brother. He's the one for you."

At the same time Louise was fascinated by his words, she was relieved that she was off the hook and didn't need to tell her side of the story. They stood up from the table and hugged each other, and she pretended to be more hurt than she actually was.

Jeremiah pulled a gemstone from his pocket and handed it to her. "I didn't have any jade, which symbolizes peace and tranquility, but I have some malachite."

She held it up to the light to admire its crystallized clumps and various sparkling shades of green.

"It's for personal strength and positive energy," he added.

"Thank you, Jeremiah. It's beautiful," she said. She looked at the stone as it sat in her hand, then folded her fingers around it, feeling it was just as valuable as the person standing before her.

Jeremiah kissed the back of Louise's hand, then touched his lips against her forehead and walked down the stairs and out the door.

Louise opened a can of beer and plopped down on the sofa in the living room, both relieved and sad at the same time. After giving herself a few moments to absorb the breakup, she made an effort to change her mood. Even though it was for the best, she still felt a slight sense of loss. She put on her Bobbi Humphrey *Blacks and Blues* album to lift her spirits and picked up the new Angela Davis autobiography that had just arrived at the library the other day, to get into someone else's groove. After a while she didn't feel like reading. She felt like talking, and called Elvira.

"Vi. You won't believe what just happened."

"What? Nana told you she wasn't entering the tomato contest next year?"

"No, chile. Jeremiah just quit me."

"So why you sounding so happy?"

"Because I was going to do it first and he just saved me the trouble."

"Hallelujah. I thought I might have to make Billy intervene and bust someone upside the head. Thank goodness I didn't have to do that and he didn't have to hurt anyone." Then Elvira lowered her voice. "By the way, I didn't tell him the whole story, what you told me the last time about Jeremiah. And I'm not gonna tell you what the little girl said to me either, 'cause she made me keep a promise."

"What did the little girl say?"

"It's funny how things happen," Elvira commented in a normal tone. "Before her brother quit you, she said she was starting not to hate you anymore, but didn't know why. 'Probably, I said, 'cause you found a friend in Medford.' She said, 'Louise seems nice enough.' Can you believe it?" Elvira raised her voice a notch, then lowered it back to where it was. "Then she said she was sorry she was mean to you and said she wouldn't mind if we set aside another time to make lemon cookies again. Ain't that something? But check this out. The next time if you offered to walk her home, she mentioned she would even consider inviting you inside. I tell you the girl is starting to turn around, turn around. There's hope for us all."

"Ruby Rose told you not to tell me all that?"

"Sure 'nough."

"That's a whole new glass of water to swallow."

"There I go again—spillin' all the beans. I shouldn't a said nothin'. Just kept my mouth shut and kept all this to myself."

"Vi, I know you can't help being generous with information, so here's another topic for you to elaborate on." Louise paused for a second. "What's it like to be married?"

"Oh, Lou, it's the most wonderful thing."

"Girl, stop lying."

"Well, it's not that way all the time, but if you're thinking about marriage, you can't go wrong with Medford. I've been saying that all along."

"Vi. You say so many things I can't keep up."

Chapter Twelve

Medford took two Swanson TV dinners out of the oven, put the aluminum plates on a tray, and sat down in front of the TV to eat. The new sitcom *That's My Mama* was coming on for the very first time in September, and any program with the word "mama" in the title was something he wanted to watch. The mama in the TV show wanted the best for her son, the same as he imagined his mama would want for him. But the TV mama was always trying to fix her son up with a woman, whereas his real-life mama wouldn't have to be concerned with that—Louise would be his lifelong mate. When the commercial came on, he went outside to get the mail. Medford looked through the envelopes, separating his father's deliveries from his. Then he saw the return address on the big brown envelope and dropped everything else to the ground. It was from the Southern Regional Box Company in Hopkinsville, South Carolina. Tearing open the envelope, he began to read the letter inside. It was short and to the point.

Dear Mr. Attaway,
In response to your inquiry, our records
indicate that our company distributed packing
crates in 1929 to several Lemon City customers:
Brunsons, Butlers and Stewarts.
We hope this information is helpful.
    Sincerely,
    Southern Regional Box Company,
    Customer Service Department

Medford slid the letter back into the envelope. None of the names stood out on paper to him, but the black-and-white photograph that he'd found in Clement's basement came to mind. Perhaps one of those names belonged to the missing face in front of the camera or to the person standing behind it, he thought. Then Medford ran back into the house to take another look at what he considered might be evidence inside his bedroom dresser drawer.

Billy was getting used to serving his pregnant wife hand and foot. Having waited seven years for this, being a doting father-to-be provided him with great satisfaction. In the past, Billy had worried about his wife putting on too much weight and now for the first time in their marriage, he actually encouraged her to eat. There were occasions when she became so full that she couldn't ingest another bite and felt like she would burst and that concerned him too, not knowing the difference between the uterus expanding and the stomach bloating because it all looked like the same area to him. All he wanted was to maintain balance in his family, and the effort was driving him crazy because he didn't have experience in this area and didn't always know what to do. Taking care of his wife was quickly becoming an extra job that made him feel like he was always working. If he wasn't on duty at the office, he was on duty at home. And if he wasn't busy being a cop in real life, he was watching them on TV just to wind down and relax. A huge fan of his regular TV show *Mod Squad*, he now had a new program to watch called *Get Christie Love*. It featured a smart, gorgeous, badass sister playing an undercover police officer who could karate-chop her way in different outfits and disguises to bring the bad guys down. Tonight she was playing a prostitute, and just as Billy was getting to the good part of the story where she was about to outsmart the perpetrator, the phone rang. He wasn't going to answer it, but after it kept ringing, Elvira shouted from the bedroom to pick it up because she was trying to get some much needed rest.

"Hello," Billy said in a whisper, trying to sound sleepy so the person calling would get the hint that he didn't want to be disturbed.

"Billy, is that you?" said a familiar voice.

"Who do *you* think you're calling?" Billy asked as if the person were stupid not knowing what number he dialed. "Who is this?" He became suspicious.

"This is Beau . . . Beauregard Taylor," said the Jefferson County Sheriff.

"Hey Beau, what's happenin', my man?"

"Billy, sorry I'm calling so late, but this is not a social call."

"It never is." Billy turned down the volume on the TV so he could at least see what was going on with Christie Love. "What can I do for you?"

"I got an APB out on a kidnapper and his victim that may be in your area."

Billy thought for a bit, wondering why this call was coming

nine months late, almost as long as it took to make a baby, but he didn't want to pause too long. "You don't say . . . what profile do you have on the suspect? . . . I'm assuming it's a him."

"It's a him, but *he's* got a *her* . . . according to the file, allegedly he kidnapped his sister. But that concept sounds pretty weird to me. Anyway, I don't make up this stuff. Seen anything unusual out your way?"

"Nope. Everything's quiet as marshmallows." Billy laughed at his own corny joke. "But I'll keep a lookout," he added seriously. Then he changed the subject. "Hey, you know, Elvira's pregnant."

"Congratulations, dad-to-be, you old son-of-a-gun," Sheriff Taylor said. "You finally stopped shooting blanks."

"Yeah, I know," Billy said, still watching TV, trying to follow the action without the sound. "Hey, I thought you were gonna retire and forget about all this police stuff."

"Yeah. Yeah. I started looking for hardware-store space last month. It's a process, ole buddy. I haven't found any commercial property that I like yet, but I'll keep trying and keep you posted."

"Well, good luck to you on that."

"Thanks, and let me know if you see something . . . a stranger in town with a little girl, ya hear?"

"You bet. Don't think I can miss anything like that."

"Give my regards to Nana and Granddaddy and to the rest of the family."

"Will do. You have a good night."

"You too."

Billy hung up the phone and returned to *Christie Love*, but the show was about to end. Since he'd missed the good part, he'd lost track of the story and gave up on watching the rest of tonight's episode. Instead, Billy called Jeremiah and warned him that the county law was catching up to his trail, which meant the state wasn't far behind. Jeremiah didn't give it a second thought. It was time for him and his sister to pack up in the GTO and head north to find Dick Gregory.

Happier than a hummingbird feeding on a honeysuckle, Nana couldn't stop thinking of reasons to celebrate. She was so excited about becoming a great-grandmother that she had a baby shower for Elvira five months in advance. On another occasion, she invited Sadie, Theola, and Vernelle to come over for tea and biscuits to mark the end of this year's tomato competition. Then she arranged for another festivity with sun tea and cinnamon rolls to commemorate the completion of her club's Dogwood quilt. She served pigs-in-blankets with beer when Clement finally beat Granddaddy in chess, and had a get-together when Louise and Medford officially decided to become a couple. Now Nana was preparing this afternoon's cookout to celebrate Ruby Rose's first piano recital. The plan was to have everyone over before the recital, then afterward go to the church to hear Ruby Rose play.

While Nana was in the kitchen, Granddaddy was in the backyard dashing lighter fluid on the coals, then striking a match to get the barbecue grill going. Using the juices that Nana had cooked when she boiled down the last of her tomatoes to make her special barbecue sauce, he basted the first round of chicken. When Billy and Elvira arrived, the first thing Nana did was cup her hands around her granddaughter's belly and put her ear to her stomach to feel close to the unborn child. Feeling a poke, a jab, and a roll-over made Nana as pleased as a snowshoe hare in winter. The other thing that made her happy was seeing Louise and Medford together again. When they arrived, Nana hugged them both, then chastised Louise for not asking her man fast enough if he wanted a glass of lemonade or a can of cold beer. Then the guest of honor arrived with her brother, and everyone made Ruby

Rose the center of attention as if she were a homecoming queen riding on a float. When everyone else arrived, the cookout came to life.

The smell of smoked hickory and barbecue drove Ole Miss Johnson outside to her garden, pretending to check on the last of her tomatoes for the season. Wondering what all the commotion was about, she saw everyone making a fuss over Ruby Rose, who was chattering faster than a cricket moving its wings to make sure it was being heard. Ole Miss Johnson decided to stay outside a little longer; her plants needed watering and she didn't mind getting some fresh air.

Nana saw Ole Miss Johnson from over the fence and decided to make her neighbor invisible. She had all the people she loved around her and she wasn't going to let the sight of wickedness spoil Ruby Rose's day.

"Ruby Rose, I'm so proud of you and looking forward to hearing you play later today," Nana stated.

"Thank you, Ma'am. I'm getting so good at playing, Nana, that I hope Jeremiah will buy me my own piano soon," she said loud enough for her brother to hear. "I've got the perfect place for it in the cottage."

Granddaddy handed Ruby Rose a hot dog. Upon hearing her comment, his eyes got big and he looked at Nana, who knowingly glanced at Billy, and they all turned to Jeremiah. Billy had told his grandparents about Sheriff Taylor's phone call and that he'd told Jeremiah it was best for him to leave Lemon City as soon as possible, but they guessed Jeremiah hadn't told his sister, probably because he had sense enough to wait until after the recital.

"Pianos are expensive, dear," Nana said. "It'll be okay to keep using the one at the church, or for that matter, you're welcome to use the one here. The main thing is that you keep practicing." Nana went over to the grill to remove two well-done hamburgers and two cooked ears of corn on the cob and put them on a plate for Elvira, handing it to her without asking, assuming she was hungry.

"I'm gonna need new sheet music," said Ruby Rose, trying to get the ketchup out of the bottle to slide on her meat. "I want to learn how to play that song 'Bridge Over Troubled Water.' It's got a piano in it."

"That's one of my favorite songs too," chimed in Louise.

"I can't buy you a piano, but I can get you sheet music," added Medford, winking at Ruby Rose.

Ruby Rose liked seeing Medford and Louise as a couple again, which was nothing personal against Jeremiah. She just thought they looked better together and belonged that way. Even though she loved her brother, Medford had grown on her faster than weeds sprawling up along a country road, and she liked seeing him happy.

"Ruby Rose," said Bootsie, sitting at the picnic table. "Let me take a look at your fingers, girl."

Ruby Rose wiped the ketchup off her hands with a napkin and extended the cleaner one to Bootsie.

"Ooh, wee," he squealed, admiring the long, narrow extensions. "You sure have got some pretty pie-ano-playing fingers. I betchu they move as fast as spider legs crawling up and down the keys."

Ruby Rose laughed at the way Bootsie said the word "piano" as if there were some kind of pie made with a filling called "ano." When she finished giggling, she thanked Bootsie for the compliment.

Clement asked Granddaddy, Bootsie, and Medford if they wanted to play poker. When Medford passed on playing to stay close to Louise because he still didn't trust Jeremiah, Theola jumped at the opportunity to partner with Clement. She admitted she didn't know how to play poker, but she told Clement she was willing to learn. Clement adjusted his newsboy hat and looked at Theola like she was crazy, volunteering to play poker without knowing the first thing about the game. He had no interest in teaching a new student, but he didn't know how to gracefully get out of the situation. He stared at Theola, with her silver streak that reminded him of a trail that a slug might leave behind on a tar-covered road, and decided she had a lot of nerve. Having no choice but to set up the card table, he took a deck from his back pocket and started explaining the rules.

Since Granddaddy was at the card table, Medford replaced him at the grill. He threw on the second round of corn and chicken and made sure the aluminum foil was sealed tightly over the casserole dish of molasses-soaked baked beans. Standing up, he had a better view over the fence, which enabled him to take a closer look at Ole Miss Johnson.

"How are things going along with the search for your mama?" Nana asked Medford, cutting into his thoughts.

Medford put the top on the grill and watched as the smoke escaped from the holes. "I'm getting closer and closer to learning the truth," he replied.

"Whatcha finding out, Medford?" asked Vernelle. "Was there anything in the old newspapers or in the church files?" She had chewed all the sugar from her Chiclet gum, retrieved a tissue from her white purse, and discreetly removed the waste from her mouth. With one swift move, the gum was gone inside the paper and stuffed into her favorite receptacle. "Did you run into someone around here that could help? Did going to the Town Municipal Offices do any good?"

Medford thought Vernelle would run him down with her questions. "Nope, but I discovered the crate that I was delivered in tucked away in my dad's basement and got a good look at it, along with some clues." Medford looked to see the reactions of anyone who was listening. Louise looked up from her potato salad; Vernelle didn't appear to believe a word of it; Sadie seemed genuinely interested in Medford's progress. Sitting at the card table, Granddaddy took a sip of beer, and Nana thought that any minute now, she would have a son-in-law to add to her list of new family members.

"I called the company that made the crates and they gave me the names of the folks in Lemon City who may have ordered them."

"When was that?" asked Vernelle.

"Nineteen twenty-nine, the year I was born."

"Um-hmm—the same year we had that lumber shortage, 'cause of that brush fire in the forest, y'all remember that."

Sadie shook her head, thinking about the fire that raged through the trees and scarred the face of the mountain.

"Who could forget it?" Granddaddy said, not expecting an answer. "Looked like someone had dropped a bomb in those hills with all that fire and smoke. If we was at war during that period of time, I'd swear the enemy had landed in our backyards."

"That would explain it," said Louise, trying to figure out the logic behind the purchase. "The reason for bypassing Rule Number Eight: 'Do business at home first, then with Outsiders you can invite into your home, as a last resort,' was because there were hardly any trees left in Lemon City. I remember y'all telling me about that."

"Any of these names ring a bell? Brunson? Stewart? Butler?" asked Medford.

"Brunson and Stewart are distant relatives fourth or fifth removed, ain't that right, Ernestine?" asked Granddaddy, trying to get his wife to confirm his memory.

Nana nodded her head, recollecting. "But Butler, now that's Ole Miss Johnson's maiden name."

"Ole Miss Johnson?" Medford looked across the yard and over the fence at the old lady. "Now isn't that a coincidence?"

As Medford examined the yard more closely, he noticed the crates she had used for packing her tomatoes for the Annual County Fair stacked high against her house. They looked like the same kind of crates everyone used every year, nothing special. The thought had never occurred to him, but he felt he should follow up on Nana's neighbor as another possible lead worth exploring.

"That's all I'm gonna say about it now. As soon as I find out, I'll let y'all know." He returned his focus to the grill and turned over the chicken so the other side could get a touch of crispy black, which was the way he liked it.

After the card game had turned into four rounds of poker and they'd all had several helpings of the afternoon's barbecue, the sun started to lower itself behind the mountains, spreading its dusty glow of orange along the sky. Realizing it was almost five o'clock, they started cleaning up and putting away the food, getting ready to leave for Ruby Rose's recital debut.

Judging by how slowly she puttered around her garden, Medford believed that Ole Miss Johnson was still outside thinking of things to do to justify her eavesdropping. Finally he got up the courage to be the first to share with her the biggest piece of gossip she'd ever heard, and to make the time spent in her garden all afternoon worth the wait. He considered he might be in violation of Rule Number Three: AIRING YOUR DIRTY LAUNDRY OUT IN THE STREET WILL SMELL UP THE NEIGHBORHOOD, but what he could possibly encounter would overturn any restrictions on odor. As a goodwill offering, he made the old lady a plate of barbecued chicken complete with side orders, covered it with aluminum foil, and brought it to the fence. He didn't quite know how to ask her his question or introduce the notion that he might be her son, but now was as good a time as any.

Ole Miss Johnson saw Medford approaching with a plate of food and met him at the fence. He stared at the old lady as if he were looking at her for the first time, and she stared back, knowing there was more on his mind than just serving barbecued chicken. Now they were standing face to face. She expected him to hand over the plate, but he never let it leave his possession. There was something he had to say, she was certain of that, but it looked like the cat had caught his tongue and ripped out his vocal cords.

Medford felt his knees begin to shake. Cocking his head to the side to take a closer look, he examined Ole Miss Johnson's profile as if her face were under a microscope. She followed his movement, wondering what he was staring at, curious about what he was looking for. He sized her up and down and she did the same with him. Her legs were long and her torso was short, just like his. Despite her height, her frame was thin, with not too much meat on her bones, and his would be too if he didn't do the kind of physical work he did every day. Her cheekbones were high like his and when he peered closer to her face, for the first time, he noticed they shared the same nose. His hair was coarser than hers, more like Clement's, and his skin was darker, more like Clement's too, but there were enough signs to convince Medford it was more than coincidence. Then he saw a portion of the familiar-looking dark spot on her shoulder, which confirmed that his notion might not be as far-fetched as he'd originally thought.

"If you get any closer, you might as well take a sniff," Ole Miss Johnson snapped. "Is what you got in your hands for me?" she added, tilting her head in the direction of the plate.

Medford slowly presented the food, all the while keeping his eyes on her face. "Sorry, Ole Miss Johnson," he said. "Please excuse me for what I'm about to do." And he pulled back the collar of her knit cardigan sweater, revealing her bare shoulder so he could see if there was anything recognizable on her skin. She smacked his hand so hard he could still feel the sting, but not until after he found what he was looking for. The spot was on her right shoulder blade, the same place as his. There was a tiny dark birthmark in the shape of a kidney bean, and he pulled down his shirt collar so that he could show her his legacy.

"What the devil you doing? You ought to be ashamed of yourself putting your hands on me." She shook her bony finger in his face. "I ought to scream right here and now . . . call the cops . . . and have you arrested . . . tell your daddy." Ole Miss Johnson was working herself up to hysteria and opened her mouth to scream at the violation, but Medford said something that made her voice stop before it reached her throat.

"I think you're my mother," he said with a straight face, holding Ole Miss Johnson in his gaze, looking at her dead-on.

"What'd you say?" Ole Miss Johnson didn't think she was hard of hearing, but there was a first time for everything and this could be the first day her ears decided to fail. She took her pinky and jiggled it around in her ear as if there were water in it.

Medford cleared his throat and repeated, "I said, I think you're my mother." He wished he had a glass of water—better yet, a shot of Johnny Walker Red—before he made the most important introduction of his life.

Ole Miss Johnson stood there with her plate in hand and almost dropped it. In a state of shock, her skin became pale as if her blood had suddenly decided to stop delivering to her vital organs. Then her breathing slowed down and she started sweating bullets. Despite looking faint, she began to squeak out a scream over and over again until she sounded like a broken siren that refused to quit, which was her way of yelling for help. Medford had lost his mind and she thought he might assault her again. Everyone who was walking in and out of Nana's house, cleaning up after the cookout, stopped what they were doing and turned their heads in her direction, curious about the racket. Medford desperately tried to calm her down, and was hoping the mother he had just found wasn't on her way to having a stroke.

Everyone gathered around the fence.

"Lurleen, what in the world is wrong with you?" Nana asked her neighbor.

Ole Miss Johnson kept yelling as if someone had turned on the switch and couldn't turn it off. Finally she started taking deeper breaths. Once she collected herself, she appeared to be ready to speak.

"He's crazy," Ole Miss Johnson said to Nana. Regaining her strength, she backed away from the fence. "As long as I've known Medford, I never known him to be crazy. The man should be carted off in a straitjacket," she added, and everyone looked at the old lady as if she had some nerve judging someone else's mental state.

"Why you calling him crazy?" asked Sadie.

"He said he thinks I'm his mama," Ole Miss Johnson replied, folding her arms across her chest as if Medford had accused her of a heinous crime.

Clement looked at his son in disbelief, but Medford didn't flinch as he stood his ground, and everyone else in attendance was awestruck.

"Why would you say such a thing, son?" Clement asked, trying to understand Medford's accusations.

"Because she is," volunteered Sadie, pulling out her dress that was stuck to the back of her legs.

"That's a helluva way to deliver a birth announcement," said Granddaddy, cracking up, shaking his head.

Ole Miss Johnson puffed up as big as a blowfish out of water. "Quit lying," she said to Sadie. "Whose side are you on, anyway?"

"I ain't on nobody's side and I ain't lying. If you look at him close, you can see he's got your eyes; look at his cheekbones . . . his nose, and looky here." She pointed down to the ground. "He's got your big feet. See, there they go . . . your size-eleven foot and his size-fifteen shoe."

The way Miss Sadie pointed out the resemblances made Louise start to giggle.

"And if I recall," added Sadie, "there's a birthmark in the shape of a kidney bean on both your shoulders. If my memory serves me correctly, it's the right one."

Medford pulled back his shirt collar so his mother could take a look. When she saw it, Ole Miss Johnson put her hands to her face.

Louise covered her mouth quickly and stopped giggling, knowing there weren't many people in town who knew about Medford's kidney bean, and it made her pay more attention to what Miss Sadie had to say.

"What do you know about this?" Nana asked Sadie, fanning herself with her hand even though it was almost fall and there was no heat in the air as the sun finally settled and disappeared from the sky.

"Medford is Lurleen's son. I've know it all his life," Sadie said to Nana, who almost fainted. It was a good thing her husband was standing close to her just in case her knees gave out.

Louise grabbed Medford to steady him with her arm.

"How could you say such a hurtful thing?" Ole Miss Johnson asked Sadie. "I have no children. You know that. How could you be so cold-hearted and cruel?" Ole Miss Johnson gave Sadie a look, trying to remember through her old friend's eyes back to that night that she spent forty-four years trying to forget.

"I was there when he was born. You know that," said Sadie, looking her old friend in the eye.

"Yes . . . yes," Ole Miss Johnson stuttered. "But you said the baby never lived . . . that it came into the world stillborn." She was afraid to let the words out of her mouth, unwilling to repeat that journey all over again.

"Maybe I shouldn't have told you that, but at that time I thought it was for the best." Sometimes Sadie regretted the decision she'd made that day, but she'd found absolution in the way Clement raised Medford and the way Medford turned out. "I was hoping you'd never catch on that Medford was your baby when he was splashed all over the front pages of the newspapers," continued Sadie. "By that time, you were all depressed, didn't want to hear nothing, didn't want to know nothing, couldn't get up out the bed, and several months later when you resurfaced, you didn't want to have anything to do with babies anymore. Then all the news died down, and thankfully you never made the connection."

Sadie turned to Medford and decided it was time he heard the truth. "Your mama wasn't married when she found herself pregnant. She concealed it well, and nobody else knew except her and me. She and Clement were messing around and one thing led to another." Sadie turned to Nana and Granddaddy. "That was a couple of years before Easely came into her life, and at the time, if you recall, I made my living as a nurse."

Granddaddy and Nana nodded their heads, remembering all the fun they had together when they were all in their early twenties.

"Hold up now. Just wait a minute," Clement stammered, looking at Sadie. "What are you trying to say?"

"You heard me. Don't act like you dumb. You're Medford's real father."

Clement fell back in his chair and Louise rushed to get him a glass of water. Then Medford plopped down, nearly missing his seat, and Louise decided she'd better get two. Everyone was dumbstruck as Sadie continued her story.

Sadie addressed Medford again. "Anyway, your daddy was a drunk." Sadie looked at Clement with disgust as details of the past came into focus. "And he needed reformation and some responsibility, something to make him sober up and straighten out his life," she continued to Medford as if she were scolding Clement at the same time. "So I wrapped you in a blanket, placed you in a sawgrass basket inside a tomato crate, and left you on his doorstep. Lurleen had passed out cold during delivery and didn't know nothing about it. So being her friend, of course I wanted to protect her so there wouldn't be any scandal in her life. At the same time, you would have a home and still grow up close to your mama—but better yet, live with your daddy."

Medford couldn't believe what he was hearing. Not only was it confirmed that Ole Miss Johnson was his birth mother, but Clement was actually his birth father too. He looked at Clement long enough for them both to start grinning at each other, and then they moved forward to embrace. After that, Clement and Ole Miss Johnson just stared at each other confused, not knowing whether to kiss or kill, so neither one of them made a move.

Then Granddaddy got tickled, remembering what Clement had said while they were playing chess at the Annual County Fair about liking *mean women*, comparing them to whiskey, and he leaned into his friend and whispered, "You got the first part of your wish. She's *mean* alright, but this is one shot of whiskey that would be too tough to swallow."

Clement gave Granddaddy a shove.

Then Ole Miss Johnson looked at her son and as she threw her arms around him, Medford felt her warm tears seeping through his shirt onto his shoulder. Ruby Rose threw her arms around Medford and his mother as far as they would go. Louise wrapped her arms around the three of them as well. Then, one by one, everyone came forward in one big, long embrace with Medford and Ole Miss Johnson in the middle. Everyone except Theola, who wondered if this meant she had to give up her pursuit of Clement because he might want to be reunited with the mother of his child, and Nana, who was sick at the thought that Louise marrying Medford would mean having Lurleen as her granddaughter's mother-in-law. Not only that, but Nana finally understood that her pregnant dream wasn't about Elvira after all; it was about her neighbor: how the baby got away from its mother and turned into a man before her very eyes.

Sadie lifted her head from the pile of bittersweet emotion, saying it was time to take Ruby Rose to the recital. But before she had a chance to turn her back and creep away from the huddle, she heard trouble stirring behind her.

"Wait a doggoned minute, Sadie Washington," snapped Ole Miss Johnson. "How dare you keep all this to yourself for over forty years."

"I did what I thought was best," defended Sadie. "That's the truth, whether you like it or not."

"I know youse slow and all that, but woman, this beats a rat's ass dipped in whip cream and served on a platter. You woulda' gone to your grave with this here secret if it weren't for Medford being curious, 'cause nobody wouldn't a thought nothing about it."

"That's the way it was supposed to be." Sadie shifted her body, ready to defend the integrity of her decision-making process.

"Miss Sadie, you prevented me from growing up with my mother," Medford said, halfway between anger and disbelief.

"You grew up with her," Sadie said, raising her voice. "She was in your life; so was Nana, so was I, so was Theola and Vernelle." She extended her arm, pointing her finger at Medford. "You look like you did okay without being with her specifically. We all took care of you, and you turned out fine."

"You know that's not the same," Clement responded.

"Well, look at it this way." Sadie took the same finger she'd used to point at Medford and swung it around to aim at Ole Miss Johnson. "If you had grow'd up with this woman, look at how mean you'd be." Sadie stretched her arm out as far as she could for emphasis. "Look at her." She raised her voice to a shout. "Would you want to turn out like that?"

For a split second, Ole Miss Johnson appeared to be raving mad—her hair out of place, the vein in her temple throbbing, and her birthmark shoulder beginning to twitch. "Sadie, you get away from me. You and me were friends. We used to be best friends. How could you do this?"

"It was the toughest decision I ever had to make. It might not have been the right one. But Lurleen, me and you was both young." Sadie began to soften, feeling guilty about the situation, but still holding on to her conviction as if it were the last one she had. "You didn't need no baby . . . but Clement, here . . . boozing it up every chance he got . . . he needed something that would change his life. Besides, the baby was half his, and he needed the infant more than you."

"Then why didn't you tell me?" asked Clement.

" 'Cause if I told you, you'd probably pass it right back on to Lurleen and never know nothing about responsibility."

Nana had held her tongue long enough. "Sadie, you should be 'shamed. Who else's baby you take away?"

"No one's." Sadie shoved her hands onto her hips. "I ain't making no habit out of baby snatching."

"Ain't that something for a nurse to be taking up as a line of business." Granddaddy smirked.

"Medford, aren't you happy you weren't adopted?" Ruby Rose tugged at Medford's shirt. "And that you know your real mother?"

"Yeah. I should be. I mean, I am. But it's shocking to know

that your own mother has been right in your own backyard, so to speak, practically in front of your face your whole life and you didn't have a clue."

"Let's go to the recital now," Ruby Rose offered Medford, her face filled with understanding. "Everything worked out. You got what you were looking for. Whatever's bothering you, you'll get over it."

"Now that's what I'm talkin' about," said Sadie, glad that Ruby Rose was helping to get her off the hook. "I doubt much is gonna change. Lurleen will still be cranky and Medford will still be Clement's son. Forgive and forget. Let's go celebrate the truth over some music. Now that Medford's found his mama, that adds something else for all of us to be happy about."

Medford looked at Louise and they smiled, knowing that the biggest part of the puzzle had been found to make it complete.

Medford asked his mother if she wanted to go to the recital, and she flatly said no. Being a new mother at sixty-two without a doubt must be stressful, he thought, but he also didn't expect Ole Miss Johnson to change overnight.

The Dunlaps and their guests left for the recital, and when it was Ruby Rose's time to play "Killing Me Softly With His Song," Sadie was so overcome with the joy of having the burden of concealing forty-four years of truth lifted off her shoulders that she started to sing. Ruby Rose was surprised that she was making an effort to sing the song the way it was played on the radio. And because Sadie kept the howling quality of her voice to a minimum, Ruby Rose was able to concentrate on the piece and not make a single mistake.

Chapter Thirteen

The next day it rained, with thunder that clapped so loudly that it sounded to Jeremiah that the sky would crack and split itself in two. He didn't know how his sister could sleep through all this racket, but he figured she was tired from her perfect performance the night before and needed to reward herself with rest, so he let her sleep. Besides, he wasn't in a hurry to deliver the news that she would wake up to. Telling Ruby Rose they would be leaving Lemon City as soon as possible, as early as this week, wouldn't be easy. To pass away the time, Jeremiah sifted through the clothes in his closet, separating the ones he would pack and take with him from the ones he would donate to the church, which he stacked in a pile on the floor.

When Ruby Rose emerged from her room, she was hungry. She made herself a sandwich and after she ate, Jeremiah asked her to remain seated because he had something to say. He pulled his chair up to the table.

"Ruby Rose, it's time." He looked at his sister and made sure his eyes didn't blink.

"Time for what?" Ruby Rose turned her head toward the clock.

"You know how we said we were just going to pass through Lemon City?" Jeremiah was hoping his sister would read between the lines so he wouldn't have to spell it out.

"Yeah. That was ages ago. Ain't you forgot about that?"

"No. I committed a crime when I rescued you and now those cops I was concerned about are starting to move in on us."

"So what does that mean?" Ruby Rose bit her bottom lip.

"That means it's time to leave Lemon City."

"No. I don't want to go." She stood up with such force that her chair fell back on the floor. "I'm going on a hunger strike just like Dick Gregory," she announced, her lip starting to quiver. No matter how hard she tried, she couldn't get it to stop. "I'm not eating ever again," she said, digging in her heels. "You don't want me to be happy. You never did. You never came to see me when I was with Mama. Then you take me away from mean Miss Molly Esther and you drop me like a hot potato for that woman. You just don't want me to have any fun. I hate you. I hate you!" Ruby Rose cried and stomped her feet before running back into her room.

Jeremiah could hear her sobs through the door. He felt bad about how his sister was feeling, and for the whole situation. Regardless of his efforts to do what was best, it seemed nothing turned out right. He had no choice but to ride out this storm. It wasn't easy raising an anchor that had just been lowered and positioned. Just as Ruby Rose was getting comfortable in Lemon City, he had to uproot her, and it was only fair to give her time to get used to the idea of being without a home.

Not knowing how to handle this kind of situation, Jeremiah called Nana for advice. Since Nana had been in a partying mood ever since the Annual County Fair, it came as no surprise to Jeremiah that she offered a celebration as a solution.

"There's a big fight coming up soon," said Nana, kicking off her Sunday shoes, just getting back from church. "Willie says it's between Muhammad Ali and George Foreman. But we'll make it a going-away party for you and Ruby Rose too. That's a few weeks away. That'll give the chile some more time in Lemon City, so you won't have to shock her into leaving right away. Meantime, she can help Elvira in her delicate state with errands and chores, and keep up her home schooling and piano lessons. I'll talk to Billy— see if he can keep Beauregard off your trail for a while longer. Billy will do what I tell him. Don't you worry. Tell the chile we're planning a party for her and Muhammad Ali. That'll cheer her up."

Jeremiah didn't know if delaying the inevitable would help or make things worse, but when he knocked on his sister's door to tell her the news, she was thrilled to have more time in town. Then she boldly announced that her hunger strike was over and immediately poured a bowl of cereal and sat down to eat again. Being happy always gave her an appetite.

Time came and went as the trees shed their leaves from summer to prepare for fall. The big match was in October. Just as everyone was glued to their TV sets to watch *The Autobiography of Miss Jane Pittman*, there wasn't a Lemonite in town who would have missed "The Rumble in the Jungle"—Muhammad Ali taking the ring to see if he could reclaim his title as heavyweight champ. The closer it got to the going-away fight party, the sadder Ruby Rose became. By the evening of the main event, Nana saw that the girl's head was drooping so low that it seemed her lips were dragging the floor. Jeremiah was right behind his sister not knowing how to handle her grief when they entered the Dunlap home, so he let Nana take over.

Quickly putting her arm around Ruby Rose, Nana guided her to the dining-room table to help herself to the chicken wings, potato salad, deviled eggs, and lemon pound cake she'd made for the occasion. When those enticements to put Ruby Rose in a better mood didn't work, she shuttled the girl off to the kitchen, mentioning that her favorite ice cream, Sealtest vanilla bean, was in the freezer, even though she knew that ice cream was the last thing on Ruby Rose's mind. She was trying to think of something to say to comfort the girl, some wise insights about growing up and meeting people in her life that would come and go. But Nana couldn't be of much help. She didn't have a point of reference about people's comings and goings, because all she had ever known was Lemon City.

Carrying a bowl of ice cream she wasn't interested in, Ruby Rose sat down at the dining-room table. The way she was playing in it with her spoon, Nana could tell she wanted to be left alone.

Then the doorbell rang and the last guest had arrived. Ole Miss Johnson showed up and everyone was happy that Nana had done the right thing by inviting her next-door neighbor into her home. Just the same, it didn't stop Nana from snorting, and Clement from grunting, when she walked through the door.

Despite Ruby Rose's need for privacy, Medford sat down next to her and lifted her chin to look squarely into her face. A moment after gazing into his eyes, she burst out crying uncontrollably.

"It's not fair. It's not fair," she said between sobs. She plopped her head down on her arms over the table. Medford rubbed her back and tried to shush away her tears.

"You found your mother, and I have none," she cried. "You're gonna settle down now, and I gotta be on the run."

Medford pulled her close to his chest. "You have your brother. *He's* your family."

"It's not the same," she said through tears. "I want to go to school. I want to take piano lessons. I don't want to leave."

Sadie heard that part about the piano, which made her want to cry too. She was going to miss the girl terribly, and she put her finger to her nose to hold back the sniffles.

As Medford held his little friend, he got to thinking. "You can always come back to visit," he said. "It's not like you have to stay away for good. You'll always have a welcome, and a round-trip ticket back to Lemon City."

Happy for the invitation, Ruby Rose wasn't completely convinced that a visit was going to be a long enough stay to do the trick.

"Come on now. Eat something," said Medford.

Ruby Rose wiped her nose with the sleeve of her sweater and stared at her bowl of half-melted ice cream, which she turned and twirled around with her spoon. Realizing Medford wasn't going to leave until he saw her eat something, she lifted the cold white mush to her mouth, and he seemed to be satisfied that he'd got his way.

Everyone gathered around the TV to watch the main event. When Muhammad Ali danced into the ring, there wasn't any breathing in the room; even the night crawlers outside seemed to stop moving out of respect. Ali was warming up, shuffling his feet, throwing punches into the defenseless air. When heavyweight champion George Foreman stepped into the ring, Ali pretended to be scared, taunting the champ with as much mouth as he had muscle. The fight took center stage in Zaire with sixty thousand spectators worldwide, and the Dunlap family and their friends felt like they had ringside seats.

Once the fight began, there was no keeping the men in the room quiet. With the cooler packed with beer next to the couch so they wouldn't have to walk to the kitchen, they had all the refreshments they needed to stay seated and root for the former champ. Ali was thirty-two years old and in tip-top shape, and Foreman was twenty-five and solid like a bull. Granddaddy was hoping that wisdom would teach the young buck a lesson and whip him into shape.

"Nice block," Billy commented as Ali dodged Foreman's punch.

"Have y'all noticed? He's not dancing around like he usually does," claimed Jeremiah.

"That's because he's waiting for George against the ropes," answered Granddaddy, "daring Foreman to come after him."

"He knows what he's doing," said Louise. "Foreman keeps snorting and swinging punches. Ali's strategy is to tire him out."

"It's the ropeadope," added Clement, opening a can of beer.

"It doesn't even seem like Foreman is hurting Ali," said Medford, keeping his eyes on the TV. "He's amazing. Look at how Ali takes those punches. It's like his midsection is steel-plated."

"Ouch . . . ooh . . . ," said Granddaddy after Ali threw a punch that snapped George's head back, and Granddaddy contracted his body and winced as if he had felt the punch himself.

"Yeah! Yeah! Yeah!" Louise yelled, each time a little bit louder, as Ali blocked several punches from Foreman, then scored a few landings of his own.

"I don't care if Foreman pulverized Joe Frazier and Ken Norton," said Bootsie. "He ain't getting a piece of Ali tonight . . . Ali is hot like James Brown and 'Papa Don't Take No Mess.' "

Everyone in the room laughed, and Nana looked at Ruby Rose, who was slumped over in the dining-room chair, looking as limp as Saint, who was curled up in her lap.

By the eighth round, the fight was over. Muhammad Ali knocked out George Foreman and lived up to his title of being The Greatest. Everyone around the TV cheered so loud that the victory startled Ruby Rose and made Saint jump and trot off into the kitchen. Elvira's head nearly rolled out of her hand, because it was way past her bedtime and she had dozed off in the chair.

Now that the fight was over, Medford went into the kitchen

and came out with two bottles of chilled champagne in his hands. He made eye contact with Granddaddy and placed the bottles on the table. Out of nervousness, he started eating a chicken wing from the platter on the dining-room table. After sucking the meat down to the bone, he began chewing on the gristle. The ligaments got stuck in his throat and he began choking uncontrollably, covering his mouth with both hands, gagging over the cake and the rest of the food on the table. He choked harder when he looked at Louise, and she ran over to him to pat him on his back.

"Don't do that!" Vernelle shouted, throwing down her white purse, rushing to Medford's side. "Let me at him." She had just learned a new choking technique in her midwife class called the Heimlich maneuver and approached Medford from behind. She grabbed him with both hands clasped together underneath his rib cage and gave a sudden hard tug slightly below his waist. It was then that the gristle propelled itself out his mouth and flew into the air, hitting Louise in the middle of her head. For the first time that night, Ruby Rose showed signs of life. She laughed and laughed until it looked like her freckles were dancing on her face and she keeled over because her stomach hurt. Medford was embarrassed and got down on one knee to apologize to Louise like he was begging for forgiveness, while Nana, Clement, and Ole Miss Johnson just shook their heads. Louise stared at him, wondering why he was being overly dramatic and wasn't getting up from the floor. She tried helping him, but he was so heavy that he couldn't be moved; it was almost as if he were stuck. The next thing she knew, he removed a tiny gift-wrapped box from his pocket and opened it. Immediately, her jaw dropped and she put both hands to her face. No one in the room had anticipated this event except for Granddaddy, who had given Medford permission to ask Louise for her hand in marriage.

"Beautiful Louise," he said, his voice wavering and his hands beginning to shake. "Beautiful Louise," he repeated to gain back some of his composure. "I've known you for most of your life and I know what kind of woman you are. Because you've got a lot of years ahead of you, I know I will respect the kind of woman you'll become. I love you and most of all I accept you for who you are, and I know this to be true, that I want only you to be my wife."

Nana burst out crying. Louise was so surprised by Medford's announcement that it looked as if her hands had become attached to her face.

"I don't want you to feel pressured into doing something you don't want to do," said Medford, knowing Louise all too well.

Louise looked at Nana, who had started crying into a napkin, and then at Granddaddy, who was nudging her with his eyes to accept his proposal. She didn't know if she was ready for marriage, but she did know that when the time came, she'd choose Medford.

"Medford," she said, and everyone in the room held their breath. "I would *like* to marry you." She said her words carefully, as if trying to remember how to construct a sentence. "At least I *think* I would." She wanted to make sure she was ready to confirm her own opinion in public. "But I would prefer to have a very long engagement first," she said with confidence. "And you have to promise to *call* me Louise; not that I don't want to *be* your wife, mind you, but that's not my identity."

"Is that a yes?" Medford asked.

Nana stopped her tears and looked up from her napkin.

"That's a yes, let's give ourselves a little more time to see," she said.

Nana didn't know what to make of that answer and wished she were standing close enough to her granddaughter to ask her if she were crazy.

Coming from Louise, that was commitment enough for Medford, and he rose from his knee and kissed her and everyone in the room who was fighting back tears, except for Nana, who had waited a long time for this moment but was confused. Ruby Rose seemed happy, as the smile had returned to her face.

Medford held Louise in his arms for a while, then whispered something in her ear, and she didn't hesitate to nod in agreement.

Everyone in the room was wondering what more they had to discuss.

"Excuse us for a minute," Louise said. "Medford and I have to talk." They went to the front porch and closed the French doors behind them.

"Ruby Rose wants to stay, Louise," said Medford. He paused, then added, "We can adopt her."

"Adoption? I don't think Ruby Rose wants to live with me. She hates me."

"She doesn't hate you. She just hates the fact that she hasn't had much love in her life. You're just the woman she needs to set her example—strong, fine, smart, and independent."

"That sounds all well and good, but you should like kids before you become a mother."

"Come on, Lou."

"I don't know. It's true. Everything is happening way too fast . . . marriage, motherhood." She looked at Medford's disappointment and didn't want to do that to him again. "I guess the good news would be, at least I'd know what I'd be getting into. For the most part, her personality has been predetermined; she's already potty-trained, she can dress herself, and she's smart. Truth is, she kinda reminds me of myself."

"Is that another yes?" Medford smiled.

"How many major decisions can one woman make in a day?"

"My lady can handle anything. That's why I love her."

"You really know how to sweet-talk a girl, don't you?"

Medford was patient, looking into Louise's eyes until he got the answer he hoped for.

"Okay. Yes." She didn't like reacting to pressure, but she thought about *The Charlotte Hawkins Brown Papers*, how Charlotte provided a place "where Negro boys and girls could combine training of a practical nature with the development of a larger sense and deeper appreciation of beauty." Louise thought she could extend some of that knowledge to Ruby Rose. She didn't know if she could meet Charlotte's goal of teaching and preparing children for tomorrow's world, but she thought she might give it a try. Besides, before Clement had found out the truth he'd had the courage to adopt Medford, and Medford turned out just fine. Push come to shove, if nothing else, a third party in her marriage might at least keep things lively and break up the monotony.

Medford grabbed Louise by her waist and lifted her off her feet as if she were weightless. He kissed her for a long time until he remembered there were people inside the house, waiting for them to return.

"There's one more thing," Medford said to everyone in the room. Then he made sure they had all quieted down and that he had their attention before turning to Jeremiah. "When we get married we'd like to adopt Ruby Rose. In the meantime, we'd like her to stay here in Lemon City and live with us."

The whole room fell silent again. Nana stopped sniffling and Ruby Rose nearly jumped out of her seat. Before Jeremiah could answer Medford's question, she ran over to her brother, nearly breaking her neck in the process, begging him to please let her stay, to please let Medford and Louise adopt her. It was like waiting for a courtroom verdict with Jeremiah speaking for the jury.

Jeremiah didn't know what to say. He had never seen hope in Ruby Rose's eyes before, only sadness beyond her years. After coming this far with his sister, he especially didn't want to leave her in the hands of strangers, but as he looked around the room, he knew that nothing was farther from the truth. These people were kinder to her than anyone had ever been in his sister's life and equally as important, she loved them too. Ruby Rose gained a lot living in this town. Besides all that, Louise was a good woman. He knew that for a fact, and there was no doubt in his mind that his Ruby Rose was attached to Medford. He looked at his sister, then focused on Louise and Medford, and saw the family that he and Ruby Rose could never be—the family that she deserved. Life on the road, on the run, was no place for a child, even if he planned to settle down on Dick Gregory's farm. After just having found his sister, it was hard to give her up, but the expression on her face and on those of the people in the room helped him come to a decision. He'd have to make a change of plans.

"We promise we'll take good care of her," Medford assured Jeremiah with Louise at his side. "We'll raise her like she was our own."

"She'll have four parents," added Nana, speaking for Granddaddy.

"She'll have six parents," said Elvira, looking at Billy while rubbing her pregnant belly, and everyone else in the room agreed to raise the child and parent by committee.

"Until Medford and I get married, Ruby Rose can live with me," offered Louise, looking at Ruby Rose for her approval. Ruby Rose smiled as wide as a mountain trail, and for the first time she gave Louise a hug.

"And Granddaddy," volunteered Medford. "I'd like your permission to build an addition to the two-family house, since Billy and Elvira will be needing the extra room and Louise and me will be needing some extra space too."

"That's plenty fine by me," agreed Granddaddy.

"Yes. We'll have to prepare for the babies that are coming."

Nana clasped her hands together and looked toward the ceiling in a gesture of prayer. Then she grabbed Ruby Rose and added, "You're my baby too."

That's all Jeremiah needed to hear, and all he needed to see.

"I want to stay," she said. "I want to have make-believe real parents."

Jeremiah smiled and lowered his body to be at eye level with his sister. "You know I'm gonna miss you." He struggled to hold back the tears even though he knew the decision he was about to announce to the room was best for her.

"I'm sorry I got you into trouble with the law," she said.

"You didn't get me into trouble. I guess my purpose was to bring you here." Jeremiah thought for a few seconds. "Nana, what about those Outsider Rules?"

"Oh, we got to fill out the paperwork and file a petition at the Municipal Building and get at least a hundred signatures from the Ladies of Mt. Zion Baptist Church. Fortunately for Ruby Rose, there are provisions. The process is more involved than getting a passport and the conversion from one religion to the next, but it can be done. You gotta have blood work, fingerprints, psychology tests, a battery of interviews, intense Rules training in classes from beginner through advance—that's why hardly anyone goes through the trouble. But when you're done with all your training you get a certificate that needs to be notarized, which is the official document to becoming a Lemonite. If the truth be known, Outsider citizenship has only occurred a few times around here. Interestingly enough, the cutoff age is twelve, so it's only happened for children, and Ruby Rose here would be going through the assimilation process at just the right time.

"Once you become a Lemonite," Nana said to Ruby Rose, "it's a lifetime commitment, so be sure you're not going to change your mind and you really, truly, absolutely, positively want to stay."

Nana breathed the kind of sigh that only comes from the exhaustion of having too much joy. "I feel like you're already a part of this family, and it would be a variation on supporting Rule Number Ten: 'Support the Community in Every Way Possible and Imaginable.'"

Jeremiah looked at his sister and could tell she wouldn't take no for an answer, and the truth was, there was no reason to tell her no. "Yes. You can stay."

Ruby Rose jumped up into his arms and kissed him all over his face. "You can visit," she said. "Can't he, Nana?"

"Sure, baby."

"Come any time," reinforced Granddaddy.

"Sure 'nough, brother," said Billy. Then he thought about what he'd said, and that if Medford and Louise were to adopt Ruby Rose, that would actually make Jeremiah his nephew. That part had the least appeal to him. Billy felt he was too young for that.

"When you pass through New York on your way to Massachusetts, be sure to visit or at least call my sister, Faye," said Louise without hesitation, as part of her Southern hospitality. "She lives in one of those brownstones in Harlem. I don't have a clue where, but I'm sure she can direct you to it when you get there." Louise found a scrap of paper and wrote down Faye's address and phone number.

Jeremiah took the paper from Louise, folded it, and put it inside his back pocket. Then he hugged Ruby Rose and they held on to each other for a long time, until she felt she had enough of his energy and could finally let him go.

"So long, folks," Jeremiah said to everyone in the room, and he went around to kiss all the women and shake hands with all the men. "Thank you for a great party, for a great stay. Thanks for everything. I hope to see all you good folks again some day." Then he addressed his sister. "Ruby Rose, I'll be back."

She waved at her brother as he walked out the door, knowing he would keep his promise and she would see him again.

Before the door closed, Billy mumbled something underneath his breath about don't call us if you have car trouble.

They heard the loud rumble of the white GTO as it backfired down Tuckahoe Road, and while the Dunlaps hoped to see Jeremiah again, if they never saw that car for the rest of their lives, it would be too soon.

Chapter Fourteen

Winter wind came whipping down the snow-capped mountains, ripping through the town, cutting its teeth against the heaviest coats, leaving its bite to chill the Lemonites right down to their bones. The only saving grace was that the energy crisis was over and the townspeople were free to turn up their thermostats and enjoy the heat. Nana spent the winter crocheting for the great-grandchild that she couldn't wait to come. Instead of using single-colored yarn, she thought she'd use multicolored so that whatever sex the child turned out to be, it would be dressed as beautifully as a rainbow stretching across a perfect sky on a clear day.

Then in the middle of winter, in February, the telephone rang and Nana received the announcement she had been waiting for. It was Billy taking Elvira to the hospital, and after Nana shouted for joy into his ear and hung up, she picked up the receiver again and started dialing everyone else.

Elvira had a baby girl, eight pounds, seven ounces, and she named the little one Aurelia Hope after Nana's daughter, who was Louise, Billy, and Faye's mother. The baby was the prettiest little thing Nana had ever seen in her life, and she could hardly wait for Elvira to finish breast-feeding in her hospital bed so she could hold the newborn and take a closer look. Granddaddy was beaming at his great-granddaughter and couldn't wait until she was old enough to teach her how to play chess.

When Ruby Rose arrived at the hospital, she was happy to see little baby Aurelia. She was thinking that Aurelia could be like her little sister, even though they would really be cousins, and when she got bigger they could play together. Nana let her hold the baby and Ruby Rose was careful, cradling her neck in the right place with her head up, smelling her newness, saying to her face with soft breath that she was lucky to have two parents who cared about her and she should be forever grateful. She squeezed her eyes shut and said a private prayer, wishing that Aurelia would be happy and grow up with love as wide as the Blue Ridge Mountains, as deep as the Shenandoah Valley, and as beautiful as the Virginia Highlands. She kissed the little baby girl on her puffy cheek that smelled like freshly made chocolate milk, then handed her back to her mother.

Nana looked through the opened door as the men were milling about and chatting in the hallway. Feeling proud of her family and cherishing the love and support that was circulating throughout the room, Nana felt blessed to be in the presence of such wonderful company, especially with the two new, young additions to the group, who she was certain would carry on with traditions and play by The Rules.

Playing by the Rules

ELAINE MERYL BROWN

A Reader's Guide

Reading Group Questions and
Topics for Discussion

1) After her sister chooses to violate Rule Number One (Never Marry an Outsider), why does Louise decide to get involved with an Outsider at the expense of losing Medford?

2) Ruby Rose grew up in an abusive foster-home environment. What ultimately happens to help her adjust to Lemon City life?

3) With the Black Power movement, the Black Feminist movement, the close of the Vietnam War, and Watergate, why does the author choose to use the backdrop of the 1970s to tell her story?

4) Louise resists falling in love with Medford. Is there anything about her that suggests she also may be running away from herself? Why is she reluctant to make a commitment?

5) The Rules are designed to protect the community of Lemon City from the outside world, but they are also guidelines for living together as a community. Are they effective in both areas? Does

their usefulness change over time? How would The Rules affect your own community?

6) Nana and Ole Miss Johnson have been rivals for years. Do you think there will ever be peace between them? What would need to occur to make this happen?

7) Have you ever dated someone who is much older or much younger than you? How did it work out?

8) Medford and Ruby Rose have a special relationship. Despite their differences, what do they have in common? As an adult, do you think you could have a significant friendship with a child?

9) Theola has a big crush on Clement. What is it about her that prevents her from approaching him with her feelings head on? In your life, who has done most of the wooing—the man or the woman? Which do you prefer?

10) Rules are sometimes made to be broken, and there are always exceptions to rules that are subject to interpretation. In which situations were The Rules somewhat flexible? How did Nana, Louise, and Medford use this to their advantage? Give some examples of times you've had to bend the rules, or laws, in your town? Was it justified?

About the Author

ELAINE MERYL BROWN is vice president of Special Markets at HBO and has held the position of creative director at Showtime Networks. She is an Emmy Award–winning writer and a director. Brown has written for national publications, including *Essence* and *Women's World*. She is the author of *Lemon City*, and she lives in New Jersey with her family. Visit the author's website at www.elainemeryl brown.com.

Don't miss the prequel to *Playing by the Rules*

Lemon City

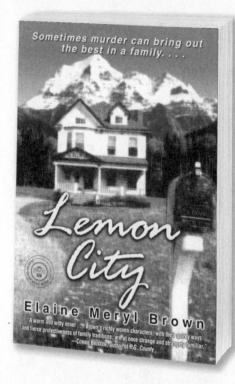

*N*ot only are outsiders breaking into Lemon City, but insiders are breaking the rules. . . . When Faye Dunlap decides to head for New York City, inspired by her new hubby's slick persona, Lemon City's patriarch steams up. But when the new hubby turns up dead during the tomato-growing contest just before Thanksgiving, the Dunlaps have to scramble to keep their tight-knit community from falling apart.

"A warm and witty novel . . . Brown's richly woven characters, with their quirky ways and fierce protectiveness of family traditions, are at once strange and strangely familiar."
—CONNIE BRISCOE, author of *P.G. County*

"Brown's inspiring, slyly amusing novel marks the debut of a welcome new voice in African-American fiction."
—*Publishers Weekly*

Read a sample chapter at www.elainemerylbrown.com

Available now in One World Paperback

 ONE WORLD/Ballantine Books